GRIM OFFERINGS

An Aisling Grimlock Mystery Book Two

AMANDA M. LEE

WinchesterShaw Publications

❀ Created with Vellum

I

ONE

"You're dead."

"No, I'm not."

"Yes, you are."

"No, I'm not. I really wish you'd stop saying that." Will Graham was falling apart. There was no other way to describe him. His brown hair stood on end, his face was devoid of color, just like the body on the bed, which he was steadfastly ignoring. He'd spent the past twenty minutes explaining – in excruciating detail, mind you – why it was impossible for him to be dead.

My name is Aisling Grimlock, and I'm a grim reaper. Because I am called out only on jobs in which the client is in fact deceased, I was running out of patience. "You're dead."

"You're handling this really well," my twin brother Aidan said, scanning Graham's packed shelves curiously. "I think this guy is a hoarder."

"I'm not a hoarder," Graham said, swatting Aidan's hand impatiently. Because only his soul remained, his efforts were ineffective and his ethereal fingers harmlessly passed through Aidan's flesh.

"Dude, you have so much stuff in here I'm surprised you can even find your way to the bathroom," Aidan said, his violet eyes flashing. The eyes, along with our shared black hair, were family traits. My three older brothers all boasted the same attributes, although I had taken to adding white highlights to my hair as a means to annoy my father – and stand out in a sea of chiseled cheekbones and strong features. "Who needs this much stuff?"

"I like to read," Graham huffed.

"No one could ever read all of this," Aidan said, removing one of the books to study the title. "I've never even heard of this. It looks like another language."

"It's Greek, you moron," Graham snapped. "Do you even know what you're looking at? Put it back. You're getting your grubby fingerprints all over the cover. That's a first edition. It's worth a lot of money."

"You're not going to get to spend it, so why do you care?" Aidan asked.

"I want you both out of my house right now," Graham announced. "You're trespassing."

"What do you think that says?" Aidan asked, shifting the book so I could get a better look.

I shrugged. "What does it matter? There aren't any pictures in there, so you're not going to be interested."

Aidan stuck his tongue out. "I read things."

"What's the last thing you read?"

"I … I read the newspaper this morning."

"The comics don't count," I argued. "I read the news section. Jerry reads the editorial page – and if I have to hear one more thing about the proposed road tax I'm going to smack him upside the head, by the way – and you read the comics."

"They have words," Aidan sneered.

"With drawings."

"You bug me."

Since Aidan had started dating my roommate Jerry, our relationship had gone from annoyed and close to annoyed and agitated. We were spending far too much time together thanks to his overnight visits to my Royal Oak townhouse. When we added work to the mix, we were both ready to blow. "You bug me."

"You bug me more."

"That's impossible," I shot back. "You're the king of annoying."

"And you're the queen of bitchy."

"Jerry is the queen of bitchy."

Aidan considered the statement. "Fine. You've got me there. You're still awful to be around these days. I can barely stand you. Do you have PMS?"

"I can't believe you just asked me that!" None of my brothers respect personal boundaries, but since Aidan and I shared time crowded together in my mother's womb – he still maintains I kicked him at every prenatal opportunity – he's especially obnoxious when it comes to invading my life.

"You're just so … crabby," he said.

"I'm not crabby."

"No, you're bitchy," Aidan said. "I thought crabby sounded nicer."

I pinched the bridge of my nose to ward off the headache beginning to build. "Can we get this over with?"

"You're the one who insists on talking to them before collecting them," Aidan pointed out. "If you'd just collect them before they opened their mouths, our lives would be so much easier."

Grim reaping is the family business, one I'd fought falling into until a few months ago. A bad economy forced me out of my job, and since Jerry insisted I still had to pay my half of the townhouse mortgage, I had been forced to go to work for my father. I was still a little bitter.

It's not as though I'm unaware of how this is supposed to go. I just feel that transitioning souls to the hereafter should be a comforting experience. Aidan doesn't feel the same way, and my other brothers make fun of me for being such a "girl" when it comes to ferrying. I still like to give clients the option of asking questions before sucking them into a scepter and transporting them to their final resting places.

Here are the basics: Whatever you believe in, that's where you go. There are a lot of variations – and how you live your life does impact how things are going to shake out. Heaven, Hell, and Purgatory are all real. If you're a douche, you're going to one of the bad ones. That's all there is to it.

"Where is he going, by the way?" Aidan asked, still shuffling through Graham's belongings. "He's got a lot of religious books here. He's obviously interested in the subject."

"Will you stop talking about me like I'm not here, please?" Graham asked, wringing his hands. "I am a person. This is my house. I want you both to leave right now."

"We can't leave," Aidan said. "You're on our list."

"What list?"

"Where is he going?" Aidan pressed. "If it's a good place, maybe he won't be so nervous."

"I'm not nervous," Graham said, shifting decisively. "In fact, I'm going to call the police right now." He strode across the room, stopping next to the desk in the corner. The phone was sitting right there, and yet he didn't reach for it.

I scanned his file more closely. Aidan must have read the look on my face. "Where is he going?"

"The Void."

Aidan smirked. "Ah, an atheist. Awesome."

"What's the Void?" Graham asked, his shoulders twitching.

"It's party central, dude," Aidan said. "Don't worry. They've got great music, and the food is to die for … no pun intended."

I shot Aidan a look. True atheists were rare. Agnostics were far more likely, and they often had a choice of where they wanted to go. This was the first time since joining the Grimlock reaping team that I'd come across an atheist. It was kind of exciting. What? Everything new is exciting at one point or another. "I've heard the Void is great, too," I offered. I was trying to be helpful. "They say it's a party atmosphere."

"I don't like to party," Graham said, hopping from one foot to the other. "I like to be left alone. I like to read, and I like to play games on my computer. That's what I like."

"Don't worry, they have *Candy Crush* in the Void," Aidan said. "Speaking of food, though, can we get this show on the road? I'm starving."

"All you ever think about is food," I grumbled.

"I like to eat," Aidan agreed. "There's a great Middle Eastern place right around the corner. They're supposed to have great hummus."

I did love Middle Eastern food. Still … . I shifted, focusing on Graham again. "Listen, I know this is upsetting. Dying is a shock, even if you're the one who died."

"I am not dead!"

Aidan had moved past mild amusement and landed on annoyance. He shuffled across the room, not stopping until he was standing at the end of the bed. "Dude, that's you. Do you see that?" He moved to the side and lifted the covers so Graham could get a better look.

Graham started rocking himself. "You're playing a trick on me."

"Why would we do that?" I asked.

"I don't know. There has to be a reason. I'm only fifty years old. Men my age don't just die in their beds." Graham was looking for reason in an unreasonable world.

"Life sucks," Aidan said, dropping the covers back over Graham's body. "It really does. I feel for you, man. You had your books and you had your iPad and you had your tricked-out laptop. All of that is gone now, though. It's time to hop on the stick. Or, in this case, it's time to hop in the stick." He removed the sterling-silver scepter from his pocket. "It's almost lunchtime. I'm sorry. We need to get this moving. I have a date tonight, and I want to get this list completed."

He was so insensitive sometimes. "Aidan!"

"What? I'm tired of being here," he complained. "If you'd just sucked him up the second we walked in, this wouldn't have become such a big issue. Now it's just annoying."

"What is that thing?" Graham asked, pointing to the scepter worriedly. "Is he going to suck me up into that thing?"

"Yes."

"No," I said, scorching Aidan with a harsh look. "Well, technically he is, but you won't be in there very long." I was trying to keep my voice even. Graham was teetering on the edge of total hysteria, and a tip the wrong way would make him a lost cause. We'd wasted this much time already, so I was hoping another five minutes would do the trick. What? I'm an optimist. Okay, that's not true. I'm a total pessimist. I still don't like being the bad guy. "We're just the transport team."

"And where are you transporting me?"

"To a hub," I said. "We'll then transfer your soul to your final resting place."

"Which is this … Void?"

"Yes," I said. "It's an awful name, but it's a really fun place. You can basically do whatever you want to do there."

"That sounds like chaos."

"That's why it's fun," Aidan said, grinning. "Come on. There's nothing left for you here. I'm sure you can get your hands on all of these books once you get settled."

Graham shifted his gaze between us. "Are you seriously telling me that everything is true?"

"You'll have to be more specific."

"Heaven is real?"

"There are a lot of different heavens," I explained. "It depends on what you believe."

"Is Hell real?"

Aidan nodded. "It's only for those who have done really terrible things, though. You don't qualify. Hoarding isn't really terrible, even if it is … unsanitary," he said, wiping dust from one of the shelves and rubbing it from his fingertips. "There are certain souls that can't be rehabilitated."

Graham obviously liked to soak up knowledge, and that's what he was doing now. "What happens to souls that can be rehabilitated?"

"Depending on what they've done, they go to Purgatory," I replied.

"And that's different from the Void?"

"Very."

"This is a lot to take in," Graham said. "I need time to think."

"You're going to have plenty of time to think," Aidan said, waving the scepter in Graham's face. "Just jump in here."

Graham shook his head. "You should never make big decisions when you're emotionally overwrought," he said. "I'm emotionally overwrought right now. How about we make an appointment … I should have some time open next week … and we'll talk about it then?"

He looked so hopeful. Part of my heart went out to him. The other part was listening to the growling in my stomach. "We can't do that."

"Well, I'm not going with you," Graham said, placing his hands on his hips obstinately. "I'm not going to go. There's nothing you can do to make me."

I exchanged a look with Aidan, resigned. "Just do it. Now that you've mentioned food, I can't think about anything else."

"Not until you say it," Aidan prodded.

I sighed. "You were right."

"And?"

"And I was wrong," I grumbled.

Aidan smiled triumphantly. "And don't you forget it." He lifted the scepter and pointed it at Graham. "Trust me. You'll feel better when this is all over with. You're going to a better place. No one hoards there."

"I am not a hoarder … you can't … ." Graham didn't get to finish his argument, because Aidan had already absorbed his essence.

When he was done, Aidan tucked the scepter into his pocket and turned back to me with a bright smile on his face. "Let's eat."

2

TWO

"This place is cute," I said, settling in a small booth and fixing Aidan with a rueful smile as he sat across from me. "Have you eaten here before?"

"I know what you're doing," Aidan said, grabbing a menu and opening it.

"What am I doing?"

"You're trying to have light lunch conversation so I won't point out that you're making this job harder than it has to be."

Ugh. He knows me too well. "I am not."

"You're also never going to admit it," Aidan said. "It's not in your nature."

"Hey, I admitted you were right at the house," I argued. "In this particular case, you were right."

"And you were wrong."

"Oh, whatever," I muttered, snatching the menu he was holding. "You just get off on being right." Unfortunately, that was another family trait.

"You're the one who can never be wrong," Aidan shot back. "Do you remember when we had family game night as kids?"

I scowled.

"Whenever you missed a question in Trivial Pursuit you had a fit and insisted the card was wrong."

"That's a total lie."

"It is not."

"It is, too."

"It is not."

"See? You're just trying to be right again," I said. "You just can't stand it when you're wrong."

"I'm always right."

"You sound just like Dad." I knew exactly how to get to him. Most siblings know what buttons to push. I was no exception. "You don't just look like him, but you act like him, too."

Aidan frowned. "You take that back."

"No."

Aidan reached over and pinched my forearm. "Take it back."

"Ow." I ripped my arm out of his grip. "That hurt."

"Oh, you're such a baby," Aidan said, grabbing another menu. "If you would just admit that you're wrong, this whole argument would be over."

"I already told you I was wrong," I snapped. "You just want me to say it again so I can pump up your ego."

"Honey, I don't need my ego pumped up by … you."

"You're about to go to a dirty place," I said, narrowing my eyes. "I told you when you started dating Jerry that I was okay with it as long as you didn't give me the details. Don't you dare start giving me the details now."

Jerry had been my best friend since elementary school. Even at such a young age, I'd known there was something different about him. He was much more interested in clothes and shoes than the rest of the boys, but he was also more sensitive and easy to talk with. When it came down to it, he'd never really given me a choice. He announced we were best friends, and we'd been inseparable ever since.

Jerry came out when we were in middle school, confirming what everyone thought they already knew. He was never ambiguous, and he was never worried about what other people thought. His mother had joined every gay parenting group she could find, and she was proud of her son and the man he'd become. The decision to embrace who he was had been harder for Aidan.

I'd always suspected Aidan was gay, but I never pushed him on it. When you have three older brothers all trying to "out-macho" one another, it's hard to be the one who is different. Aidan was only a few minutes older, but he acted as though he had years of maturity to lord over me. Our brothers had always been protective of both of us, but I got the brunt of it.

When Aidan finally came out, the whole family embraced him. My mother knew. I saw it on her face. She didn't care, and she made sure that

Aidan never felt like an outcast. It was harder for my father, but he sucked up any ill feelings he had about the announcement and hugged Aidan close.

In the years since, Dad not only embraced having a gay son, he also did the one thing Aidan needed above all else: He treated him exactly as he did his other sons.

I was a different story. There were specific rules when you were a girl. After my mother died while trying to collect a soul in a fire, my upbringing had been … unique.

I was a teenager when I lost my mother, and dating in a house filled with men and boys was uncomfortable. Those who were brave enough to try were hounded until they fled. It takes a strong man to put up with the Grimlock family. I thought I'd found him, but now I wasn't so sure.

"Where is your mind?" Aidan asked.

When I glanced up, I found him studying me. "Nothing," I said, turning back to the menu. "I was just thinking about how different you and Jerry were back in the day. It's weird to think of the two of you being together."

"I thought you were okay with it?"

"I am."

"That's not what you were thinking about," Aidan said after a moment. "Well, it might have started out that way. That's not where it ended, though."

He knows me so well it's frightening sometimes. "I was just thinking about … Graham. Do you think he'll be happy in the Void?"

"You weren't thinking about Graham," Aidan said. "You were thinking about Griffin."

I stilled. Griffin Taylor was a Detroit police detective I'd crossed paths with several weeks before. I'd been initially attracted to him, his dark hair and eyes calling to me. Of course, when you're in a supernatural line of work like I am, it's hard to forge a lasting relationship. Griffin eventually stumbled over the truth. We'd fallen into bed, and then he'd fallen into his own void as he took a step back to think. After almost dying together, he'd decided he didn't care what I did for a living and that he wanted to be with me.

We'd spent one blissful week together, and then he'd been called away on an undercover assignment. I hadn't seen him in two weeks, although we did share sporadic texts. He couldn't give me the details of his case, and I didn't feel comfortable texting the details of my day. We were at a crossroads.

"I was not thinking about Griffin," I lied.

"Is he still undercover?"

I scowled. "Yes."

"Has he called you?"

"He's texted a few times." I averted my gaze and scanned the restaurant. "Where do you think the waitress is?"

"He's got a job to do, Aisling," Aidan said. "I'm sure he doesn't like being away anymore than you like him being away."

"Since when are you on his side?" I asked. "You were still calling him Detective Dinglefritz three weeks ago."

"I don't like anyone who defiles my sister," he replied.

"Defiles?"

"You know what I mean," Aidan said. "The walls in that townhouse are thin. I've heard the … defiling."

"You know that means I hear you and Jerry, too, right?"

Aidan smirked. "Yes, but that's a lot more fun for me."

I rubbed my cheek. "I'm a little worried," I admitted.

"What are you worried about?"

"He hasn't called in two weeks."

"He might not be able to," Aidan said. "Didn't you say the case popped up out of nowhere and that it was serious?"

I nodded.

"Well, he might be in real danger if he does try to call you," Aidan said. "Have you ever thought about that?"

Only every night while trying to fall asleep. "Why do you think I haven't been pitching a fit?" I was known for being able to freak out with the best of them.

"So, instead of pitching a fit and getting it out of your system, you've decided to be pouty and morose?"

"I'm not pouty."

"Oh, you're so pouty it's not even funny," Aidan said. "I've put up with it because I know you're depressed, but it's time to snap out of it. You've only been dating the guy a few weeks – and you haven't even seen him two of those weeks."

"Wow, way to make me feel better," I grumbled.

"No one needs the sarcasm," Aidan chided. "I'm trying to help."

"Well, you're doing a really crappy job of it," I said. "You don't even like Griffin."

"I don't dislike him," Aidan corrected. "I just want to make sure he's good enough for my baby sister."

"I'm not your baby sister," I pointed out. "We're the same age."

"I'm older, and wiser."

"You're like three minutes older than me."

"I'm a lot wiser, though." Aidan's grin was charming, and hard to argue with.

"I'm fine," I said. "Griffin has gone out of his way to understand my job. I owe him the same, don't I?"

"You do," Aidan agreed. "That doesn't mean you can't feel sorry for yourself."

"I don't feel sorry for myself."

"Then what do you feel?" Aidan asked. "Sometimes it's like I know you better than I know myself. Other times, like now, I'm not sure what's going through your head. You're hard to read. I think it's because you spent so much time hiding what you were doing from a bunch of prying eyes and ears when you were growing up."

"I'm not really feeling anything."

"Well, when you want to talk, I'm here," he said. "I do wish that waitress would show up, though. I'm starving."

Sensing that the conversational crisis was over, I fixed my gaze on the spot where Aidan's was suddenly locked. I expected to see a waitress, one Aidan would flirt with shamelessly. Instead, the figure sitting across the restaurant was a familiar one.

His hair was a little longer, but his handsome face and strong jaw was the same. He was dressed down in simple jeans and a button-down shirt, but his smile was warm and amiable as he chatted up the woman sitting next to him at the table.

She was beautiful. Her hair was long and brown, her face angular and pleasing. She seemed enraptured by whatever story Griffin was telling, and when he placed his hand over hers she gripped it warmly.

My heart flopped, and my face started to burn as I took in the scene. I swallowed hard.

"Well, I guess his job isn't all that was keeping him away," Aidan said, his tone grim. "I'm going to kill him. Check the list. See if his name is on it."

I couldn't find words, and my heart was hammering so hard all I could hear was blood rushing through my ears. I stumbled to my feet, trying to find focus. I had to get out of here.

In my efforts to escape, I stumbled into a waitress as she attempted to deliver food at the table next to us. I mumbled an apology, and the waitress managed to hold onto the tray – but barely. "Excuse me!"

I felt Aidan's hand on my arm, but I jerked away. "I have to get out of here."

"I'll go with you," Aidan said. "Just hold on a second. I want to have a talk with Detective Dinglefritz."

"I have to go." I moved away from Aidan, glancing up momentarily to make sure I didn't inadvertently run into anyone else. When I did, my eyes met Griffin's across the restaurant expanse. His face drained of color when he saw me.

Griffin jumped to his feet and pointed his muscular body in my direction while I struggled to keep my head from flying off my shoulders. Aidan must have read the look on my face, because he stepped between us and cut off Griffin's angle of approach.

"Go outside," Aidan ordered.

"Aisling." Griffin's face was unreadable.

"Go," Aidan prodded.

"I was going to call you," Griffin said. "I just wrapped my case this morning."

"Don't bother, detective," Aidan snapped. "Don't bother ever calling her again."

Griffin's face registered confusion until he glanced over his shoulder. The woman he'd been dining with appeared concerned, but she wisely remained silent. I'd hate to have to rip her hair out in such a public setting.

"It's not what you think," he said.

Aidan pushed me. "Go outside," he repeated. "I'll handle this."

"Aisling, don't go," Griffin said.

Aidan grabbed his shirt roughly, stopping him in his tracks as he tried to follow me. "Stay away from my sister," he warned. "You just … stay away from her."

3

THREE

"Oh, come on, Bug. Don't hide in there all night."

Aidan had dropped me at home after our disastrous aborted lunch, promising to finish the final two names on the list himself. In my head, I knew I should suck it up and finish the list with him. It was my responsibility, too. In my heart, I just didn't have the energy.

Because it was the middle of the afternoon, the townhouse was empty. I handled my disappointment the best way I knew how: I crawled into bed and slept the afternoon away. Several hours later, I heard the front door open. I knew Jerry was home, but I couldn't face him, so I remained hidden.

I don't know when, but sometime during the afternoon Jerry had been made aware of what happened. He'd been periodically stopping at my bedroom door ever since to check on me. It was starting to get annoying. "I don't want to come out."

"If you don't come out, I'm going to come in," Jerry warned.

"I locked the door."

"I'll kick it in."

I snorted. Jerry was fit. He worked out every day, and now that he was dating Aidan he wasn't doing it just to cruise guys on the weight benches. But he still couldn't kick in a door. Even if he could, the mess would drive him crazy. "You will not."

"I'll have Aidan do it when he gets here," Jerry said.

"Are you going to make him pick up the mess when he's done?"

"Of course."

I sighed. "I'm really not in the mood, Jerry."

"Come on, Bug," he prodded. "I need to see you. I keep picturing you doing horrible things in there."

"I would never hurt myself," I scoffed.

"That's not what I'm talking about," Jerry said. "I can't find the scissors, though. You're not cutting your hair, are you? Your face isn't the right shape for short hair."

I groaned and buried my face in a pillow. "Go away."

"No."

"Jerry, I don't want to talk," I said. "I just want to go to sleep and pretend this day never happened."

"You've been sleeping all day, Bug." He'd given me the nickname when we were kids, a fierce fight I'd had with my brothers over the fate of ants on a sidewalk giving him the inspiration. It had stuck even though I couldn't stand it. "Come on. I have a whole stack of *The Golden Girls* Blu-rays waiting for you."

Jerry abhors clichés, for the most part. He still insists *The Golden Girls* is the best show ever made – and he's not averse to paisley. Go figure. I couldn't argue with him on this front, though. *The Golden Girls* was downright hilarious. "I'm not in the mood."

"Aidan is bringing pizza."

My stomach growled at the mention of food. I hadn't eaten since Jerry had shoved a muffin in my hand on my way out the door this morning. He owns a bakery in downtown Royal Oak, and he's always experimenting at home. This morning's pomegranate-nut blend had been good – but it wasn't enough to sustain me for the whole day. "Where did you order it from?"

"Your favorite," Jerry cajoled. "Papa John's."

Dang. I did like that butter sauce they give you for crust dunking. I tossed the covers off and climbed out of bed, resignedly opening the door and finding Jerry's concerned face waiting for me.

"Oh, you poor thing." Jerry pulled me in for a tight hug, his tall body swallowing my more diminutive one as he tried to smother the sadness out of me. "I hope he gets a horrible disease and his thing falls off."

I hoped that, too. "It's fine, Jerry," I said, patting his back. "It's not like we were dating all that long."

Jerry pulled away, brushing my flyaway hair out of my face so he could study me. "It's not fine. He's a very bad man."

"It's not like we'd ever promised to be monogamous," I pointed out, pushing past him and padding into the living room. I'd changed into my favorite fuzzy pajama pants and oversized T-shirt when I got home. Since it was just going to be the three of us tonight, I saw no sense in cleaning myself up. "He has a right to see whoever he wants."

"Oh, you poor thing," Jerry clucked again. "You're too sad to be mad." He held his hand to my forehead. "You're not sick, are you?"

I jerked my head away. "I'm not sick."

"Hey, when Troy Dancy cheated on you in high school you didn't shed one tear," Jerry said. "Instead you vandalized his car and set his letterman's jacket on fire."

"He shouldn't have left it in an unlocked car," I said. "And I haven't been crying."

Jerry ran his finger over my cheek. "Your eyes are red and puffy."

"Maybe I was smoking pot?"

"If you had pot we'd be doing that right now instead of this," Jerry said. He gestured to the couch. "Come and sit with me, Bug. We'll do some mud masks tonight. You'll feel better in no time."

I pursed my lips. Jerry had his own recipe for masks, and my face felt like satin when he was done. "I'd rather eat the pizza."

"You can't get fat now," Jerry said. "You need to look hot so you can snag another man. I'll put a nice deep conditioner on your hair, too."

"You're going to fix my problems with deep conditioner?"

Jerry smiled. "Yes. I'm going to wash that man right out of your hair."

I couldn't help but smile. There was a reason he was my best friend. We settled on the couch, Jerry pulling me tight as he started in on some second-season episodes. "I think you should start taking on Blanche's approach to life," he said after a few minutes.

"You want me to sleep with everyone who pays me a compliment?"

"Yes," Jerry said. "I'll buy some extra condoms tomorrow."

I snorted. "I think I'm done with men."

Jerry snuggled closer. "You can't be done with men. You're too sarcastic to be a lesbian. None of them would ever put up with you."

Thankfully, the sound of the front door opening grabbed our attention before I could come back with what I'm sure would have been a biting retort. Aidan dropped his keys on the kitchen table as he spread out the pizza boxes. He looked concerned when he finally braved a look in my direction. "How are you?"

"I'm fine," I said, quickly averting my gaze. "We're watching *The Golden Girls*. What could possibly be wrong?"

"Ais … ."

"She's fine," Jerry said, cutting him off. "We're going to eat, and then I'm going to make a special mask to pull the puffiness from her face. Then I'm going to deep condition her hair."

"Yeah, that will makes things better," Aidan grumbled. "Wait … are you saying you're going to wash that man right out of her hair?"

Jerry's face brightened. "That's exactly what I said."

"You two are freaky," I muttered.

Aidan brought one of the pizza boxes to the couch and sat down on the other side of me. "Eat something," he ordered. "You look dead on your feet."

"Have you checked your list? I might be on it."

Aidan's face was grave. "That's not funny."

"Well, I'll put on my clown wig and do a little dance later," I said. "That will be funny."

Aidan ran his hand down the back of my head. "I'm still willing to kill him. You know that, right? I'm sure we can find a way to hide his body."

I waved him off. "It doesn't matter. I don't want to talk about it anymore."

"Well, don't dismiss the idea outright," Aidan said. "If the mask and conditioner don't make you feel better, I'm sure property destruction or murder will."

"I'll think about it," I said, grabbing a slice of pizza from the box.

Aidan was just about to grab his own slice when there was a knock on the door. "Are you expecting anyone?"

Jerry shook his head. Aidan disappeared. I heard him vigorously swear once he opened the door. "You've got to be kidding me!"

"Is she here?"

I froze when I heard the voice. Griffin.

"No, she's not," Aidan said. "I told you at the restaurant that I didn't want to ever see you again. You need to stay away from my sister."

"Is she in there?"

"No."

"I think she is."

"She's not."

"Just … let me see her."

"Where's your other girlfriend?" Aidan asked. "Why don't you go and bother her? No one here wants to see you, Detective Dinglefritz."

The sounds of scuffling assailed my ears, and Jerry straightened to try to peer around the wall that separated the living room from the entryway. "Do you think they'll take their shirts off and wrestle?"

I rolled my eyes. After a few moments, Griffin pushed into the living room. His hair was disheveled, and he pulled up short when he saw me sitting on the couch. He scanned the room quickly, taking in my pajamas and bedhead, and then pasted an apologetic smile on his face. "Well, I'm glad to see you're not doing anything destructive."

Aidan appeared at Griffin's back, his face murderous. "Don't talk to her. You've done enough."

"Mind your own business," Griffin shot back. "Aisling, I want to talk to you."

"We're watching *The Golden Girls*," I said, forcing my face to the television.

"And then we're doing mud masks and deep conditioning," Jerry added.

Griffin pursed his lips. I had the distinct impression he was trying to stop himself from laughing. I didn't find the situation particularly funny.

"So, you didn't stick around for lunch earlier," he said. "I had someone I wanted you to meet."

"Yeah, I'm not into threesomes," I said.

"Well, that's good," Griffin said. "I don't think my sister is either."

I stiffened. "What?"

"Oh," Jerry said, his face relaxing. "That was your sister. See, I knew he couldn't really be a bad man."

"Maya," Griffin confirmed. "She's a nurse at Presbyterian Hospital. That was a convenient place for us to meet for lunch. I haven't had a chance to see her in a few weeks and when I texted her that I was done with my assignment, she wanted to have lunch."

"Oh, he's making that up," Aidan protested.

"Why would I make it up?" Griffin asked.

"Because you got caught." Aidan crossed his arms across his chest petulantly.

I was confused. Part of me wanted to believe him. The other part wanted to kick him in his special place.

"How come you didn't tell Aisling you were done with your assignment?" Jerry asked.

That was a very good question. I tilted my chin and watched Griffin, curious about his answer.

"Because I was planning on surprising her with a bottle of wine and dinner tonight," Griffin replied. "I didn't expect to just run into you at a Middle Eastern restaurant in the middle of nowhere."

Aidan bumped shoulders with Griffin as he pushed around him and sat back down on the couch. "Don't believe him," he said.

"You're starting to piss me off," Griffin said, extending his finger in Aidan's direction. "This has nothing to do with you."

"Oh, right, my sister getting her heart broken has nothing to do with me," Aidan said.

"I didn't have my heart broken," I mumbled.

"You spent the whole afternoon in bed, and Jerry could only lure you out of your bedroom with *The Golden Girls* and pizza," Aidan countered.

"Well, that explains the outfit," Griffin said.

"And the hair," Jerry said, running his hands over my head to smooth the snarls.

Griffin smiled. He could tell I was still leery, but he didn't appear to be going anywhere. He shrugged out of his coat and dropped it on the chair by the table. "Is there enough pizza for me?"

"No," Aidan said.

"Yes," Jerry said. He prodded me with his hip. "Don't you have something you want to say to him, Bug?"

"Like what?" Aidan was still incensed.

"Like she's sorry for overreacting," Jerry supplied. "And she's sorry her brother is such a ... tool."

"Hey!"

I couldn't help but smile. I was sorry. Kind of. I still blamed Griffin for keeping me in the dark.

Griffin strode over to the couch and nudged Aidan with his knee. "Move over."

"No," Aidan said. "I was here first."

"And I haven't seen my girl in two weeks," Griffin said. "I want pizza, and I'm even willing to watch *The Golden Girls*. I am not willing, however, to put up with your crap."

"You're kicked out."

"You can't kick someone out," Griffin said. "It's not your place."

"He's right," Jerry said. He patted the couch on the other side of him. "Come sit here with me. Let Griffin sit next to Aisling."

Aidan was furious, but he did as he was told. After a few minutes of quiet munching and television watching, I could feel Griffin's eyes on me. I finally found the courage to meet them.

"Are you okay?" he asked.

"I'm not sure," I said.

"Do you want to expand on that?"

"I feel a little ... stupid."

"It was an honest mistake," Griffin said, resting his hand on my knee. He was testing me. He wanted to see if I would pull away.

"I feel a little pathetic, too."

"Because you pouted all afternoon and look like you should be at a slumber party instead of on a date?"

I scowled.

"Don't worry about it," Griffin said. "I grew up with sisters. I'm used to stuff like this."

"Shh." Aidan pressed his finger to his lips and pointed to the television.

Griffin shot him a dark look and then held his hand out to me. "How about we get some sleep and start over with a fresh perspective tomorrow morning?"

It was a gracious offer. He was letting me off the hook. I just had one thing to make clear to him. "If you ever cheat on me, I'll burn your letterman's jacket." Griffin looked confused.

"And your car," Jerry said.

Griffin shook his head, nonplussed. "Duly noted." He grabbed my hand and pulled me to a standing position. "Not that this isn't fun, but I haven't slept in thirty-six hours and I can't take much more of ... this."

Despite the harsh looks Aidan flashed me as I crossed the room, I followed Griffin. Maybe some sleep would do us both good. It certainly couldn't hurt.

4
FOUR

I woke up the next morning, for the first time in two weeks, with a warm body draped over mine.

"Morning, baby." Griffin pressed his lips to my neck as he cuddled me. "Feeling better?"

That was a loaded question. Unfortunately, I am not a morning person. It takes me time to digest anything before I've had a cup of something caffeinated. "I'm fine," I murmured.

Griffin's hands were on my waist, and he forced me to roll over so he could study my face in the early morning light. "You look better," he said. "Your hair is out of control, though."

"It always is."

"You usually braid it before you go to sleep."

"I'm surprised you remembered that."

"I was gone two weeks, Aisling," he said. "I didn't fall off the face of the Earth."

"That's not how it felt to me," I grumbled.

Griffin snuggled closer. "I know. I didn't know I would be out of touch that long. I'm sorry. The assignment was only supposed to last a few days, a week tops. Once I was in, though, I had to stick it out. I wanted to call you, but every time I got a chance it was in the middle of the night. I didn't want to wake you.

"If it's any consolation, I dreamed about that braid every night," he said.

It was some consolation. Good grief, when I did I become the kind of girl who gets a thrill out of a boy saying gooey things?

"I missed you, Aisling."

I sighed. Here was my opening. "I missed you, too."

"Good," he said. "Now, how about we forget about yesterday and you can welcome me home with something a little nicer than your brother's incessant whining?"

I smiled. "What did you have in mind?"

"I'm glad you asked."

AN HOUR LATER, WE MADE OUR WAY TO THE KITCHEN. WE WERE both still in our pajamas – well, boxer shorts and a T-shirt for Griffin – but I had managed to run a brush through my hair.

"Well, good morning." Jerry greeted us with a mischievous smile and two mugs of coffee. "And how are you two doing this morning?"

"Good," Griffin replied, sitting on the opposite side of the table from a glowering Aidan. "We're both good."

"Aisling doesn't need you to answer for her," Aidan said.

"Oh, please, we heard the headboard against the wall," Jerry said. "We know they had a good morning." He cuffed the back of Aidan's head lightly. "Eat your pancakes. I made them special for you."

"No, you didn't," Aidan said. "I like peaches in my pancakes. You put blueberries in these. That's Aisling's favorite."

"Why are you being such a sourpuss, Snickerdoodle?"

I couldn't stop from laughing as I sat in the chair between Griffin and Aidan. "Yes, Snickerdoodle, why are you so sour this morning?"

Aidan arched an eyebrow. "So you've just forgiven him?"

I shrugged. "Why wouldn't I? It was just a misunderstanding."

"That's exactly right," Jerry said. "Griffin, do you like blueberry pancakes?"

"Sure. That sounds good," Griffin replied.

"Bug, yours will be ready in a minute."

"Good," I said. "I'm starving."

"I bought you pizza last night," Aidan pointed out.

"What's your deal?"

Aidan stiffened. "Nothing."

"Well, you're acting like you have a deal."

"You are," Jerry said.

"I don't have a deal," Aidan said. "I'm just surprised that you automatically believe that woman was his sister. He could be lying."

"I'm not," Griffin said. "Maya is my sister. She's been my sister for, oh, twenty-six years now."

"And I'm sure you have proof of that?"

"Are you asking whether I have her birth certificate in my wallet?" Griffin challenged.

"That would be helpful."

"I don't," Griffin said.

Aidan shot me a triumphant smile.

"However, when I told Maya about Aisling – which was before she ran out of the diner yesterday, mind you – she insisted on all of us getting together for dinner," he said.

I faltered. "She did?"

"She wants to meet you," Griffin said, smiling as Jerry slid a heaping plateful of food in front of him. "This smells wonderful."

"I aim to please."

"And you do," Griffin said, forking a bite into his mouth. "This is great. I can't believe you're all not fat with food like this."

"We go to the gym a lot," Jerry explained.

"I don't," I said.

"Aisling doesn't," Jerry corrected. "She just has one of those metabolisms that allow her to eat a horse and not have it land on her hips."

Griffin smirked.

I was still dwelling on the dinner bombshell. "What did you tell her?"

"What did I tell who?"

"Your sister," I said.

"I told her we would have dinner with her," Griffin said, pouring more syrup on his pancakes, seemingly oblivious to my newfound panic. "It was right before I got my assignment. I figure we can pick out a time and get together in the next few days."

"But … ."

"What's the problem? I've had dinner with your family," Griffin pointed out. "I've had breakfast with them, too. Your family is a lot more hostile to me than Maya will be to you."

"People don't like me," I said.

Griffin frowned.

"Especially other women," I added. "I think it's because I was raised with men. I don't have proper social skills with women."

Aidan snorted. "She's not lying about other women not liking her. I can't think of one friend she's ever had who was female."

"She didn't need female friends," Jerry said. "She had me."

"I'm sure it will be fine." Griffin wasn't ruffled.

"But … she saw me freak out in that restaurant yesterday," I said. My mind was whirling with scenarios. Had Maya laughed when Griffin explained the situation? Did she think I was pathetic? More importantly, how had my hair looked? I searched my memory.

"So? I told her what I thought was wrong. She understood. She didn't understand Aidan's little fit, but she understood why you ran out."

"Little fit?" Aidan glared at Griffin. "Little fit? Standing up for my sister is not a 'little fit.'"

"Do you have something you want to say to me?" Griffin asked pointedly. "If you do, I really wish you'd just say it."

"Fine," Aidan said, leaning forward.

"Aidan," I warned.

"It's fine," Griffin said, waving off my concerns. "I want to hear what he has to say."

I wasn't convinced, but Aidan wasn't going to be dissuaded.

"The first time we met you, I'm not going to lie, I didn't like you on sight," Aidan said. "You were a cop, and where we come from you don't hang around with cops. Still, you seemed to genuinely care about my sister."

"I do."

"Then you had sex with her and bolted the next morning," Aidan continued. "When you showed back up, you were all business and you didn't even apologize."

"I did apologize," Griffin said. "I was just confused. It was a lot to take in."

Aidan blew an inelegant raspberry. "I actually thought you might be a decent choice for her, but then you took off for two weeks and couldn't even bother to call her," he said. "You abandoned her."

"I couldn't call her where I was," Griffin said. "I was … being watched … every day."

"And what were you doing every night?"

"Wishing I could call her and missing her," Griffin replied, guileless.

Aidan's face shifted, if only marginally.

"The only time I was alone was the middle of the night," Griffin said. "I thought about calling her, but I didn't want to wake her. Did I make the wrong decision? I'm starting to think so. Waking her would have been better than letting her suffer. I didn't realize that's what I was doing. The assignment was supposed to take only a couple of days."

"Still .... ." Aidan wasn't ready to admit defeat. "You should have called her the minute your assignment ended."

"I thought she was at work," Griffin said. "I was planning to go home, take a nap and then surprise her last night. What else have you got?"

Aidan's jaw worked, but no sound came out.

"I don't think he has anything else," Jerry said, rubbing Aidan's shoulders to soothe him.

"Good," Griffin said, returning his attention to his pancakes. "These are really outstanding."

"What should I wear?" I asked.

Griffin slid his eyes in my direction. "For what?"

"For dinner," I snapped. "What kind of outfit will make your sister like me?"

Griffin barked out a coarse laugh. He leaned over and cupped the back of my head and gave me a quick kiss. "I love that your mind can handle only one thought at a time. I find it very ... refreshing."

"That wasn't an answer."

"We'll go shopping, Bug," Jerry said. "I've been dying to update your wardrobe. We'll donate all those Converse shoes to Goodwill."

"Don't you dare touch those shoes," I growled.

"See, her mind does work when it wants to," Jerry teased. Aidan was still pouting in his chair, so Jerry opted to continue engaging me in morning conversation. "What are your plans today? We could go shopping this afternoon."

"We have four names," I said, reaching for the iPad on the baker's rack. "I'm not sure how long it will take. I'll try to be quick."

"Can't you and Aidan split the list?" Jerry asked. "We're going to need a few hours. You need a pedicure, too."

I thought I'd just been insulted. "Hey!"

"You're a beautiful girl, Bug, but your feet look like claws sometimes."

Griffin smirked. "I think her feet are cute."

"Thank you," I said. I glanced at Aidan. "Can we split the list today? Is there anything bad on it?" Technically, I was still in training. Once I passed my father's rigorous final test I would be on my own every day.

Aidan sighed as he took the iPad from me. After perusing the four names, he shook his head. "There's nothing on here that looks too hard. We can split them."

"Yay!" Jerry clapped his hands and jumped up and down.

"Is that safe?" Griffin asked. "I'd much rather envision Aisling shopping all afternoon than whatever it is that you guys usually do, but I'd also rather she have backup if she needs it."

"She'll be fine," Aidan said. "She's capable of collecting a soul on her own."

"Yes, but what about the ... ?"

"We haven't seen any wraiths since the incident at the cemetery," Aidan said. "I think they fled after Genevieve died."

Genevieve Toth was a centuries-old witch who had lived off the essence of innocents. She'd employed wraiths – fallen human beings who prolonged their lives by sucking souls from others – to do her dirty work. Detroit, with its many abandoned homes, provided a great hiding place for them.

After a bloody showdown, one that ended with my father killing Genevieve, the wraiths that remained had scattered. I couldn't help but be a little relieved.

"That's good, right?" Griffin pressed.

"It is," I said.

"Good," Griffin said, clasping my hand. "I'd hate to think about you running into trouble."

"Oh, don't worry, most of the time collecting souls is really boring," I said. "The guy we got yesterday was more worried about leaving his stuff behind than anything else."

"I told you he was a hoarder," Aidan said, his eyes flashing.

"I don't think he was technically a hoarder," I said. "It was more that he simply liked to collect stuff."

"Oh, jeez," Aidan complained. "Now that Detective Dinglefritz is back and you're fornicating like bunnies you're back to believing you're never wrong."

I grinned. "I never am."

"Of course you're not, baby," Griffin said, shooting a smug look in Aidan's direction. "No woman ever is."

5

FIVE

I parked my car a block from my second client's apartment building and killed the engine. I had a half hour to burn before he expired, and rather than returning home I opted to wait it out with my iPad.

What a difference twenty-four hours makes. At this time yesterday I was cursing Griffin's existence and crawling into bed to sleep my pain away. Today I was trying to finish work early so I could go shopping with Jerry – a terrifying extravaganza no matter what we're looking for – and I was actually basking in Griffin's return.

I had no idea how it had happened but somehow I'd become … a woman. I couldn't help but wonder if that meant I would start crying at those sappy Christmas commercials.

My phone rang. The screen told me it was my father. Uh-oh. "Hey, Dad."

"Where are you?"

"It's good to hear your voice, too."

There was a momentary silence. I could practically see him rolling his eyes and collecting himself. Cormack Grimlock had raised five children. Four were boys, and he understood how to deal with them. There were fist bumps, high fives and the occasional screaming throwdowns. He tried to take a different approach with me. It didn't always work.

"I'm sorry," he said. "How are you, my beloved daughter?"

"I'm great, thanks. How are you?"

"I'm just peachy, light of my life," he said. He sounded as though he was gritting his teeth.

"Well, I'm so happy to hear that," I said, refusing to give him an out. "What do you think about this weather we're having?"

"I love this time of year," Dad replied mechanically. "Summer is great. Who doesn't love summer?"

"Technically, it's still spring," I said. "It won't be summer for another two weeks."

"Are you trying to kill me?"

"Is it working?"

"You're the reason my hair is going gray. You know that, right?"

My father still had a full head of black hair. Sure, he was graying at the temples, but it only made him look more distinguished. He blamed all of us for his gray hair whenever we gave him cause to yell. I was used to it. "I thought Aidan was the reason you were going gray."

"That was last week."

"It was Redmond the week before," I pointed out.

"And I'm sure it will be Braden and Cillian before the week is out," Dad said. "You're the one doing it right now."

I sighed. "Fine. What's going on?"

"Where are you?"

"I'm in Detroit," I said. "I'm waiting for Morgan Reid to die so I can go up and collect his soul."

"And where is Aidan?"

I faltered. If I admitted the truth, would I be throwing Aidan under Dad's bus? "He's … um … staking the place out."

"Huh."

"He is."

"I just got a call that Aidan has a flat on I-94," Dad said. "Do you want to change your statement?"

"Am I under oath, judge?" I teased.

"Aisling," he growled.

"Fine," I grumbled. "We split the list."

"He told me. I just wanted to ask you why you think it's okay to go out on your own when you're still a trainee."

Oh, good, he was in serious mode today. "They're both nothing," I said. "I already got the guy at the retirement community. This Morgan Reid guy is just a normal guy who is going to die of … ." I scanned the file. "A knife to the chest." Crap. I should have read the file closer. He has a fit when I'm not properly prepared.

"You stay in that car until you're sure that whoever kills him is gone," Dad ordered. "Then you scamper your butt up there, suck his soul without any conversation … I mean it, young lady … and then you scamper right back out of there."

"There's going to be a lot of scampering going on."

"I'm not joking," Dad said. "The last thing we need is police involvement."

"Oh, crap," I mused. "I wonder if this will be Griffin's case?"

"Yes, and we're going to have a talk about him later, too."

I scowled. "What did Aidan tell you?"

"He told me everything."

Somehow I doubted that. "You know he has a grudge where Griffin is concerned, right?"

"I do know that," Dad said. "I just don't think you realize why he's holding that grudge."

"What do you mean?"

"It's not my business."

"Since when?"

"This is between you and your brother," Dad said. "I learned a long time ago that you two need to work your issues out on your own. You've got a … unique … relationship. I think it's because you're twins.

"Personally, it frightens me how co-dependent you two are," he continued. "Your mother convinced me to let you two handle certain things on your own, though, and this is one of those things."

"Fine."

"Good."

"Great."

"What are you going to do, Aisling?" Dad wasn't about to let me off the phone until I placated him, so I played the game. When I recited his instructions back to him he sounded marginally better. "Okay. Call me if you have any problems."

"I definitely will."

"Aisling?"

"Yeah?"

"I do love you."

His words warmed me. "I love you, too."

"You're still my least favorite child right now."

I scowled. "Thanks."

"Text me when you're done," Dad said. "I won't be able to relax until I know you're out of there."

"Yes, sir."

"I know you're rolling your eyes."

He always did. "Bye, Dad."

"Bye."

I WAITED FIVE MINUTES AFTER THE TIME NOTED IN THE FILE AND then exited my car. Morgan Reid lived on the fifth floor. I could take the elevator, and run the risk of being caught on a security camera, or climb the five floors to his apartment.

I seriously considered the elevator. Since this was a murder scene, though, I finally broke down and started climbing the stairs. Four excruciating minutes later, I exited the stairwell and scanned the hallway.

It was the middle of the day, so everything was quiet. I strode down the hallway and paused outside Reid's apartment, pressing my ear to the door. I couldn't hear anything. That must mean he was dead.

I pulled the universal skeleton key from my pocket. We're all assigned them when we join the team. I pressed it into the lock. The keys are magically imbued – and no, I don't know who does it; they just appear. I started to push the door open.

When I realized the door was opening much too quickly, I jerked the key back and jammed it into my pocket. I was ready to run. This had to be the murderer.

The face that appeared in the doorway, surprise washing over his handsome features, didn't look like a murderer. In fact, he looked like my victim. Crap. Morgan Reid was still alive. How was that possible?

"Can I help you?"

I had no idea what to do. Lying seemed my best option. "I'm sorry, are you Mike Morrison?"

Reid shook his head. I could feel his eyes moving over my body, and he exuded a predatory sexual nature. "Unfortunately, I'm not."

"Oh, no," I said, biting my lower lip and giving into the performance. "I must have the wrong apartment. I could swear he told me it was five-fifteen."

Reid pointed at his door. "I live in five-fifteen."

"Do you have a roommate?"

"No." The dimple on Reid's cheek came out to play as he studied me. "Why are you looking for this Mike Morrison?"

"Oh … he had an ad on Craig's List. I answered it."

Reid's smile widened. "What kind of ad?"

I realized what he was asking. What a sick pervert. "He's selling a couch."

Reid's face fell. "Oh, that's too bad. You look like … fun."

I shot him a look. I could see why someone was about to murder him. "Well, I guess I got the wrong address. I should be going."

Reid reached out and snagged my arm. "Wait … ."

I jerked it away. "I'm on a tight schedule today." I had to call my brother and figure out what was going on.

"Why don't you come in?" Reid offered. "I could make some coffee or something."

"Sorry, I can't." I started moving down the hallway, my mind busy. I avoided the elevator again, out of habit, and plunged into the stairwell. I could feel Reid's eyes on my back during the short trek. I already had my cellphone out of my pocket by the time I hit the front steps of the apartment building.

"Hello."

"Redmond?"

"Who else would answer my cellphone?"

In some ways, my relationship with Aidan is the closest familial tie I have. In others, it's my relationship with Redmond that stands out. As the eldest brother, he takes his responsibilities seriously. His responsibilities often involve protecting his four younger siblings. When it comes to me, he is especially intense.

"Something happened," I said, pacing in front of a tall elm tree in the courtyard.

"What? Did Detective Dinglefritz hurt you?"

"No! What has Aidan been telling you?"

"He told us what happened yesterday," Redmond said, his voice even. "I don't happen to believe that he's lying. I think he really likes you. That doesn't mean I want him … touching you. It's gross."

"Thanks. It's always good to hear that I'm gross."

"I didn't say you were gross."

"Are you saying he's gross?"

"I'm saying the things you two do together are gross," Redmond said. "I'm your brother. I don't like thinking of things like that. Sue me."

"Maybe later. I have a different problem right now."

"Hit me."

I laid out my afternoon. When I was done, Redmond was as confused as I was. "Wait, he's not dead?"

"No, he hit on me. Speaking of gross, he thought I was answering a Craig's List ad for … well, you know."

"Oh, well, maybe I'm the one who is supposed to kill him," Redmond mused. "Sick piece of … ."

"Redmond!"

"What?"

"What should I do?"

"I don't know," he said.

That wasn't the answer I expected. Sure, maybe there was some hero worship involved, but Redmond always had answers. "You don't know?"

"I'm equally stunned," he said. "I just … where are you?"

I told him the address.

"Okay," he said. "Stay in your car. I'll be there in a few minutes. I'll call Dad."

"Tell him I followed every single rule," I said.

"He's not going to be angry, Ais."

"He's always angry with me. He says I'm his least favorite child."

"You were his favorite last week," Redmond replied. "That wheel never stops turning. I'm on my way. Just … don't do anything until I get there."

"Okay," I said. "Redmond?"

"Yeah?"

"Thank you for coming."

"Kid, I'll always come for you," he said. "Never, ever doubt that. I'll be there in ten minutes."

"Okay, I'll just wait in my … ." The sound of a scream in the nearby alley stopped my sentence. It sounded like someone was dying. Maybe Reid was just running late. "Wait. I hear someone screaming. I think he's in the alley, though. Maybe the file changed and the update just hasn't come through."

"Don't go there, Aisling," Redmond warned.

"I'll be quick," I said. "I have a shopping date with Jerry. Don't worry. It will be fine."

I disconnected the phone, but not before I heard one more outburst from Redmond. "Aisling, don't you dare go into that alley! You have no idea what is down there!"

It would be fine. My day was about to get back on track.

I had no idea how wrong I was about to be.

6

SIX

By the time I hit the alley, the screams had subsided. There was, however, another noise. It took me a moment to realize what I was hearing, but when I did I was horrified. The person who screamed wasn't dead. Not yet. Someone was gasping for air, and the ragged and wet sounds coming from the man's chest were horrifying.

I couldn't stop myself from trying to help. It wasn't my job, but there was so much blood, and the dark eyes of the man on the ground were terrified. I knew there was nothing I could do – and one glance at the prone figure told me this was not Morgan Reid – but I did what I could.

"I … just hold on." I pressed my hands over the gushing wound. He was losing a lot of blood. I realized, with both of my hands busy, I couldn't call 911. My father was going to have an outright fit when he heard what I'd done, but it was too late. I was in this.

I glanced over my shoulder, my gaze landing on a young woman peering down the alley. She must have heard the screams, too. She was too frightened to investigate, though.

"Hey, I need you to call for help," I said.

The woman just looked at me.

"Do you speak English?"

After a moment of staring, her blue eyes focusing on my blood-covered hands, she finally opened her mouth. "Y-yes."

"Call 911. Tell them we have a victim who has been stabbed, and he's losing a lot of blood." I shifted so I could meet the man's glistening eyes. "What is your name?"

"Grant," he rasped. "Grant Spencer."

There was blood at the corner of his lips. I knew that wasn't a good sign. It signified internal injuries. "Mr. Spencer, do you know who did this to you?"

His eyes were starting to go glassy and his breathing was more ragged. I'd seen enough death to know the truth: It wouldn't be long now.

"I … it didn't look like a man."

I frowned. "What do you mean?"

"It was tall. It was wearing some black cape thing. It was white … except for the claws."

My heart rolled. He was describing a wraith. "Did it say anything to you?"

"No."

"Did it … try to take anything out of you?" There was no graceful way to ask the question. How do you ask a dying man if a big, scary monster tried to suck his soul out?

"I don't know." Grant's eyes were sliding shut.

"Good journey," I murmured. I pulled the scepter from my pocket and held it ready. The second his soul started to detach from his body, the familiar shimmering edges tugging away from the solid form of a discarded husk, I absorbed it and shoved the scepter back inside my pocket so it was hidden away.

I would have preferred more time to talk to Grant, but emergency personnel were on their way. That meant the police were on their way, too. I didn't have time to sit around conversing with a displaced soul.

I forced myself to a standing position and studied my bloody hands. You wouldn't think someone who is trained to deal with death would be traumatized by the act of dying, but I was. When I turned to face the end of the alley, I found the woman was back and staring at me.

"Did you make the call?"

She nodded. "Is he … ?"

"Yeah," I said. "He's dead."

GRIFFIN LOOKED AS THOUGH HE WANTED TO THROTTLE ME. I suppose it was a foregone conclusion that he would be the one called to the scene. My luck is almost always bad. Still, I knew his reaction was going to be a cakewalk compared to the verbal smackdown my father was going to lay on me later.

"So, I need to know what you were doing here."

The woman asking the question was a new face. She'd exited the same vehicle with Griffin. Since he usually worked alone I was surprised by her appearance. It didn't help that she had long auburn hair, legs that went on for miles and she kept smiling at Griffin as if he were the hottest man ever born. I didn't like her. What? I'm not jealous.

"I was just in the area," I said, searching for an alibi. "I'm supposed to be meeting my brother for lunch. I was sitting in my car fiddling with my iPad when I heard a scream."

Griffin rolled his eyes.

"Where were you going to have lunch?"

I frowned. I had no idea what restaurants were in this area. "We were going to decide when he got here, Officer … ?"

"Detective Andrea Black," the woman supplied.

"Detective?" I shot Griffin a narrow-eyed look.

He sighed. "We can't interview her."

Andrea's shoulders hopped. "Why?"

"Because she's … my girlfriend."

His admission stunned me. He'd never referred to me that way before.

Andrea looked me up and down. "This is your girlfriend?"

"For now," Griffin said pointedly. "We can't interview her, though. It's a conflict of interest."

"That's only if she's a suspect," Andrea pointed out. "And, as long as I do the interviewing, I'm not sure what the problem is?"

I waited for Griffin's response.

"I … ."

"Do you think your girlfriend killed him?"

"No," Griffin protested.

"Then what's the problem?"

Griffin shifted uncomfortably, his dark eyes flicking over me as he considered the question. "I guess there's not a problem."

"Good," Andrea said. "So, what is your full name?"

"Aisling Grimlock."

"What's your middle name?"

"That's top secret." I hate my middle name.

Griffin made a face. "It's Agnes."

"Who told you that?" I was going on a brother hunt as soon as I was cut loose from this crime scene.

"Your birth certificate," he said dryly.

"Oh. I need to get that thing amended."

"Is there something wrong with the name Agnes?" Andrea asked, her green eyes flashing.

"Yes, it sucks."

Griffin bit his bottom lip and rubbed his hand through his hair. "Just answer the questions."

"You're very crabby," I said.

"You found a dead body in an alley," he countered. "Again."

"I have horrible luck. I'm really a victim in all of this."

Griffin reached to grab my arm. I was sure he was going to shake me. A shared look with Andrea had him retracting his fingers.

"So, you were just waiting for your brother to arrive?" Andrea pressed. "Why did you agree to meet here?"

That was a very good question. "I have a bad sense of direction," I replied. "My brothers say I can't find my way out of a paper bag. I got lost and had to call my brother with my location. He's coming to find me."

"How many brothers do you have?"

"And which one is coming?" Griffin asked.

"I have four brothers," I said. "And Redmond is coming."

"Oh, good grief," Griffin muttered. "Is he going to be all … ?"

"All what?" Redmond stepped up on the curb behind Griffin.

"Oh, good, you're here," Griffin grumbled.

"And you're the brother?" Andrea asked.

"I am." Redmond sent Andrea a devilish grin. All of my brothers are attractive, and they're all willing to flirt with a woman to get her on their side. Redmond was no exception, and since he was the oldest he had the most practice. "And who are you?"

"This is Detective Andrea Black," I said. "She's … with Griffin."

"She's my new partner," Griffin corrected.

"How new?"

"Today is her first day," Griffin said. He wagged his finger in my face. "And don't go there. You're the one in trouble today."

"She can't be a police officer," Redmond said, smiling. "She's too lovely to be a police officer."

Andrea's face flushed, a mixture of embarrassment and pleasure riding high on her sculpted cheekbones.

Griffin scowled. "You people are unbelievable."

"Mr. Grimlock, can you tell me why you were meeting your sister here?"

Redmond's smile remained in place. "She gets lost a lot," he said. "She has a negative sense of direction. She couldn't find her way out of a paper bag."

"That's exactly what she said," Andrea said.

"Go figure," Griffin said.

"What's your glitch?" Redmond asked, fixing Griffin with a dark look.

"I'm pretty sure it's your sister."

"You should thank your lucky stars she deigns to date you," Redmond shot back.

"Yes, that's just what I was thinking."

"My sister is a catch."

"I didn't say she wasn't," Griffin said. "I'm just considering whether I want to throw her back." I stilled, his words hitting home. His face softened when he saw the change in my demeanor. "I'm just joking," he said.

"You shouldn't joke about things like that," Andrea said. "It's not nice."

"It's definitely not," Redmond agreed. "See, your new partner has beauty and brains."

"You were supposed to be shopping with Jerry," Griffin grumbled.

"I'm supposed to meet him in an hour."

"She had a date with another man?" Andrea was confused.

"Jerry is her roommate."

"And that doesn't bother you?"

"No," Griffin said. "Jerry is in a relationship with … ."

"Our brother," Redmond supplied.

"Oh," Andrea said. "That's very progressive."

"And annoying," I interjected.

"Okay, we need to get back on track," Griffin said. "This whole thing is giving me a headache."

"Welcome to my world," Redmond said. "Aisling could be a walking advertisement for aspirin."

"Hey!"

"Detective Taylor is right," Andrea said. "I just have a few more questions. Witnesses have already reported that you didn't start down the alleyway until you heard the screams, so you're not a suspect."

"Thankfully," Griffin muttered.

I ignored him. "He was already on the ground when I got there. There was another girl … ." I searched the crowd and pointed when I caught sight of her. "I asked her to call 911, and I just kind of … sat with him."

"Was he conscious?"

"Yes."

"What did you do?"

I stared down at my hands a moment. After the crime scene team collected forensic evidence I'd been allowed to wipe them off. There were still streaks of dried blood, though. "I tried to stop the bleeding. I knew it was too late, but … I didn't know what else to do."

"You did the right thing," Andrea said, her tone gentle. "Did he say anything?"

"I asked his name," I replied. "He said it was Grant Spencer."

"Did he say who attacked him?"

"No," I lied. "He seemed confused. He … just kind of died."

Redmond reached over and pulled me close. "That must have been horrible."

"It was."

Griffin studied us both for a moment, but remained silent.

"Well, I think that's all we need," Andrea said. "I'm sure if I have further questions Detective Taylor has your number."

"I do," Griffin said. "I'm just going to walk Aisling to her car. I'll be back in a minute."

"I'll stay and talk to Detective Black," Redmond said.

"Oh, no you won't," Griffin said, grabbing Redmond's elbow. "You two have a lunch to get to."

Redmond scowled, but he let Griffin lead us across the street. Once we were out of earshot, Griffin unleashed a string of curses that would have made my father proud on a poor golf day. "What really happened?"

"Just what I said."

"Was he on your list?"

I shook my head.

"So, why did he die?"

"I have no idea," I said.

"Whatever happened, it screwed up the list," Redmond said. "Spencer wasn't supposed to die, and the guy who was supposed to die here is still alive. We don't know what's going on. We have to talk with Dad."

"He's going to kill me."

"He is," Redmond agreed. "He says he gave you very specific instructions."

"Well, I guess I'm going to remain his least favorite child for the foreseeable future."

Redmond smirked. "He still spoils you rotten. You'll survive."

"Am I to assume you'll be at Grimlock Manor this evening?" Griffin asked, his face unreadable.

"I don't see how I have much of a choice," I said.

"Okay," Griffin said, glancing over his shoulder to take in the scene again. "I'll find you there later." He gave me a quick kiss, despite the eye daggers Redmond was silently shooting him. "Keep her out of trouble," Griffin ordered.

"Oh, yeah, task me with the impossible," Redmond muttered.

"I'm not joking," Griffin said. "I'd like her in one piece. Dating her if she's dead is going to be a problem."

"You could just not date her at all," Redmond suggested.

Griffin gave me a quick hug. "That's not going to happen either," he said. "You need to get over it."

I watched him stride back over to Andrea, a small smile playing at the corner of my lips.

"Oh, you're so mushy," Redmond said. "It's gross."

I pinched his arm. "You're gross."

"No, you're gross."

"You're the grossest."

Redmond slung his arm across my shoulders. "We need to get out of here," he said. "Whatever happened today was a total cluster of crap. We have to figure out what is going on, and how we can fix it."

"I just want to know why it keeps happening to me."

"I think it's karma," Redmond said.

"What?"

"It's because you're so gross."

"You're gross."

"You're both gross," Griffin snapped. He was watching us from across the road, and he didn't look pleased. "Don't you two have somewhere to be?"

I saluted. "Yes, sir."

Griffin fought the urge to smile, and lost. "Go home, please."

"You've got it, Detective Dinglefritz," Redmond said.

Griffin's smile evaporated. "You people drive me crazy. You really do."

7

SEVEN

"I can't believe you're blaming this on me!"

My father was so angry his eyes practically glowed. He sat at his office desk, with my brothers scattered amongst the leather couches in the middle of the room, and he hadn't stopped lambasting me since I walked into the house.

Grimlock Manor isn't really a house. It's more a small castle on Grosse Pointe's Lakeshore Drive. Even in a neighborhood teeming with big houses, Grimlock Manor stands out. It's ostentatious, but beautiful.

My father employs a full-time staff, and all of my brothers have remained under his roof. Of course, that might have something to do with the fact that he high-fives them when they expound on their sexual exploits. He loves to hear about them. On the flip side, he tried to lock me in my room for an entire month when I was eighteen when he caught me making out with a boy in a car. There's a real double standard in the Grimlock house, and it was on full display tonight.

"What were you thinking?"

"I was thinking that my client was running late," I said. "I figured he was the one dying in the alley. In case you forgot, I did manage to collect a soul."

"One that wasn't on the list," Dad pointed out.

"Technically it was on the list," Cillian said, winking at me supportively. "It was just a late addition."

"Yeah, Dad, if you really think about it, Aisling was being overly diligent," Braden offered. "She was a superstar today."

All of my brothers have the same features: strong jaw lines, striking eyes and sly grins. While Redmond and Braden opt to keep their hair at a medium length, Aidan crops his shorter, but Cillian's is longer and flows around his shoulders. Even with the differences in hair length, they're an impressive sight when gathered together. Since they appeared to be trying to take up my cause, I was doubly impressed with them this evening.

My father didn't feel the same way. "Stop making excuses for her."

"I'm not making an excuse," Braden said. "What did you expect her to do?"

"She should have called me."

"Yeah, because that would have gone over well," Redmond said. "I'm sure you wouldn't have yelled at her or anything."

"I don't yell," Dad snapped.

"You always yell," Cillian said.

"Well … that's neither here nor there," Dad sputtered. "She ran into an alleyway, and she could have been hurt."

"She wasn't, though," Redmond pointed out.

"There was a wraith there," Dad said. "What would have happened if she had run into the wraith?"

"She didn't, though," Redmond said, sighing. "She did what any of us would have done. She knew I was on the way. You can't treat her differently because … ."

Dad furrowed his brow. "Because of what?"

"Because I'm a girl," I finished.

Dad sighed. "I'm not treating her differently because she's a girl. She's a trainee."

"Oh, whatever," I scoffed.

"You're on thin ice, young lady."

"Oh, good, I didn't miss the verbal sparring portion of the evening's entertainment." Griffin let himself into the office and headed straight for me. He gave me a quick kiss and hug, and then settled in one of the wingback chairs across from my father's desk. "How much longer are you going to yell at her?"

"Did you just enter my office without knocking?" Dad was flabbergasted. No one did that. Not even his children.

"I heard the yelling from the hallway," Griffin said, nonplussed. "The maid seemed too nervous to knock. I didn't want you to lose your train of thought."

"See, he was being considerate." I was understandably nervous.

"You're trying to distract me," Dad said, shifting his attention back to me. "I want to know what you were thinking when you followed the sound of a scream down a dark alley?"

"It wasn't dark."

"Don't make me ground you," Dad warned.

"I don't live here."

"That won't stop me from grounding you."

Redmond snickered. "He's always wanted to use that dungeon in the basement."

Griffin's eyes lit up with interest. "You have a dungeon here?"

"Yeah, we were all threatened with it when we were kids," Cillian said.

"Can we forget about the dungeon?" Dad snapped. "Well, not you Aisling. You might have to spend the night in there."

"She's got a date tonight," Griffin said. "You can't put her in the dungeon."

I was impressed with his bravado. "I do?"

"You do," Griffin said. "We're having dinner with my sister."

I faltered.

"Oh, look at her," Braden said, grinning. "She's trying to decide whether she'd rather be locked in the dungeon."

"Well, that's not an option," Griffin said. "If I have to eat meals with you people, she's got to eat meals with Maya. I wanted to put it off for a night, but this is the only night Maya has open for the next few days."

"Is Maya hot?" Cillian asked.

"She is," Aidan supplied.

"You all keep your filthy paws off her," Griffin warned. "She's not your type."

"How do you know we have a type?" Redmond asked. "And, besides, we let you put your filthy paws on our sister."

"You let me?"

"We tolerate it."

"Everyone stop talking about filthy paws in conjunction with my daughter," Dad ordered.

"Yeah," Cillian teased. "Make sure you wash your hands before you paw our sister."

"Do you think that's funny?" Dad asked.

"Yes."

"You're the one who is going to be in the dungeon tonight."

Cillian rolled his eyes. "Whatever. Can we get back to business? Aisling apparently has a date, and the rest of us are going to that new sports bar on Woodward. We have to pick up Jerry at seven."

"You're taking Jerry to a sports bar?" That wouldn't end well.

"He'll be fine," Aidan said.

"After the tenth time he's referred to all the butt slaps as foreplay you're going to rethink that statement," I promised.

"Can we please spend five minutes talking about our problem?" Dad exploded. "I don't want to hear another word about dates … or bars … or butt slapping."

"Well, there goes my weekend," Redmond quipped.

"You're going in the dungeon, too," Dad said.

"Well, as enlightening as this conversation has been, I have to agree with Mr. Grimlock," Griffin said.

"Call him Cormack," Cillian suggested, his eyes twinkling.

"Or Dad," Braden interjected.

"Call me Mr. Grimlock," Dad barked. "What did you find out about this Grant Spencer?"

Griffin slid a look in my direction. "Well, he wasn't a good guy. He's a got a record longer than my arm, and it includes pandering, drug dealing and attempted murder."

I swallowed hard. "Are you saying I risked everything to comfort a jerk?"

"I'm sorry," Griffin said, grabbing my hand. "There's no way you could've known."

"There's one way," Aidan said. He was paging through a file on his iPad. "It says here that Morgan Reid was supposed to be murdered by Grant Spencer."

The room fell quiet.

"Well, that explains a few things," Redmond said. "Reid was saved because a wraith happened across his murderer in the alley and killed him. What are the odds of that?"

Griffin shifted. "Wraith? You didn't mention seeing a wraith."

"I didn't see it," I said. "That's what Grant described to me before he died."

"You said he didn't say anything other than his name," Griffin pointed out.

"How was I supposed to give a description of a wraith in front of your new partner?"

"She's hot, by the way," Redmond said. "Is she single?"

"She'd better be a lesbian," I grumbled.

Griffin rolled his eyes, but snagged me around the waist and pulled me down on his lap as he considered the most recent development. "I thought you said all the wraiths left the area?"

Dad's eyes were focused on Griffin and the way he was holding me. It was as if his eyes could not look elsewhere.

"I guess we were wrong," Aidan said. "This is the first time we've heard of any wraith activity since Genevieve died."

"We shouldn't jump to conclusions," Cillian said. "Wraiths have always existed. Just because we have a rogue one now, that doesn't mean it's tied to Genevieve Toth. It could be a coincidence."

"He's right," Braden said. "Genevieve and the wraiths managed to hide in Detroit for so long because of all the abandoned buildings. That's still a legitimate reason for wraiths to be drawn to the area."

"I don't like it," Redmond said. "It seems too coincidental that a wraith showed up at another one of Aisling's assignments."

"He has a point," Aidan said.

"You were supposed to be there," Dad said, his eyes stuck on Griffin's hand as it massaged my hip.

"So now this is my fault?" Aidan challenged.

"It's nobody's fault," Redmond said. "It happened. We couldn't have foreseen it. Now we have to move on with the new information we have. We can't keep going in circles. Did the autopsy on Grant Spencer give you any leads?"

Griffin shook his head. "He was stabbed twice. The first wound was fatal, but someone clearly wanted to make sure he didn't survive."

"Have you found anything out about him besides his record?"

"No," Griffin said. "Technically, Andrea is the lead on this one."

"And she's a lesbian, right?" I prodded.

Griffin kissed the side of my face. "Yes."

"Oh, really? I'm totally bummed," Redmond said.

"Good."

I narrowed my eyes. "He's lying. She's not a lesbian. He's just saying that so you don't hit on her and I don't get jealous. By the way, I am not a jealous person."

All four of my brothers snorted in unison.

"I'm not," I said, crossing my arms over my chest. "I am a very even-tempered and trusting person."

"You thought he was sleeping with his sister yesterday," Cillian said.

"I didn't know she was his sister," I shot back. "There's a difference."

Braden grinned. "You're jealous. Admit it."

"Bite me."

"You bite me."

"All of you can go and … bite yourselves," Dad said, his face grim. "Except you two." His eyes were still fixed on Griffin's hand. "There will be no biting where you two are concerned."

"Ha, ha," Aidan sang.

I flipped him off discreetly.

"I saw that, young lady," Dad said. "Seriously, what are you doing with your hand?"

Griffin's face was blank. "What?"

"Your hand," Dad said, pointing. "Where does it keep going?"

"To her back," Griffin said. "I was just … ."

"Oh, I know what you were doing," Dad said. "You're definitely the one going in the dungeon."

Redmond snickered. "See, Ais, even when you're at the bottom of the list you're still the one he worries about the most."

"That's because she needs to be watched," Dad said. "Someone could take advantage of her … virtue."

"She lost that in high school," Aidan said.

Redmond covered his ears, while Cillian and Braden barked out short laughs.

"You're all going to be the death of me," Dad said.

"Have you ever considered you're going to be the death of us?" I asked.

"No." Dad was all business again. "We need to start investigating this in an orderly fashion. We have to keep an eye on our lists. If Morgan Reid pops up again, I want to be informed the second it happens."

"Does that happen a lot, people falling off and then returning to the list?" Griffin asked.

"No," Dad said. "We don't have enough to go on to look in another direction, though. For now, that's all we have."

"Okay," Griffin said. "I'll keep you in the loop on the Spencer investigation."

"Thank you," Dad said, getting to his feet. "Now, let's eat dinner. I'm starving."

My stomach growled and I realized I'd missed lunch for the second day in a row. "What are we having?"

"You're going to dinner with me," Griffin said. "Did you forget?"

"Of course not." I was hoping he would. "I don't have anything to wear to dinner, though."

"You have a whole closet of clothes upstairs," Aidan said.

I glared in his direction.

"Good," Griffin said. "Why don't you go up and get dressed? You have twenty minutes. I'll wait for you here."

Well, that was it. There was no way out of this. I was officially going to have dinner with Griffin's sister. May the gods have mercy on my poor, tormented soul.

8

EIGHT

"I think my skirt is too short."

"Your skirt is fine."

"No, it's too short. I look like a streetwalker."

Griffin sighed, exasperated. "I happen to like it. I wasn't sure you had legs." He thought he was teasing me, relaxing me, but he was driving me insane.

"What is that supposed to mean? Are you making fun of my Converse?"

"Will you please calm down?" Griffin asked. "You're … unraveling."

We were in his Explorer, sitting in the parking lot of a kitschy restaurant in downtown Ferndale, and I was just about at my wit's end. Dead bodies don't bother me. Absorbing souls doesn't bother me … well, most of the time. Meeting Griffin's sister was almost more than I could bear, though. "She's not going to like me."

"Why do you think that?"

"Women don't like me," I said. "They either look at me as competition or the obstacle standing between them and one of my brothers."

"Well, you won't be in competition with each other and she's not going to date one of your brothers," he said. "It's going to be fine. I've already told her all about you. She thinks you sound fascinating."

"You've told her all about me? All?"

"Not all," Griffin clarified. "Your family's secret is safe with me. I told you that."

"What did you tell her I do for a living?"

"I went with your antiquities lie," he replied. "That seemed as good an answer as anything else – and it's kind of true."

"And she's a nurse, right?"

"Yes."

I chewed on my lower lip as I stared out the window. "She's not going to like me."

Griffin growled. "Okay, we're done with the self-pity, Aisling," he said, throwing open the driver's side door. "Get out and get moving."

"I'll just wait here."

"No, you won't."

"But … ."

"Get out now."

I was out of options. I reluctantly pushed open the door and jumped out, smoothing my black skirt and glaring down at my uncomfortable heels as I shuffled them against the pavement. Griffin kept one eye on me – in case I ran – and another on the parking meter as he fed coins into it.

After a few moments, I realized I was still standing by myself, and when I lifted my head I found him watching me with a curious look on his face. "What?"

"Nothing," he said. "I've just never seen you like this before. I'm not sure how I feel about it."

"What do you mean?"

"You're usually pretty sure of yourself," Griffin said. "That's one of the things that drives me nuts about you, but it's also one of the things I really like about you. I just don't understand why this is such a big deal."

I narrowed my eyes. "Really? Are you just saying that or are you playing a game?"

"I'm really at a loss."

"Fine, I'll lay it out for you," I said. "If your sister doesn't like me, it's only a matter of time until you dump me."

Griffin moved his jaw, opening and closing it, but no sound came out.

"That's what I'm worried about," I said.

"Baby, I don't know where you would get an idea like that," Griffin said. "It's not true, though. First, I think Maya is going to like you. Do I think you're going to be best friends? No. Your life is far too … chaotic … for her to fit into it.

"Whether Maya likes you or not, though, it won't change how I feel about you," he continued. "I don't understand why you think it would."

I faltered. "Because that's how it works in my family."

"Really? None of your brothers like me and you haven't dumped me," he said. "Or is that just what's going to happen down the road?"

"Of course not," I scoffed. "I don't care what my brothers think. They're never going to like anyone I date. That's a brother thing. It's different with sisters."

"I'm still confused."

"When a sister doesn't like her brother's girlfriend, she keeps whispering in his ear until he dumps her," Aisling said.

"Have you done that with your brothers?"

"Of course."

Griffin pursed his lips. "How many of your brothers' relationships have you torpedoed?"

"All of them."

"Have you ever liked any of the women your brothers have dated?"

I searched my memory. "Two or three."

"And yet they're not still around," Griffin pressed. "Has it ever occurred to you that your brothers just aren't ready to settle down?"

"I … ." Huh.

"Yeah, here's the thing, Aisling; when you really like someone it doesn't matter what anyone else thinks," Griffin said. "I happen to really like you. You drive me crazy, and I think most of your family should be committed, but I'm still fairly attached to you.

"When it comes down to it, I don't care what my sister thinks, and I don't care what my mother thinks – and you are eventually going to have to meet her, too," he continued. "I also don't care what your father thinks or what your brothers think. I wasn't aware they were part of this relationship."

"They're not," I hedged. "I just … ." I didn't know what to say. Anything I added to the conversation now would just make me sound pathetic.

"You're nervous," Griffin said. "I get it. You're not going in there alone, though."

"I know."

Griffin held out his hand. "Come on. I promise this is going to be okay."

I sucked in a deep breath and nodded, lacing my fingers with his and letting him lead me inside. The good news is, nothing could be worse than his first meal with my family. We'd already hit rock bottom.

"SO, YOU'RE THE FAMOUS AISLING. I CAN'T TELL YOU HOW GLAD I AM to finally meet you."

I extended my hand and shook Maya's, forcing a bright smile onto my face. Maya was already seated by the time we arrived, and the waitress immediately took our drink orders. I needed some bourbon and I needed it now. "Famous? I'm not sure how to take that."

Maya's eyes were thoughtful as they studied me. "You're the first woman Griffin has brought home in … forever."

"Forever?"

"I can't remember the last time I met a girlfriend of his actually," Maya said. "I'm sure he's had a few over the years, but you're the only one he's mentioned. In fact, when he started talking about you I was surprised. I figured he was a bachelor for life."

Griffin shifted uncomfortably. "Can we not harp on this? Aisling is nervous enough as it is."

"You were nervous to meet me?" Maya asked, tickled. "Why?"

"I just … ."

"Aisling's family runs a little differently than ours," Griffin explained. "She's never been to a civil meal before. She didn't know they existed."

Maya giggled. "Is that so? I heard you have a really big family. Four brothers, right?"

"Yes."

"Younger? Older?"

"Three older."

"And one younger?"

"Isn't Aidan technically older than you?" Griffin pressed.

"We're twins."

"He was still born first."

"Oh, you have a twin brother," Maya said. "That's so cool. What was that like growing up?"

"Co-dependent," I replied honestly.

Maya was confused. "What do you mean?"

"I mean that we're probably a little too attached to one another," I said. "We … don't have a lot of boundaries."

Griffin snorted. "That's putting it mildly, and none of your brothers have boundaries."

"Well, wait. Aisling was the youngest," Maya said, trying to be helpful. "I can see how her brothers would be overprotective."

"They're militant," Griffin said.

"Oh, are they being mean to you?" Maya pinched Griffin's cheek, mocking him. It was the first time I'd seen hints of closeness between them. It was kind of cute.

"They're not mean to me."

Maya looked to me for confirmation.

"They're mean to him," I said. "They don't really mean to be. We're kind of all mean to each other. It just comes naturally to us."

"Oh, do you fight a lot?"

"We … spar."

"Their dad has a dungeon he threatens to put them in when they mouth off," Griffin said. "I just found that out tonight. I want to see that dungeon, by the way."

"You're not missing much," I said. "It's just a locked room in the basement. Redmond lobbied to move down there when he was a teenager, but I think it was because he wanted to smoke pot and bring girls home without getting caught."

"I'm sorry, how do you have a dungeon in a house?" Maya asked.

"It's not a house," Griffin said. "It's a castle."

"Castle?"

"It's one of those big mansions on Lakeshore Drive," he explained. "It looks like a castle."

"That's so cool," Maya said. "Did you pretend to be a princess when you were little?"

"No, I was always the knight," I said. "My friend Jerry was the princess."

Griffin snickered. "Please tell me he wore a tiara."

"My mother had one left over from her beauty queen days."

Griffin stilled, focusing on me for a second. "Your mother was a beauty queen?"

"She was." I was never going to live this down.

"Oh, did she put you in pageants when you were in high school?" Maya asked.

"Um … ."

"Ow! What did you do that for?" Maya rubbed her shin under the table. "Why did you kick me?"

"It was an accident," Griffin said.

"No, it wasn't."

"He didn't want you to mention my mother," I supplied.

"Oh, I'm sorry," Maya said. "I didn't realize it was a sore subject."

"It's not," I said. "My mother died when I was in high school. We just don't … talk about it a lot."

"That's horrible," Maya said. "I didn't know."

"It's okay," I said. "It's not a big deal. And, no, she didn't put me in pageants before she died. I think she knew that wasn't my thing."

"How did she die?"

"Maya," Griffin warned.

"It's okay," I said, waving off his concerns. "She died in a fire."

"That must have been so hard for you," Maya said. "I mean, you were clearly outnumbered by all of the boys in your family, and then to lose your mother … ."

"I consider myself lucky to have known her for as long as I did," I replied truthfully. "And it's not like I was alone after she died. I'm very close with my father and brothers, and … well … I'm a firm believer that things work out how they're meant to."

"That's a healthy way to look at things," Maya said. "Griffin didn't do you justice when he described you, by the way. He said you were pretty, but you're really … exquisite."

My cheeks started to burn. "I don't think that's the right word."

"It is," Maya said. "Your hair is gorgeous, and I like the white streaks. They really make you stand out. Your eyes, though, they're just amazing."

"Those run in the family," I said.

"Oh, does everyone in your family have them?"

I nodded.

"They all look alike," Griffin said. "It's freaky."

"Well, I hope to meet them some day," Maya said. "I have to say, you're nothing like Angelina described."

I froze, my glass of water pressed to my lips. "Angelina?"

"Angelina Davenport," Maya said. "We take a yoga class together once a week. When Griffin mentioned your name, I happened to mention it to her and she said the two of you graduated together."

"We did," I said carefully.

"Why does that name sound familiar?" Griffin asked.

"Um … well … do you remember the night that Jerry, Aidan and I were arrested for the brawl at the gay club?"

Griffin chuckled. "Yeah. That's the morning I realized I couldn't get enough of you. You were so … feisty. You kept going after that woman in the lobby … what was her name?"

I pursed my lips. "Angelina Davenport."

"Oh."

Maya's face was conflicted. "You were arrested for fighting with Angelina?"

"No, I was arrested for kicking her ass," I corrected.

Angelina Davenport was my mortal enemy. No, I'm not being dramatic. She'd tortured me in high school, constantly making fun of my hoodies and Converse, and then she'd gone after Cillian the minute she developed boobs. After dating her for a few months, despite the nasty insults I hurled at her whenever she was in our house, Cillian discovered she was cheating on him and dumped her.

Angelina had spent the intervening years trying to get Cillian back. Since I loved my brother, that forced me to beat the crap out of her every chance I got. What? No one hurts a member of my family, especially a guttersnipe like Angelina Davenport. "So, what did Angelina say about me?"

"She said you were … spirited," Maya said.

"I'm betting she used more colorful language than that," I pressed. "I've ripped entire chunks of her hair out at one time or another, and I once cut a big hole in the seat of her jeans during gym and she walked around for an hour with her ass hanging out until someone finally told her."

"She said you were an evil bitch and that I should get my brother away from you as soon as possible," Maya admitted. "I wanted to meet you for myself to see if that was true. The stories she told me were … troubling."

"And?"

"I haven't decided yet," Maya said.

That seemed fair.

Griffin grabbed my hand. "It doesn't matter," he said. "We're not having this discussion again. I've met Angelina Davenport, and she's a horrible person. I don't care what she says about Aisling."

"I didn't mean anything by it," Maya protested.

"Well, then you shouldn't have brought it up."

"It's fine," I said. "I can guess the things Angelina said about me. I'd like to say it all stems from her breakup with Cillian, but it started long before then. We've hated each other since we laid eyes on each other in middle school."

"May I ask why?" Maya asked.

"She used to terrorize my friend Jerry," I said. "She made fun of him for being … different."

"Because he's gay?"

I nodded. "She went after Aidan in high school, too. There's really no love lost between us. I hate her."

"Well, at least you're honest," Maya said. "She's been really nice to me, though."

"Was that before or after she found out you were Griffin's sister?"

"What does that matter?"

"Just wait."

"I'm not sure I like what you're insinuating," Maya said. "Angelina is a friend of mine. I'm loyal to my friends."

"Then you're going to have to learn the hard way," I said. "And you will."

Griffin rubbed his forehead and sighed. I couldn't tell what he was thinking, but it couldn't be good. "Where is that waitress with our drinks?" he asked.

Where indeed?

9

NINE

"Are you going to say anything?"

"Nope." I inserted the key into the lock and pushed open the door of the townhouse.

Griffin followed me inside, contemplative. "Are you sure?"

"There's nothing to say," I said, shrugging out of my coat. "It went pretty much as I expected."

"I'm really sorry," Griffin said. "I had no idea she knew Angelina. She never mentioned it."

"It doesn't matter," I said wearily, removing the clip from the back of my hair and letting the long tresses fall down my back. I rubbed the sore spot where the barrette had been digging in for the past three hours.

Griffin pushed my hand away and replaced my fingers with his, rubbing. I groaned appreciatively. "That feels good."

"Sit down on the floor in front of the couch," Griffin ordered. "I think you've earned a shoulder rub tonight, and I think we need to talk."

I stiffened involuntarily.

"Wipe that look off your face right now," Griffin chided. "Sit down."

I did as instructed, kicking off my shoes and stretching my legs out under the coffee table. Griffin settled behind me, pressing my body between his knees as he started rubbing my neck. It felt heavenly.

Griffin chuckled when I groaned. "If you keep making noises like that this is going to be a short massage."

I clamped my mouth shut.

"I want you to tell me about Angelina," Griffin said after a beat, digging his fingers into the tight bundle of muscles between my shoulder blades.

"What do you want to know?"

"All of it," Griffin said.

"It's not a very interesting story," I said. "We were in different elementary schools, so everyone was kind of thrust in each other's worlds in middle school. She had this clique of little … harpies. They were horrible.

"They went after Jerry that very first day," I continued. "I'm not sure how to explain Jerry in middle school. He was … ."

"Exactly the same as he is now?" Griffin suggested.

"Kind of," I said. "Jerry always knew he was different. His mother – you should meet her by the way – knew he was different, too. She encouraged him to be whatever he wanted to be."

"The way Jerry tells it, he took one look at you and decided you were going to be his best friend for life," Griffin prodded.

"He decided I was a fashion victim and that I needed him."

Griffin barked out a laugh. "Lean your head down." He brushed my hair out of the way so he could kiss my neck, and then he proceeded to grind his fingers into my flesh. "What did Angelina do to Jerry?"

"Typical stuff," I said, moaning a little despite myself when he found a sensitive spot. "She tortured him by putting dresses in his locker. She would write hateful little messages with nail polish on his locker and in his books. She called him 'Jerry the Fairy.'"

"That must have been hard for him."

"He took it better than I did," I said. "I … didn't like the way she looked at him."

"Which was?"

"Like he was somehow beneath her."

"So what did you do? Other than cutting holes in her pants, that is."

"Oh, I wrote her cellphone number on the bathroom wall at my dad's Knights of Columbus meeting hall," I replied. "I said she was always open for a good time, so she had, like, fifty old dudes calling her for a month straight."

Griffin snorted.

"I put red paint on her pants in art class one day and told everyone she'd started her period," I added. "It was typical kid stuff most of the time."

"Until?"

"I don't know when things really got out of control," I said. "In high school, she'd go after every boyfriend I had. I didn't have a lot of them. No one wanted to date me because of my brothers."

"I can see that."

"Then … well … maybe we should just stop now?"

"Tell me," Griffin urged.

"I told the football team she had herpes and that she was trying to pass it on to all of them," I said. "They all refused to date her, especially after all those pamphlets from Planned Parenthood fell out of her locker."

"Pamphlets?"

"Venereal disease is very serious."

"Continue."

"She didn't take it well, and when she decided to get back at me she was … inventive," I said. "She had one of her friends tell me that Jerry was crying in the high school at the Homecoming game senior year. When I went looking for him, I didn't find Jerry."

Griffin stilled his fingers. "What did you find?"

"She'd told Shawn Lassiter that he was going to meet her, and he was expecting some … special attention," I said. "Then she locked me in the locker room with him and I was stuck there all night. Oh, and he was naked. She took his clothes."

"Did he hurt you?"

"No. He was a wuss. When my father and brothers found me the next morning, though, it wasn't pretty," I said. "I think they would have killed him if they had the chance. The cops were called. Angelina denied everything. Shawn took her side because he was hoping he would still get some action."

"Well, that was a bit much," Griffin said. "How did you retaliate?"

"What makes you think I retaliated?"

"I've met you."

"I put a sonogram picture in her locker and made sure everyone knew that the janitor was the one who knocked her up."

Griffin shook his head. "How was that fair to the janitor?"

"I admitted what I'd done before he got in trouble," I said. "It was just ten minutes of hilarity."

"And then what happened?"

"We just kept going after each other," I said. "The final straw was when she went after Cillian."

"I don't understand why he dated her."

"She's pretty," I said. "She convinced him that she was a good person."

"And then she cheated on him?"

"Yes."

"And you've been fighting ever since?"

"Yes."

"What stories do you think she told Maya?"

"It doesn't really matter," I said. "She has no reason to lie. The truth makes me look just as bad. She'll just leave her part in the whole mess out of it. I'm not exactly proud of everything I did."

"Do you regret any of it?"

"Nope."

Griffin blew out a sigh and rested his chin on top of my head. "Maya will figure out what Angelina is on her own. I'm sorry this happened, though. I had no idea this would blow up."

"It's fine," I said. "I probably deserve a little ire. I did some truly awful things to Angelina."

"It sounds like you two did some truly awful things to each other," Griffin said. "I remember teenage girls in middle and high school. The things you two did to each other – that locking-you-in-with-a-teenage-boy thing notwithstanding – don't sound any different from what the girls in my school did to each other."

"Yeah, but I'm betting the girls in your high school aren't still doing them," I said.

"Probably not," Griffin conceded. "I can't fault your loyalty, though. You love your brothers, and Angelina hurt Cillian. I have a feeling your brothers would kill me and hide the body if I did something to you."

"Aidan was making plans before we found out Maya was your sister."

Griffin reached his hands down under my rear and lifted me up to the couch, settling me on his lap and nuzzling his nose against my cheek. "I would never cheat on you. I hope you know that. I don't do things like that."

"Okay."

"And you wouldn't cheat on me, right?"

"No way," I said. "I would never find another guy as hot as you."

"Oh, you're so sweet," Griffin teased, brushing his lips against my jaw. "I didn't know you could be so sweet."

"I'm a very sweet person."

"I think you are," Griffin said, shifting our bodies so we could stretch out on the couch. "I think you're a rampant pain in the ass, but you're also sweet."

"I'm not really sweet. You know that, right?"

"You are," Griffin said, tickling my ribs. "You're so sweet I think you've earned a reward this evening."

"Wasn't that the massage?"

"Oh, sweetheart, that was just … foreplay."

Well, the evening was looking up.

"I DIDN'T SAY THAT THE BUTT PATTING WAS EROTIC," JERRY SAID, striding into the room huffily. "I said that it could be construed as erotic. That's not the same thing."

"It's not erotic."

"It is if you do it right."

"I can't believe we're still … ." Aidan pulled up short, and when his eyes met mine I could almost see the murderous intentions rolling through his mind.

"What's going on?" Jerry asked, pushing past Aidan. When he saw Griffin and me on the couch – our clothes strewn about the floor – he wasn't nearly as bothered as Aidan. "It looks like you two had a good evening."

"I thought you weren't supposed to be back until later?"

"Yes, well, Aidan says I'm an embarrassment in a sports bar," Jerry said. "You know me; I don't ever want to stay where I'm not wanted."

"I get that."

Griffin shifted next to me, making sure the blanket covered both of our naked bodies, and then fixed Jerry and Aidan with a blasé look. "How was your night otherwise?"

"Fine," Jerry said. "How was your night?"

"It was a lot better five minutes ago."

I studied Aidan. "What's wrong with you?"

"I think I'm having a stroke. I'm just waiting for my head to implode. I'm kind of curious which one of you will be responsible for absorbing my soul."

"Something tells me you'll live," Griffin said. "Hey, Jerry, can you hand me my boxer shorts?"

Jerry retrieved them from the floor, looking them over before he relinquished them. "The paisley is a nice pattern."

"Um … thanks."

Griffin slid into his boxer shorts and then propped himself up on his elbow. "Are you two just going to stand there staring?"

"I'm trying to decide where to hide your body," Aidan said.

"Well, can you do that in the other room?"

"Why?"

"Because Aisling needs to get dressed."

"Oh, that's okay," Jerry said, sitting down on the opposite end of the couch. "I've seen her naked more times than you have."

Griffin lifted an eyebrow.

"He's gay," I said.

"Still … ."

"I don't want to see her naked," Aidan said.

"Then go in the other room."

"You go in the other room."

"I've already seen her naked," Griffin said. "I'm hoping to see her again in a few minutes."

"That's it … you're banned from the townhouse."

"Whatever," Griffin grumbled. "You're becoming increasingly unhinged."

He had a point. I'd never see Aidan so … flummoxed. "Seriously. It's fine." I pointed to the floor. "Hand me my panties."

"I'm not touching your panties!"

"Oh, good grief," Jerry said. He leaned down and scooped up the flimsy black patch of fabric, tossing it to me haphazardly after looking it over briefly. "You shouldn't wear a thong, Bug. They cut you funny. You should wear those cute little panties I pointed out at Victoria's Secret last week. They would look much better on your figure."

Griffin shook his head. "You go underwear shopping together?"

"That's what best friends do," I said, fumbling under the covers to pull my panties back into place. "Can someone hand me my bra?"

"Where is it?" Jerry asked, scanning the floor.

"I don't … oh, it's on the table over there. I guess it kind of … flew."

"Aidan, it's by you," Griffin said. "Can you please hand your sister her bra?"

Aidan glanced at the lacy material next to him, then up at me. He opened his mouth, and then snapped it shut. "I can't look at you ever again." He stalked toward Jerry's bedroom. "You've completely ruined my sister!"

Once the door slammed, Jerry reclined on the couch. "Does anyone want to watch *The Golden Girls*? He's going to be in there pouting for hours and I can't deal with any more drama tonight."

"What happened?"

"Oh, you make one little comment about how you always wanted to wear a cheerleading uniform and men just … flip out. It's just so ridiculous."

"Poor Jerry."

"So, where did we land on *The Golden Girls*?"

"We're going to bed," Griffin said. "And I don't care if you've seen her naked before, look the other way until we're in the bedroom."

"Fine," Jerry said. "You don't have to be such a prude, though."

"I am not a prude," Griffin said, climbing up from the couch.

I kept the blanket wrapped around my front as I followed Griffin to the bedroom. It was gaping in the back, but I didn't really notice.

"You're totally a prude," Jerry said. "Hey, Bug?"

I stilled.

"I'm making an appointment at that spa for us this weekend," he said. "You totally need to get your butt buffed."

Griffin scowled. "It's like living in a circus."

"Come on," I said, pushing him forward. "If you're a good boy, I'll let you play with the clown car."

"That's the only reason I'm still here," Griffin grumbled.

"See you in the morning, Bug."

10

TEN

"I don't care what Jerry says. You don't need to buff your butt."

Griffin's hands were warm as he snuggled up behind me the next morning.

"I thought you were appalled because Jerry has seen me naked."

"I've thought about it, and it really doesn't bother me."

I waited.

"Okay, it bothers me," Griffin conceded. "I guess I'll just have to get over it. Jerry is your best friend, and it's not as if he's sexually attracted to you."

"He's definitely not attracted to me."

"Have you seen him naked?"

"Yes."

"Does he like ... walk around naked?"

"Absolutely not," I said. "Jerry thinks putting your naked bits on furniture other people use is tacky."

"So, does he think what we did last night was tacky?"

"I'm betting he's cleaning the couch as we speak."

Griffin laughed. "He's funny. I can see why you two are so close."

Something about his wistful tone tugged at my heart. "Who is your best friend?"

"I don't really have one."

That was sad. "Never?"

Griffin shrugged. “I have friends. I just don’t bond with people like you do.”

“I’m not bonded to anyone but Jerry.”

“You’re bonded to Aidan.”

I frowned. “I don’t know what his deal is,” I said. “Right before we saw you with Maya he was the one trying to make me feel better by saying you were probably just busy with work and it wasn’t your choice not to call me.”

“I’m really sorry about that,” Griffin said, rubbing my hip with his finger. “Just for the record, if I have to go undercover again I’m not going to hesitate to wake you up.”

“Do you think you’ll have to?”

“Probably,” Griffin said. “It’s part of my job. Does that bother you?”

“I would be a hypocrite if it did,” I said. “You’ve been pretty understanding about all of my stuff.”

“I don’t know if ‘understanding’ is the right word, but I’m trying to be better,” he said. “I just never imagined any of this stuff was real. Now that I know it is, it’s kind of … .”

“Terrifying?”

“Interesting,” Griffin corrected. “I’m not going to lie, though. Your constant appearances at crime scenes are going to cause problems.”

“I didn’t know that was going to happen.”

“I know you didn’t,” he said. “I just need you to be more careful. At a certain point, I might not be able to save you.”

“Well, hopefully it won’t be an issue again,” I said.

“Hopefully.”

The sound of his growling stomach filled the room.

“Are you hungry?”

“I could eat.”

“Let’s get dressed,” I said. “I could eat, too.”

“Aren’t you worried about Aidan being at the breakfast table?”

“Nope,” I said, climbing out of bed. “He needs to get over himself. I have no idea what his problem is.”

“I think he’s just protective of you,” Griffin said. “I’m not taking it personally.”

“Don’t,” I said. “He’ll calm down.”

“Let’s hope so. I can only take so many dirty looks before I punch him in the face.”

"GOOD MORNING."

Jerry was fluttering around the couch with an aerosol can in his rubber glove-covered hand when we exited the bedroom. "Don't sit on the couch. I'm fumigating it."

I shot Griffin a knowing "I told you" look.

"Do you think I have cooties?"

"Your bare butt was on my sofa," Jerry said. "It's just unsanitary. Although, to be fair, I'm mildly curious to see what it looks like."

Griffin blanched. "Excuse me?"

"I'm kind of a butt connoisseur."

"I don't even know what to say to that."

"Go and sit your butt down at the kitchen table," Jerry ordered. "I have French toast in the oven."

"Yum," I said. "Peaches and walnuts?"

"And powdered sugar."

"This is why I love you," I said, giving him a quick kiss on the cheek.

"I'm not kissing you," Griffin said. "I'm going to eat the French toast, though."

"You'll kiss me some day," Jerry said. "People just can't stop themselves."

"I'm willing to bet that never happens."

"Never say never."

I scanned the room. "Where is Aidan?"

"He's getting ready," Jerry said. "He'll be out in a second." He led us into the kitchen. "You need to stay off that couch for six hours."

"Fine."

"You're kind of … fussy," Griffin said, pouring coffee into two mugs and sliding one across the counter in my direction.

"I'm not fussy," Jerry said. "I'm a perfectionist. Why do you think I want to get Aisling's butt buffed?"

"I think you just want to throw me off my game."

"Well … she still needs to be buffed."

"You leave her butt alone," Griffin said, shooting me a lazy grin. "I like it the way it is."

My mind was still on my brother. "Was Aidan better this morning?"

"I don't know what his deal is," Jerry said. "He won't talk about it. He says nothing is wrong."

"Do you believe him?"

"No. You know your brother, though. He'll hold it all in until he completely blows, and then we'll have to pick up the pieces."

"Well, I hope he blows soon," I said.

"Me, too," Jerry said, grinning slyly.

I smacked him. "Don't be gross."

"Sit down," Jerry ordered. "You two need food in you after your … long night."

I narrowed my eyes, but Griffin ignored him. "Yeah, lay this French toast on me."

"Do you have to work today?"

"Nope. I'm off. Because I was on for two straight weeks I get to make my own schedule for the next few weeks."

Well, that was interesting. "Does that mean we can spend a whole weekday in bed?"

"Don't you have to work?"

"Are you really turning me down?"

"You're right. That was a stupid question. Let's eat the French toast and go right back to bed."

I wrinkled my nose. "I have to work."

"You're such a tease."

"Hey, I put out with the best of them."

Jerry grinned. "You two are cute. I want to bottle you up and sell you over the Internet."

The sound of a door opening caught everyone's attention. Aidan strode into the kitchen. His greeting was muted, but he settled at the table to wait for his breakfast.

"How are you this morning?" I asked.

"I slept well."

"Have you looked over our list today?"

"No."

"Are you going to be monosyllabic all day?"

"Yes."

"Are you going to pretend I'm not talking no matter what I say?"

"Pretty much."

"Oh, good," I said. "Did you know, when Aidan was in high school, he once dressed up as Marilyn Monroe for a costume party? He even shaved his legs."

"I did not!"

"See, I knew you couldn't hold out," I said, poking his arm.

"I'm not ready to talk to you yet," Aidan said. "Just … let me get some caffeine and we'll talk later."

"Great. I can't wait."

Someone knocked on the front door and then entered. That could only mean one thing: One of my brothers had come calling. My father refused to visit the townhouse. He said it made him feel claustrophobic. Cillian followed his nose into the kitchen. "Is that French toast I smell?"

"You're just in time," Jerry said, smiling widely.

"Cool." Cillian sat at the table and glanced around. "Why is no one looking at each other?"

"We're looking at each other," I said, proving my point by gazing at Griffin.

"Aidan isn't looking at anyone," Cillian said.

"He had a long night."

"Oh, is he still mad about the cheerleading thing? I thought it was kind of funny."

I kind of wished I'd been there to see it. "That's probably it."

"Oh, that's not it," Jerry said. "When we came home ... ."

"Jerry," I warned.

"He's going to find out anyway," Jerry said. "This family can't keep a secret. When we came home last night, Aisling and Griffin were naked on the couch. Aidan is scandalized and he's not talking to anyone."

Cillian stilled. "Naked?"

"They'd just had sex," Jerry said, carrying the pan of French toast to the table and setting it on the waiting trivets. "Don't worry. The couch is being aired out even as we speak. It will be sanitized in a few hours. Everyone dig in."

"I think I lost my appetite," Cillian moaned.

"Oh, get over it," I said. "I walked in on Jerry and Aidan pawing each other on the couch a little more than a month ago and I didn't pitch a fit."

Jerry challenged me with a look.

"What? I didn't."

"You screamed that you were blind and ran outside," Jerry said.

"Where you were promptly attacked by a wraith," Aidan interjected.

"That wasn't what happened," I said. It was totally what happened. "Still, I didn't freak out like you did last night. You claimed you were having a stroke."

"This whole family is too dramatic," Griffin said, digging into his French toast. "It's a good thing the food is great. Otherwise, I'm not sure I would be able to put up with the constant sniping and whining."

"We don't whine," Aidan and I said in unison.

"They don't," Jerry said. "They … complain shrilly."

"Is that different?"

"It's all about the presentation," Jerry said. He cuffed Griffin on the back of the head. "Eat your breakfast. Stop stirring the pot." He pointed a finger in my direction. "You, too."

I turned my attention to Cillian. "Not that I'm not happy to see you, but is there a reason you're invading our breakfast table this morning? Is Dad not feeding you?"

"Well, we've had a change to the lists for today," Cillian answered. "Dad sent me here so we could tackle your list together."

"Why can't I go with her?" Aidan asked.

"You're going, too."

"That must be some list," I said. "Three of us?"

"It's not a long list," Cillian said. "It's just that … well … Morgan Reid is on it again."

It was as if all the air had been sucked out of the room. "Are you serious?"

"Unfortunately," Cillian said. "Dad is worried a wraith is going to show up, so he wants us all to go out together today. Reid is the only one on our list."

"Hey, that means we can spend part of the day in bed," I said, turning to Griffin excitedly.

"No, it doesn't," Cillian said.

"Oh, not you, too."

"You're my baby sister," Cillian said. "To me, you're a good girl."

"That's such a double standard."

"I'm not denying that," Cillian said. "In the back of my mind, I know you're an adult. In my heart, though, you're the same little girl who cried when the gardener accidentally mowed over your stuffed dog."

"Fine," I said. "We're not going to spend the afternoon in bed. We're going to go to church."

"Good girl."

I rolled my eyes until they landed on Griffin. "Do you want to go to church with me later?"

"I'm going to go with you on your assignment."

I stilled. "I don't think that's allowed."

"Why not?"

"I … ." I turned to Cillian for help.

"Wasn't he there when you killed the wraith at the retirement home?" Cillian asked.

"Yes."

"What does it matter if he's there for this one? It might actually be helpful if something goes wrong."

"But … do you want to see what we do?" I asked.

"I do," Griffin said. "I'm kind of curious."

"This one probably won't be like a normal one," I said.

"I can live with that," Griffin said. "I'd just feel better knowing you weren't blindly walking into trouble with no one watching your back."

"What do you think we're going to be doing?" Aidan challenged.

"Probably still avoiding eye contact."

Aidan scowled.

"I think it's a good idea," Cillian said. "The sooner he understands what we do the easier it will be on Aisling."

"He hasn't been hard on me," I said.

"Just hard in … ."

I interrupted Jerry. "Don't finish that filthy sentence."

"How did you know what I was going to say?"

"Because I know you," I said. I glanced at Griffin, still unsure. "If you want to come, I don't see why you can't. You just can't get in the way. You know that, right?"

"I have no intention of getting in the way," Griffin said. "And, when we're done, I'll take you out for a nice lunch and then we'll … go to church."

"Very good," Cillian said. "Okay, someone pass me the syrup."

11

ELEVEN

"Hand me some chips," I ordered.

"No, you said you didn't want chips when we stopped at the gas station," Aidan said. "You can't change your mind now."

"Oh, give me some chips!"

"No."

From the passenger seat of Aidan's car Cillian reached over and cuffed his brother. "Will you give her some chips?"

"Do I have to spell it out for you?" Aidan asked, irked. "N.O."

Cillian studied him for a moment and then he reached over and grabbed the bag of dill-pickled delight from his lap and handed it to me. I shoved a handful in my mouth, meeting Aidan's gaze in the rearview mirror as I chomped on them noisily.

Griffin rolled his eyes from the backseat. "Is this how all of your stakeouts go?" We were sitting outside of Morgan Reid's apartment building. We'd arrived early so we could get a handle on who was going in and out of the building.

"Pretty much," Cillian said.

"Very professional," Griffin deadpanned.

Because I'd shoved so many chips in my mouth I was having trouble swallowing. I slapped Aidan's shoulder and pointed toward his bottle of water.

"No."

I mimed coughing.

"It serves you right."

Cillian sighed and snatched the bottle of water. "What is it with you two?"

I swallowed half the bottle for good measure before handing it back. When Aidan took it, his face was murderous. "Oh, man, you backwashed!"

"I don't backwash," I argued.

"I'm going to beat the crap out of both of you," Cillian warned. "What is going on here?"

No one answered.

"Is this because you saw her naked?"

"I didn't see her naked," Aidan said. "Don't give me nightmares."

"Hey!"

Cillian shifted in his seat, his gaze bouncing between us. "Why are you two acting like this?"

"We're acting how we always act," I grumbled.

"No, you're not," Cillian countered. "I haven't seen you two act this … poorly … since middle school."

I crossed my arms over my chest. "Ask him."

"I'm asking both of you."

"They've been fighting for days," Griffin said. "I think it's because of me."

"What did you do to Aidan?"

"I didn't do anything to Aidan," Griffin replied. "He just has attitude with me. I understood when he attacked me because he thought I was cheating on her. I have no idea what his problem is now."

"I don't have a problem," Aidan sniffed. "She's just acting like … a beyotch."

"Oh, good grief," Cillian said. "It *is* like you're back in middle school."

"Did they fight a lot in middle school?" Griffin asked.

"It was unbelievable," Cillian said. "Dad finally had to put them in different wings of the house because they kept hurling statues at each other."

"That sounds … expensive."

"It was," Cillian said. "They got over it eventually. I'm not waiting three years for you two to start getting along again. Just be forewarned."

"Then don't listen to us," Aidan snapped.

"I'm going to have Dad put you in the dungeon," Cillian warned. "You're seriously on my last nerve. Either tell me what's wrong or move on."

"She's irritating me."

"How? She just asked for some chips."

"And she backwashed in my water," Aidan pointed out.

"Oh, I'm totally done," Cillian said, popping open his door. "We need to break up into teams. Aisling, you're coming with me. Griffin, you can go with Aidan."

"That's a terrible idea," I said.

"No one asked you," Cillian said.

"I happen to think it's a terrible idea, too," Griffin added.

"Well, here's my problem," Cillian said. "My father ordered me not to let Aisling out of my sight. You could come with us, but that leaves Aidan alone."

"I'm fine with being alone," Aidan said.

Cillian ignored him. "I need Aisling with me."

"I came to watch her," Griffin argued.

"Fine," Cillian said, running his hand through his hair, exasperated. "Sit in the car. I don't care. Come on, Aisling."

I shot Griffin an apologetic look. "He's technically my boss."

"Go," Griffin said. "Let's get this over with. I can't take much more time with your family right now."

"Oh, but we really love you," Aidan snapped.

"Hurry," Griffin reiterated.

"DO YOU WANT TO TELL ME WHAT'S WRONG WITH YOU AND AIDAN?"

Cillian led me behind the apartment building, studying every alcove and bush as we moved.

"He's being mean to me."

"He's being mean to you?"

"I don't know why," I said. "At first I thought he was just doing it to bug Griffin. Now I think there's something else wrong with him."

"Maybe he has PMS?" Cillian suggested.

"That's not funny," I said. "You can't call him a girl because he's gay."

Cillian snorted. "I like how you still stand up for him even though he's being mean to you."

"I'm not standing up for him," I corrected. "I'm standing up for gay men everywhere."

Cillian cupped the back of my head briefly. "Okay," he said. "You two are going to have to figure this out, though. If he's got a problem with Griffin then … ."

"Then what? I'm not breaking up with Griffin because Aidan is crying like I broke his favorite doll."

Cillian made a face. "You can say that, but I can't ask if he has PMS?"

"I wasn't trying to slur him," I said. "This whole thing just reminds me of when I broke his doll."

"That wasn't a doll," Cillian said. "It was an action figure."

"If you can take its clothes off and dress it up, it's a doll."

"No, that's not true," Cillian argued. "It was an action figure. It had a gun."

"And bracelets."

"That was a walkie-talkie."

"It was a doll."

"It was an action figure."

"Is this a private argument, or can anyone join in?"

I froze when I heard the voice. Cillian glanced behind me, his face unreadable. "Can I help you?"

"That was going to be my next line," the voice said. "Who is your friend?"

I clenched my jaw and turned, meeting Morgan Reid's gaze evenly as it landed on me.

"Well, hello again," Reid said.

"Hi."

"Is this Mike Morrison?"

"Who?"

"Isn't that the name of the man you said you were looking for yesterday when you stopped by my apartment?" Reid pressed.

How could he possibly remember that? "Um, yes," I said. "This is Mike Morrison."

Reid smiled at Cillian. "And you're selling her a couch?"

"I am," Cillian said.

"In the bushes beside the building?"

"We decided to get some exercise first," I interjected.

"I see." Reid obviously didn't believe me. "You do realize you two look almost exactly alike, right?"

"I think he's making fun of your hair," I said to Cillian.

"I wasn't," Reid said. "I was pointing out there's more than a passing resemblance between the two of you."

"That's because he's my husband," I said.

Reid waited.

"Why would I look like you if I was your husband?" Cillian was exasperated. "That makes even less sense than me selling you a couch."

I fought the urge to strangle him. "I'm … not sure."

"Are you two on a stakeout or something?" Reid asked. "Are you cops?"

I wrinkled my nose. "Do I look like a cop?"

"You look smoking hot," Reid said.

"Hey," Cillian warned. "That's my … wife."

Reid rolled his eyes. "What are you two really doing here?"

"We're … um … thinking of moving into the building," I said.

"Together?"

"We're very close."

"Because you're married?"

"I'm her brother and she's considering moving here," Cillian said, pinching my wrist viciously. "She really liked the building yesterday when she was here to see the couch."

"Did you buy the couch?"

"No. It looked like someone died on it," I said.

"And now you're considering moving into the building." Reid pressed.

He's so suspicious. I have a very honest face. I don't deserve this. "I am."

"And you brought your brother to look it over?"

"He wants to make sure it's safe," I said.

"Why didn't you just say that in the first place?" Reid asked.

"Because … ."

"Because she's a woman," Cillian answered for me. "They like to play games."

Reid's face softened. "Is that what you're doing? Do you want to play a game with me?"

Cillian shifted uncomfortably. "I'm going to check around the rest of the building," he said. "Why don't you guys … stay right here?"

I shot him a look. "What?"

"I … just stay here," Cillian muttered. "I need to look around the rest of the building."

"But … ."

"You'll be fine," Cillian said.

"Why wouldn't she be fine?" Reid asked.

"Because you look like you have eight hands," Cillian said, moving toward the back of the building. He paused long enough to fix Reid with a serious look. "If any of those eight hands land on my sister I'm going to beat the crap out of you. You've been warned."

"You look like a fun guy," Reid said, his face full of faux brightness.

"You have no idea," Cillian said, disappearing around the back of the building.

"So, tell me a little about yourself," Reid said, not missing a beat. "If you're going to move into the building, we should be … friendly."

I'd rather make friends with a professional cheerleader. "Oh, well, I'm pretty antisocial."

"You don't look antisocial."

"I am."

"You don't look it."

"Looks can be deceiving." What is this guy's deal? Does he think he's charming? He's got "creeper" written all over him. It's right before "tool" and right after "douche" in the loser's dictionary.

Either Reid didn't notice my overt dislike or he didn't care. I was leaning toward the latter. "So, do you have a boyfriend?"

"Yes."

"Why isn't he helping you look for an apartment?"

That was a very good question. "He's here," I said. "He's with my other brother. They're looking around, too." I wanted Reid to realize Cillian wasn't his only worry. I had no idea why.

"That sounds cozy."

"It is."

"Are you serious with your boyfriend?"

"She is."

I jumped at Griffin's voice, but I also was relieved. "Hi, honey!"

Griffin narrowed his eyes. "Dear," he drawled. "I've been looking for you."

"Well, you found me." Thankfully.

"What happened to your brother?" Griffin wasn't sure what was going on but he obviously knew better than to blow our cover. He wasn't a novice.

"He's looking around the building," I said. "He's not sure he'd feel safe with me living here."

Griffin caught on. "I agree with him. I've been watching the people going in and out. I don't think you'd like it here."

"Hey, I live here," Reid said.

"Oh, honey bear, this is Morgan Reid. He lives in the building."

Reid stuck out his hand. "It's nice to meet you."

Griffin's face was immovable. "It's nice to meet you."

Something was bothering me about this situation – other than the obvious. Reid was supposed to be dead already. Again. Instead, he was wandering around outside of his apartment building. Who does that? Okay, who does that besides me?

"You know what, snookums, I'm going to run around and see if I can find … my brother," I said. I didn't want to reveal any names. "Why don't you stay here and quiz Mr. Reid on the building?"

Griffin arched an eyebrow. "Well, baby doll, maybe I should go with you?"

"No," I said, glancing around. "Someone should probably stay here and keep Mr. Reid company, you sexy beast."

Griffin ran his tongue over his teeth. "But I want to spend some quality time with you, sweetie pie."

The names were starting to get out of control, and yet I couldn't stop. "You'll be fine for two minutes, Tootsie Roll."

Griffin scowled. "If you're not back in two minutes, pain in my ass, I'm going to come looking for you."

"Great," I said and bolted in the direction Cillian had gone moments before.

"Wait! I thought we were going to get to know one another?" Reid called after me.

"You can get to know me," Griffin said, his tone grim.

I left Griffin to handle Reid as I scanned the back of the building. It was empty and there was nowhere to hide. I jogged around the next corner, and the scene was straight out of a horror movie. Cillian was on the ground, his face devoid of … anything. A wraith loomed over him, its face inches from Cillian's, and I realized it was trying to suck his soul.

"Hey!" I raced forward. I had no idea what I was going to do, I only knew Cillian was vulnerable.

The wraith straightened as I approached. It was hidden in the shadow of the building, and the opening between the building and the nearby fence was narrow. There wasn't a lot of room to navigate, but I had to get to Cillian.

"You get away from him," I ordered.

"Aisling." The voice was a hiss. "Aisling Grimlock."

It knew my name. That was … freaky. Hopefully it was afraid of me. "Get away from my brother."

"Must not kill her," the wraith hissed. "She's not supposed to be touched."

I couldn't figure out who the wraith was talking to. "That's right. You don't want to touch me," I said, closing the distance between us. "Now step away from my brother."

"Pretty prize."

"Listen, creepy, I don't have time to deal with you," I said, extending my finger. "Get away from my brother."

The wraith glanced back down at Cillian. "He's mine."

"No, he's not."

"Mine. Mine. Mine." The wraith made a move to go back to Cillian.

I felt helpless. I knew I couldn't let the wraith touch me. If it did, I would be incapacitated. A wraith can suck the energy out of a reaper with just a touch. I scanned the ground at my feet and picked up the only weapon available: a rock. The one good thing about growing up with four brothers is that you're not allowed to throw like a girl. I hurled the rock as hard as I could, hitting the wraith in the middle of its forehead.

The creature reared back, its long hands splaying over its forehead as confusion washed over it. "Mine!"

I took another step forward, this time scooping up an errant brick that had detached from the side of the building. It was big and I wasn't sure I could hit my target with it, but I hoped the wraith didn't know that. "I'll bash your head in," I warned.

The wraith was obviously torn, and the second it turned its attention back to Cillian I knew I was out of options. I hurled the brick and scored a direct hit. The wraith tilted to the side as it listed against the building. I put myself between Cillian's prone body and the wraith. I scooped the lobbed brick back off the ground and slammed it into wraith's head. It didn't fall, but it did … scream. Kind of. I pounded the brick into its head as many times as I could. My arm was tiring when the wraith's body stiffened – and then exploded into a pile of dust.

I fell back, surprise and exhaustion washing over me. I didn't give myself time to recover. Instead, I crawled to Cillian and checked him for signs of life. He was breathing, but barely.

Griffin and Aidan found me seconds later.

12

TWELVE

"Is someone riding with him to the hospital?" The impatient paramedic glanced down at us from the back of the ambulance.

"I am." I climbed up and settled on the bench next to Cillian's gurney. He was unnaturally pale and I didn't like his shallow breathing.

"We'll be right behind you," Griffin said, his face grave. "We're going to have to answer some questions."

I bit my lower lip and nodded.

"We'll be right behind you," Griffin repeated.

"I'll call Dad." Aidan's voice was low. "Just … stay with him."

It hadn't taken long to explain the situation to Griffin and Aidan when they happened upon Cillian and me. Unfortunately for us, someone heard the wraith's scream, so we had to make up an explanation on the spot to explain Cillian's status. Apparently there was an errant mugger in the area, at least that's what Griffin reported to the uniformed officers who arrived a few moments later. Aidan and I had no choice but to back him up.

I had no idea what happened to Morgan Reid; he must have managed to sneak away in the melee. He wasn't my concern now.

The paramedic shut the ambulance door and the driver took off like a shot. I gripped the handles on the bench as the ambulance careened around a curve.

The paramedic continued checking Cillian, who was deathly still. "Did he hit his head?"

"I don't know."

"I don't see any injuries," the paramedic said.

I didn't know how to respond. I couldn't tell the man that a supernatural soul devourer with red claws and white skin had tried to suck the life out of my brother. "I just found him on the ground."

"And you saw the guy who attacked him?"

"Not really," I said, shrugging. "I saw a dark figure in a hoodie escape through the gate. I didn't get a good look at him."

"You're probably lucky that he didn't get too close to you," the paramedic said. "You could have been seriously hurt."

I wasn't feeling particularly lucky. I gripped Cillian's hand. It was cold. "Is he going to be okay?"

"He's your brother, right?"

I nodded.

"I don't know," the paramedic replied, his face earnest and honest. "I have no idea what's wrong with him. We'll know more when we get to the hospital."

I reached up to brush Cillian's hair from his face. Of all my brothers he was the most even-tempered. He was the last one to fly off the handle and it took him longer to anger than everyone else in our family, but that didn't mean he was quiet. I'd never seen him this still before. "He'll be okay," I said. "He has to be."

"WHERE IS HE?"

Cormack Grimlock is a formidable man on a normal day. On a day when one of his children is in danger, though, he's terrifying. I heard Dad's voice before I saw his face, and when his furious countenance fell on me as he rounded the corner into the waiting room I shrank.

My legs were shaking when I got to my feet. "They're working on him now."

Dad pulled up short when he saw me. "Are you okay?"

"I'm fine."

"Where is Aidan?"

"He had to stay at the scene with Griffin to answer questions."

"Griffin?" Dad's eyebrows nearly flew off his forehead. "Why was he there?"

I glanced around nervously. We were starting to draw curious looks. "Dad, you have to calm down."

"You calm down!"

"Let's all calm down," Griffin said, striding into view and pulling me in for a quick hug. "You need to stop yelling, Mr. Grimlock."

"I am not yelling."

"I could hear you in the parking lot."

"You could not."

"He's right, Dad. You need to zip it," Aidan said, moving to Dad's side. "People will start to talk if you don't, and we don't need to draw attention to ourselves."

Dad growled in response, but let Aidan pull him down into a chair.

"Where are Braden and Redmond?" Aidan asked.

"They're on their way," Dad said. "They were in Dearborn."

I rested my head on Griffin's shoulder as we sank into chairs. Griffin had directed us to a spot near Dad, but not too close.

Dad leaned forward, quieter now. "What happened?"

I told him the story, being careful to keep my voice low to ward off prying ears. When I was done, Dad looked as though he wanted to hit something.

"He'll be okay," I said. I had no idea whether I was saying it to make him or me feel better.

"You attacked it with a brick?"

The question took me by surprise. "I didn't have any other options."

"And what would have happened if it had gotten its hands on you?"

"I don't know," I said, anger starting to bubble. "Should I have just sat there and let it kill Cillian?"

Griffin rubbed my knee. "That's not what he's saying."

"No, it's not," Dad said. "You just … you could have been killed, too."

"He's not dead." Not yet.

"Aisling, I am not faulting you for being brave," Dad said, fighting to rein in his temper. "You should have called for Aidan and Griffin. You should never have taken on that situation yourself. Why do you think I wanted Cillian there for backup?"

"Because you think I'm incompetent," I said.

"I do not."

"You do, too," I shot back. Anger and worry over Cillian were eroding all hints of reason from my brain. "No one else had to be on probation as long as me."

Dad scowled. "Oh, here we go."

"Is now really the time for this?" Griffin asked.

"It seems all we have is time," Dad shot back. "You listen, Aisling. I can only deal with one thing at a time. Right now, I'm dealing with your brother. That doesn't mean I want you to do something stupid and get yourself hurt. This is exactly why I didn't want you in this line of work."

I stilled. "What? When I told you I wasn't going to be a … antiquities dealer … you practically disowned me."

"I did not."

"You did so."

"I did not."

"You did so."

"I did not."

I turned to Aidan for help. He looked as though the last place he wanted to be was in the middle of this conversation. "You did yell at her," he said finally.

"I only did that because you all expected me to yell," Dad said, crossing his arms over his chest. "I was secretly relieved."

"Why?" I was flabbergasted.

"Because you weren't in danger in an office setting," Dad said. "You were off in your own little world. The worst thing I had to worry about then was whether you'd ever date anyone because you spent all of your time going to gay bars with Jerry."

"But … you were always so disappointed."

"Aisling, I've never been disappointed where you're concerned," Dad said. "Well, that's not true. When you were arrested for stealing that car as a teenager I was disappointed."

"I did not steal that car," I hissed. "I borrowed it from Kelly Kolchak. It's not my fault she was too drunk to remember, and when her parents caught us she totally threw me under the bus." I glanced at Griffin. "That is exactly why I don't get along with other women."

He smirked. "Don't worry. I saw the stolen-car charge on your record the day I met you," he said. "It's not like it's news to me."

I scowled. "I did not steal that car."

"I'm sure you didn't, baby." Griffin rubbed his hand over my shoulders. "Listen, I know there is a lot of drama where this family is concerned. A lot of drama."

I shot him a look.

"I do not think now is the time to air all of your dirty laundry, though," Griffin said. "You're all upset about Cillian. I get that. We just have to … wait."

"In case you haven't noticed, this family isn't good at waiting," Aidan said.

"Oh, I've noticed."

Braden and Redmond picked that moment to arrive, and after an initial flurry of questions we all settled in for the wait together. After a very uncomfortable ten minutes, Redmond couldn't take it anymore.

"Do we know what happened to Reid?"

"I was talking to him when I heard the scream," Griffin said. "I didn't really think about watching him. I thought Aisling was in trouble."

"No one is blaming you, man," Redmond said, rubbing the back of his neck. "I just think it's suspicious. Why was he outside?"

"I'm wondering if the wraith was supposed to kill him," Braden said. "Maybe Cillian got in the way?"

"No," I said. "Reid should have been dead before Cillian and I even separated."

"And why did you separate again?" Dad asked.

I narrowed my eyes.

"I'm not asking because I want to attack you," Dad said. "I'm asking because I'm trying to understand what happened."

"Once Reid showed up, he wouldn't stop asking stupid questions," I said. "Since we knew he was supposed to be dead already, Cillian was worried and he wanted to take a look around the building."

"So, he left you with a potential murder victim?"

"Don't you dare say anything bad about him," I warned.

Braden sighed heavily and leaned back in his chair. "How long are we supposed to wait?"

"If you all promise to behave I'll see if I can get some information," Griffin offered.

"How are you going to find anything out?" I asked. "We're his family. We should be the first ones to hear updates."

"Did you forget who works here?"

I knit my eyebrows together. It took me longer than it should have to figure out who he meant. "Maya."

"She's on duty," Griffin said. "I'm willing to ask her to check on Cillian."

I jumped to my feet. "Let's go."

Griffin was unsure. "Maybe you should stay here."

"Why?"

"You know why."

"Why?" Redmond asked, curious.

"His sister doesn't like me," I said.

"She didn't say that," Griffin protested.

"She takes yoga classes with Angelina Davenport," I supplied.

Four Grimlock faces twisted into identical grimaces of dislike.

"Wow, that was impressive," Griffin said. "I just … why don't you wait here? I won't be gone long."

I was desperate for information about Cillian. "But … ."

"Stay here, please," Griffin said.

"Fine."

He brushed a quick kiss against my forehead and then focused on my brothers and father. "Do not attack her while I'm gone."

"Why would we attack her?" Braden asked.

"If I understood why you guys do half the things you do, I would be one of the wisest men in all the land," Griffin said. "Just … sit here and try to get along with one another."

"Yes, sir," Braden said, mock saluting.

"It's cuter when your sister does it," Griffin said, slipping out of the waiting room.

Once Griffin was gone, Aidan bounced up from his chair and settled in the one next to me. He wrapped his arm around my shoulders. "He's going to be okay."

I nodded, fighting off tears.

"He's going to be fine," Aidan repeated. "You saved him."

I could only hope he was right.

13

THIRTEEN

Griffin returned a few minutes later. "Maya's going to see what she can find out."

It wasn't much, but it was all we had to hold on to at this point.

Griffin eyed Aidan for a second, seemingly surprised that he was sitting next to me, but he let it go and sat at my other side. "Did everyone get along while I was gone?"

"Contrary to popular belief, we don't always argue," Redmond said.

Griffin waited.

"That's just the way we communicate on a normal day," Braden supplied.

"I know," Griffin said, grabbing my hand.

"That's how all siblings get along," Redmond said.

"I don't get along that way with my sister."

"Then you're doing it wrong," Aidan grumbled.

Griffin shot him a look. Aidan had the grace to avert his eyes.

"I can't believe they've made us wait this long," Dad said, rocking in his chair. I knew he wanted to pace, and he had a few times, but he kept returning to the same spot after a few minutes. It's hard for a man like my father to just sit and wait. It's not in his nature. He was almost at his limit.

"They probably can't figure out what's wrong with him," I said. "The paramedic mentioned him not having any injuries in the ambulance."

"What did you say?" Redmond asked.

"I said I didn't see the attack," I replied. "I figured it was the safest answer."

"You're smarter than you look," Aidan said, tightening his hand on my shoulder.

I was too tired to acknowledge the remark. After a few more minutes of silence, Maya appeared in the doorway. She looked different in her scrubs. She was still pretty, but she appeared so much more approachable. I liked her better in the scrubs.

"This is Maya," Griffin said by way of introduction. "This is Braden, Redmond, Mr. Grimlock and Aidan. You remember Aisling."

"Yes," Maya said, her eyes full of sympathy. "I'm sorry to meet you all under these circumstances."

"How is Cillian?" Redmond asked.

"Well, he's holding his own," Maya said. "He's breathing on his own and his brain function seems normal."

"That's good, right?" Aidan asked.

"It is," Maya said. "He still hasn't woken up. And he appears to be running a low-grade fever. The doctors can't find any injuries. It doesn't appear he sustained a blow to the head. Until he regains consciousness, they're … baffled."

"Why haven't they told us that?" Dad asked.

"Well, Mr. Grimlock, I'm not sure," Maya said.

"Call me Cormack."

Griffin scowled.

"Cormack, I think they're just trying to make sure they have all the information possible before speaking with you," Maya said. "We try to be very diligent here."

"I'm sure you're a professional," Braden said, winking.

Griffin extended his finger in Braden's direction. "Don't even think about it."

Braden's face was a mask of faux innocence. "What did I do?"

"Leave her alone," Redmond said. "You don't have a chance anyway." He waved at Maya.

Her face was unreadable as she regarded my brothers. "Uh-huh."

"Ignore them," Griffin instructed.

Maya turned to Aidan. "Don't you want to flirt, too?"

Aidan was nonplussed. "I have a boyfriend."

"Oh, you're the twin brother," she said.

"I see Aisling has been talking us up," Redmond said. "What did she say about us?"

I couldn't believe they were hitting on a nurse – on Griffin's sister, of all people – while Cillian was unconscious in another room.

"She said that you were codependent and unnaturally attached to each other," Maya replied honestly.

"I am not codependent," Braden said.

"Aidan and Aisling are codependent," Redmond corrected. "The rest of us are normal."

"You modeled the dress I had to make in home economics when I was in high school," I reminded him.

"I secretly did that," Redmond said, pointing and firing an imaginary gun in my direction. "Secretly."

I rolled my eyes.

"I don't wear dresses," Redmond clarified for Maya's benefit.

"I'm sure you don't." Maya appeared genuinely amused.

"I don't."

"Oh, give it up," I snapped.

Maya shifted her attention to me. "The people at the nurse's station are talking. They said you were the one who found your brother."

"She was," Griffin said. "She's upset."

"It's good you found him so quickly," Maya said. "If you hadn't, who knows what would have happened?"

"Thanks," I said.

Aidan tugged on my hair. "I thought you said she didn't like you?"

"Who said that?" Maya asked, straightening.

"Aisling did," Redmond said.

"I never said that," Maya protested.

"She's friends with Angelina," I reminded them.

Braden and Redmond made faces.

"You know Angelina is evil, right?" Aidan asked.

"She's my friend," Maya said, uncomfortable. "She's never been anything but nice to me."

"She's a snake," Redmond said.

"She's the devil," Braden interjected.

"She's a complete and total bitch," Dad said, not mincing words. "If she got run over by a truck we'd all band together to bail out whoever hit her."

Maya was taken aback.

"They really dislike Angelina," Griffin said.

"So I've noticed," Maya said. "I guess now would be a bad time to tell you she's in the hospital and asking about Cillian then?"

My heart jumped. "What?"

Maya looked as though she wanted to suck the words back into her mouth. "I … she said she heard that he was here and wanted to see him. I'm not sure how she found out."

I stood. "Where is she?"

"Aisling," Dad warned. "Now is not the time for a hair-pulling contest."

"It's always time for a hair-pulling contest," Aidan said. "I'll hold her down."

"I'll get the scissors," Braden said, moving toward us.

"Let's go get her," Redmond said.

"You four are not starting a brawl in this hospital," Dad ordered.

"I'm going to have to agree with Cormack," Maya said. She glanced at Griffin. "Do you want to chime in here?"

"I'm mildly curious to see what will happen," Griffin admitted.

"What?"

"The woman is a viper," he said. "If Aisling wants to fight, I'd rather she get it out of her system now. That will make her more … pliable … later tonight."

Dad reached out and cuffed Griffin on the back of his head. "That is my daughter you're talking about."

Griffin rubbed his head ruefully. "You guys hit a lot."

"You're all really aggressive," Maya said.

"Of course they are. They should all be locked up." My old nemesis had slipped in the family waiting room.

I shifted my gaze to focus on Angelina. She stood behind Maya, her face a mask of anger. "Go away, harlot."

"Don't you dare speak to me, Aisling," Angelina snapped. "You should have called me the second he was admitted to this hospital. I had to hear from a client when you should have called me."

"Why?"

"Because … you know why."

"No, I don't."

"Because … we're in love," Angelina said, her lower lip jutting out.

"No, you're not," I shot back. "You dated years ago … and for like six months. You cheated on him and he dumped you. He hasn't bothered speaking to you since. How is that love?"

"Maybe she's gone crazy," Redmond offered.

"You shut your mouth, Redmond," Angelina said. "We all know you're going to take Aisling's side."

"Of course I'm going to take Aisling's side. She's my sister."

I sent him a pointed look.

"And she's always right," Redmond added.

"She is not always right." Angelina stomped her heeled shoe on the tiled floor. "She is a horrible person. Do you know the things she did to me in high school?"

"How about the things you did to Jerry?" Aidan countered.

"I never did anything to Jerry," Angelina said.

"You called him 'Jerry the Fairy.'"

"So? He is a fairy. You need to get over that. God made Adam and Eve, not Adam and Steve," Angelina said. "It's not my fault you're all godless heathens. Well, except for Cillian. You've all just snowed him."

Maya balked. "Wait a second … ."

"Listen, I know you have to pretend to like her because she's sleeping with your brother, but he won't be able to take her for long and then he'll dump her," Angelina said. "I have to pretend to like fairies all the time. I've even been to gay bars. They buy houses, though, so I don't have a lot of choice in the matter. The good news is, you won't have to be nice to her for long."

"Rip her hair out," Redmond instructed.

"I'll shove a sock in her mouth so no one hears her scream," Braden said.

"I hate you all," Angelina said. "Maya, what can you tell me about Cillian?"

"Nothing," Maya said. "You're not family."

Angelina was stunned. "I'm his … soul mate."

"You're my ass's soul mate," I shot back. "You stay away from my brother."

Griffin snagged me around the neck and pulled me flush with his chest. "Calm down."

"You are not welcome here, Angelina," Dad said, fixing her with a hard look. "You need to leave."

"You're not the boss," Angelina challenged. "Not here. This is a public place."

"Omigod! What is she doing here?" Jerry had arrived. He stalked into the waiting room and glared at Angelina. "Who invited the Devil?"

"She invited herself," I said.

"Oh, look, it's Jerry the fairy," Angelina said.

I did it without thinking it through. Mostly. I lashed out and smacked her across the face. Hard.

Angelina took an involuntary step back, her hand on her reddening cheek. "You … ."

"That's enough," Maya snapped.

"I want her arrested," Angelina said, pointing to me. "She assaulted me."

"I didn't see anything," Griffin said.

Angelina turned to Maya expectantly. After exchanging a quick look with her brother, Maya squared her shoulders. "I didn't see anything either."

I was surprised by the show of solidarity.

"You're all going to be sorry you messed with me," Angelina hissed.

"Honey, we're already sorry you wore that hideous suit," Jerry said. "The clearance rack is no place to shop, Angelina. How do you expect to sell houses when you look like you're homeless?"

Angelina waved her finger in Jerry's face. "You may be a faggot, but you don't know everything about fashion. Stop being a cliché."

I reached out to slap her again, but Griffin snagged my hand before I could. "Get out," I seethed.

"You can't make me leave."

Maya sighed and reached over to grab my wrist, directing my attention to her. "Why don't you come with me? I'll see if I can get you in to see your brother."

"That sounds like a great idea," Griffin said.

"I want to see him," Angelina said.

"You're not allowed to see him," Maya said. "Not only are you not a family member, but you seem to be a family enemy. My best advice for you is to go home."

"I am not going home until I see him."

"Fine," Maya said, nonplussed. She jerked on my arm. "Come with me."

Reluctantly, I followed her. Once we were away from the waiting room and near the nurses' station Maya held up her finger to still me. She motioned for the security guard who was drinking coffee and chatting with the receptionist. "Steve, can you come here, please?"

Steve shuffled over to us. "I was just having a cup of coffee."

"I don't care about that," Maya said. "There's a woman named Angelina Davenport in the waiting room. She's causing a disturbance. She's not related to anyone here and she's upsetting people who are here for legitimate reasons. I need you to show her out."

Steve nodded. "I'm on it."

I slid an appraising look in Maya's direction. "Thank you."

"I don't think your family needs more stress," Maya said, primly. "Now, I don't want you to think it's okay to slap someone across the face."

"It's not the first time."

Maya ignored me. "You need to learn to use your words."

"I can't use the words good enough for her in a public setting."

Maya smiled, sympathetic. "Let's go see your brother."

"HE'S SO PALE," I SAID, MOVING TO CILLIAN'S BEDSIDE.

"Nurse Taylor?" The doctor watching me didn't look thrilled with my appearance.

"Dr. Mackenzie, this is his sister," Maya explained apologetically. "They've been waiting for word. I thought it might be good if he had a familiar voice here to try to wake him."

Mackenzie looked me up and down. "I see the family resemblance."

"There are four more of them in the waiting room," Maya said.

"Okay," Mackenzie acquiesced. "Try talking to him. We're not sure why he's still unconscious. He doesn't have a head wound. And if he fainted, he should have regained consciousness by now."

I took Cillian's hand in mine and smoothed his hair off his forehead with my other hand. "Did you hear that? They think you fainted."

Cillian didn't stir.

"Try again," Mackenzie instructed. "Talk about something that would … I don't know … upset him."

I wracked my brain. "How freaked out are you that Ben Affleck is going to be Batman?"

Mackenzie shot me an odd look.

I sucked in a breath. "Angelina was here," I said. "She insisted on seeing you. I didn't rip her hair out, but I did smack her across the face. Then Maya … she's Griffin's sister, by the way, had her escorted out by security. I'm kind of sad I missed it, but I'm hoping Aidan filmed it on his phone to show me later."

Still nothing.

"Dad told me he never wanted me to join the family business," I tried again. "He said that he only worried about me before because I kept going to gay bars with Jerry."

Cillian's eyes fluttered. I leaned forward excitedly.

"You know you're going to be his favorite for at least a week straight if you wake up right now, don't you? You'll get chocolate cake every night, and blueberry pancakes every morning."

Cillian's mouth opened. "Blueberry pancakes are your favorite." His voice was hoarse, and he hadn't opened his eyes yet, but he was back. I wanted to cry, I was so relieved.

"I'll eat as many mushroom omelets as you want if you open your eyes right now," I offered, gripping his hand tighter. "I'll even eat the ones with the funky mushrooms."

"Morels aren't funky," he said, forcing his lavender eyes open to focus on me. I'd never seen anything so beautiful. "They're delicious."

"Hi," I said, tears spilling out.

"Hi, baby sister. How are you?"

"Better now."

"Good," Cillian said.

Mackenzie moved up to the other side of the bed. "Do you know where you are, son?"

Cillian glanced around the room, his eyes finally falling on Maya. "Heaven?"

I rolled my eyes. "Really? You're going to hit on the nurse now?"

"I have to use my ailment while I can," Cillian said, winking. "Women love to dote on an injured man."

"That's Griffin's sister."

"I don't care," Cillian said, pressing his eyes shut briefly. "She's hot."

I let loose with a shaky laugh. "You're going to be okay."

"Of course I am, Ais," he said. "I could never leave you."

14

FOURTEEN

"What happened?"

After an hour of doctors hovering around Cillian and asking an unending series of questions, my family – and Griffin and Jerry – were left to our own devices.

"I don't really remember," Cillian said, rubbing his forehead to clear the cobwebs. "It's all … fuzzy."

"What's the last thing you remember?" Dad asked.

"Morgan Reid," Cillian said. "He found us next to the building."

"That's good," Dad said. To no one's surprise, he was doting on Cillian. "What do you remember about the conversation?"

"He's a pig," Cillian said. "He was hitting on Aisling."

"He is a pig," Griffin grumbled.

"And that was after we told him we were married," Cillian added.

Redmond made a face. "Gross."

I stuck my tongue out at him.

"He didn't believe us," Cillian said.

"You look too much alike," Dad said, soothing.

"Especially with your hair," Redmond teased. "It's very feminine."

"Don't you dare pick on your brother's hair," Dad ordered.

Redmond raised his eyebrows once Dad turned his back and mouthed the word "wow" as he smiled at Cillian.

"I remember leaving Aisling with Reid," Cillian said. "I didn't want to, but I was worried. I couldn't figure out why he wasn't already dead."

"I think someone is hiring people to kill him," I said.

"Why do you think that?" Griffin asked.

"One murder might be random," I replied. "Two murders in two days? That's design."

"See, you are smarter than you look," Aidan teased.

"She has a point," Dad said. "The guy who tried to kill Reid yesterday had a lengthy record. That means he wasn't a novice. You have to be gutsy to go after a guy two days in a row."

"Or desperate," I said.

"What do you mean?"

"Maybe Reid has dirt on someone," I suggested. "He doesn't seem like the kind of guy who's above blackmailing someone. Why else would someone go after him? He's not married. I mean, if he were married I could see his wife wanting to kill him, but his file says he's single."

"Did he touch you?" Griffin asked pointedly.

"No."

"Did he want to?"

"He definitely wanted to," Cillian said. "The dude just feels slimy."

"Let's get back to this afternoon," Dad prodded. "What happened after you left Aisling with the human piece of filth?"

"It's probably a good thing I almost died, huh?" Cillian said, his eyes twinkling through the weariness. "I'd be in big trouble for leaving you if things had gone differently."

"That's exactly right," Dad said. "What happened after?"

"I … I just remember rounding the building," Cillian said. "I didn't see anyone right away. It was more like … I could feel someone moving in behind me. I didn't see anyone. There were hands on my shoulders, and then everything went black."

"He couldn't have been down long," Redmond said. "Wraiths can kill us in less than a minute if they want to."

"Aisling must have been there within a few seconds," Aidan said.

"You found me?" Cillian's eyes landed on me. "How did you … ?"

I shot him a reassuring smile. "I'm tougher than I look."

"But how?"

"She beat it to death with a brick," Redmond said.

Cillian's eyebrows shot up. "A brick?"

"There was one on the ground."

"How did you get close enough to hit it with a brick without it putting its hands on you?"

"I threw the brick at it first," I said. "While it was stunned, I grabbed the brick and beat its head in until it dissolved into dust."

"I … I remember something," Cillian said, his face grave. "It talked to you."

"I thought you were unconscious?"

"Wait, it talked to you?" Aidan was on his feet. "You didn't tell us that."

"I kind of forgot," I admitted.

"You forgot the wraith talked to you?" Redmond was incensed. "How does that happen?"

"I was worried about Cillian."

Dad held up his hand to silence everyone. "Okay, calm down."

We all waited.

"Seriously, how could you forget the wraith talked to you?" Dad exploded.

I shrank back, bumping into Griffin as a never-ending sea of lavender eyes landed on me. He put a reassuring arm around me. "Do we have to yell at her?"

"This is big," Braden explained. "Wraiths rarely talk. I mean, I guess they talk to other wraiths, but I've never heard of one speaking before."

"I didn't know they could speak," Redmond admitted.

"What did it say?" Dad pressed.

"I don't … it said my name," I said, flummoxed at the memory.

"It recognized you?"

I nodded. "It said that I couldn't be touched."

"Be more specific," Jerry said, speaking up for the first time. "Did it want to touch you in your naughty place?"

"Jerry!" Dad was beside himself.

"There are different kinds of touching," Jerry said. "They've done after-school specials about it. Watch something other than *Downton Abbey* for a change."

I couldn't hide my smirk. "It didn't want to touch me that way. It did recognize me, though."

"What else did it say?" Braden asked.

"It just kept looking at Cillian and saying 'mine.' I was waiting for it to call him 'my precious' and jump into the fiery pits of Mount Doom while cuddling him close to his chest."

Jerry made a face. "It's a good thing you're pretty, because most men would not tolerate a *Lord of the Rings* geek in their bed."

I glanced at Griffin.

"I don't care what kind of a geek you are," he said. "It does help that you're hot, though. It helps more with your family than anything else."

Redmond grinned as my father scowled.

"We still don't understand why the wraith was in the area," Cillian said. "We're not even sure it was the same wraith that killed Grant Spencer. Of course, we can't be sure a wraith killed Spencer at all.

Griffin wasn't happy with the insinuation. "You're saying there are more wraiths here, aren't you?"

"I think we have to assume that," Dad said.

"And why would they recognize Aisling?"

"I don't know," Dad said. "Maybe they recognize us all."

"It didn't appear to recognize Cillian," Griffin pointed out. "They seem to specifically be fixated on Aisling."

"Let's not jump to conclusions," Dad said.

"You're always the one who jumps to conclusions," Griffin argued.

Dad made a face. "Calm down."

"You calm down," Griffin shot back.

"You calm down."

"Everyone calm down," Jerry snapped. "We can't freak out."

I tilted my head as I regarded him. "Really?"

"I don't freak out, Bug," Jerry chided. "I calmly ascertain a situation and then enthusiastically voice my opinion. That's not the same thing."

I rolled my eyes. "We need more information," I said.

"I know where to get it," Redmond said, his eyes resting on me. "And you have to come with me."

"Where?" Dad asked.

It took me a second to grasp what he was suggesting, and I immediately started shaking my head. "No way. That woman hates me."

"Who hates you?" Griffin asked. "And, by the way, I'm not sure I buy that 'every woman in the world hates me' motto you keep espousing."

"Women hate me," I said. "It's a fact."

"You're going to Madame Maxine, aren't you?" Dad asked.

Redmond nodded.

"I'm not going to see that woman," I said. "She always tells me awful things about my future."

"Who is Madame Maxine?" Griffin asked.

"She owns a magic shop on Woodward," Braden explained.

"She's a psychic," Aidan added.

"She always tells me I'm going to be rich and famous," Jerry said, beaming.

"Why don't you like her?" Griffin asked.

"I already told you. I don't like her because she tells me awful things about my future."

"She said that you were wasting your time when you became a secretary," Redmond interjected. "How was that awful?"

"It was the truth," Jerry pointed out.

"Shut up, Jerry," I grumbled.

"You need to be there," Redmond said. "She's more forthcoming when you're there."

"She loves you," I said. "She thinks you're the greatest thing since the iPad. She's mean to me."

"I am the greatest thing ever," Redmond said. "The iPad isn't even in contention. She's not mean to you. She's … matter of fact."

Griffin's gaze bounced between Redmond and me. "Why does she have to go?"

"Madame Maxine likes to see her," Redmond said.

"Is she in any danger?"

Redmond shook his head.

"Then I think you should go," Griffin said.

Oh, great, now he was turning on me, too. "You're just letting me go? I thought you wanted to watch over me?"

Griffin smirked. "I have no doubt your brother will protect you from this Madame Maxine. As long as you're not taking on a wraith, I'm happy."

"But … ."

"It will only take an hour, Ais," Redmond prodded. "We need information."

One look at Cillian's wan face told me I was outnumbered. I crossed my arms over my chest. "Fine. If she tells me one bad thing … ."

"You'll listen and have a fit, like you usually do," Redmond finished. "We should go now. The shop will close in two hours."

Griffin ran his hand down the back of my hair and gave me a quick kiss. "I'll meet you at your place. I'll bring pizza."

"I don't want pizza," I sniffed.

"I'll get Chinese."

"I want Crab Rangoon … and spring rolls."

"Fine."

"And sesame chicken."

"Fine."

"And fried rice."

"I've got it, Aisling." Griffin pinched the bridge of his nose.

"We'll put together a list," Jerry said, patting Griffin's arm. "We like choices when we have Chinese."

"I can't wait," Griffin deadpanned.

The door to the hospital room opened and Maya entered. "How is everyone doing?"

"We're fine," Griffin said.

"I want to go home tonight," Cillian said.

"The doctors want you to stay overnight for observation," Maya said. "I think you probably should."

"He is," Dad said.

Cillian opened his mouth to protest.

"When you get home I'll have the cook make whatever you want," Dad said. "You're staying here tonight, though. We're not taking any chances."

Braden shot him a thumbs-up. "Don't worry. I'll stay here with you."

"Oh, good, you two can cuddle together and watch television," I teased.

"We're not you and Aidan," Braden shot back.

"I think the patient needs rest," Maya said. "I don't think an overnight guest means he's going to get rest."

"Yeah," Cillian said, smiling weakly. "I'm sure Maya will be willing to soothe me if I have any bad dreams."

"You stop that right now," Griffin ordered.

I pressed my eyes shut briefly. Things were back to normal. Everyone was okay. Now we just had to keep everyone that way.

15

FIFTEEN

"Come on."

Redmond held open the door to Tea & Tarot and waited.

"She's going to be mean to me," I said, pushing a faux pout on my face as I regarded my eldest brother. My brothers don't often fall for my emotional manipulation, but Redmond is the one who gives in easiest.

"She's not going to be mean to you."

"She is."

"She's not."

"She is."

Redmond growled. "Get your behind in this store!"

I made an exasperated sound in the back of my throat and strode through the door, stopping long enough to fix Redmond with a pathetic look. "You're the meanest man I know."

Redmond flicked the end of my nose. "I give in to you most of the time because I can't tell you 'no,'" he said. "But we need information. Cillian almost dying trumps you feeling uncomfortable."

"Fine."

Redmond pushed me the rest of the way across the threshold. Because the door had been open so long we'd drawn the attention of the proprietress. Madame Maxine floated from behind the counter, her floor-length skirt billowing as she crossed the room.

"Redmond Grimlock," she said, giving him a big hug. "It's been too long."

"It's only been a month and a half," he said.

"That's still too long," Maxine said. She turned her attention to me. "Hello, sourpuss."

I scowled. "Madame Maxine."

"You look … pouty."

"I'm not pouty."

"You look pouty."

"Well, I'm not."

"You look it."

Redmond clamped his hand on my shoulder. "We've had a long day," he said, glancing around the shop. Thankfully, it was empty. "Cillian was attacked by a wraith in Detroit this afternoon."

Maxine's face turned serious. "Is he all right?"

"Aisling got to him before the wraith could kill him," Redmond said.

"Did it run?"

"Aisling killed it."

Maxine gave me an appraising look. Her overlong hair was tucked in a messy bun, strands of gray shining under the overhead lights. "How did you kill it?"

"I beat it to death with a brick."

Maxine was impressed. "I didn't think you had it in you."

"She's being mean!"

"She's not being mean," Redmond said, exasperated.

"You're too sensitive," Maxine said. "That's always been your problem."

"Oh, are you going to tell me I'm going down the wrong path again? Isn't that your shtick?" Maxine had told me on two different occasions that I was due for a world of hurt before finding happiness. I hated her for it.

"No, you're done going down the wrong path," Maxine said, moving over to her tarot table. "You'll still make some missteps, but that's life."

I faltered. "What?"

"You're on the right track now."

"See, Ais, you were worrying for nothing," Redmond chided. "I told you."

"Oh, shut up," I grumbled.

"You were on the wrong path when you were trying to separate yourself from your destiny," Maxine said. "That's not a problem anymore. It will take time, but you will find yourself."

"Well, great."

Redmond shot me an admonishing look. "We need to know what you've heard about wraiths in the area."

"Not a lot," Maxine admitted. "Some people have claimed to see them, but no one has seen them in groups like before. The sightings have been sporadic. I thought that meant things were back to normal."

"We can't be sure, but we think there has to be more than one in the area," Redmond said. He recounted the past few days for Maxine while I watched nervously.

While he told the story, Maxine shuffled the tarot cards. When Redmond finished the story, she handed the cards to me. "Cut them."

"No way," I said. "I don't want to hear anything bad."

"Aisling," Redmond growled.

"Cut them."

I sighed, exasperated. I reached out and grabbed the deck, holding it close to my chest to hide my actions from Maxine before handing the cards back. Maxine flipped the first card up and studied it.

"What do you see?" Redmond asked.

Maxine ignored him as she continued to flip cards. When she had them assembled to her liking, she finally turned her attention back to us. "Things are shifting."

"Well, great," I muttered.

"You have more than one enemy," she said. "One you know. One you will … struggle with."

"What does that mean?" Redmond asked.

Maxine shrugged. "The future isn't written, and what I'm seeing here is clouded. Things are going to be in … flux."

"So, you're saying you don't know," I said.

"I'm saying that your family is at a crossroads," Maxine corrected. "Aisling is at the center of the crossroads."

"Is she in danger?" Redmond asked, instantly alert as his gaze shifted to the front door.

"You're all in danger," Maxine said. "You're also poised for greatness."

"How do we fight our enemy?" Redmond asked.

"You have to wait for it to show itself," Maxine replied. "When it does, decisions have to be made quickly."

"What does that even mean?" I sputtered.

"You're the one who will have to make the decisions," Maxine said, fixating on me. "You're the one who holds the key."

"I can barely keep track of my car keys," I said.

"Don't second-guess yourself," Maxine cautioned. "Your first instinct will be the right one."

Well, I was done here. "I'm hungry," I announced.

Redmond shot me a chastising look. "When?"

"Not today. Not tomorrow. Soon, though."

"So, I have time for dinner?" I knew I was being petulant. I couldn't seem to stop myself.

Maxine's expression wasn't dark, as I expected. The sympathy washing over her face was almost enough to bring me to my knees.

"You're going to be all right," she said after a moment. "You're stronger than they give you credit for. When the time comes, that's what you need to remember. Push everything else out of your mind."

"I'M NEVER GOING BACK THERE AGAIN!"

I slammed the front door of the townhouse for dramatic emphasis as I made my grand entrance, expecting the three occupants to fawn over me. I was disappointed.

Griffin glanced up from the chair at the edge of the living room. "Hello, dear."

"What happened?" Aidan asked.

"She was a pain in the ass, as I predicted," I said. "Oh, wait, maybe I'm a psychic now."

"Get some dinner," Jerry instructed. "We've been keeping it warm in the oven."

I pulled up short. "Have you guys already eaten?"

"You know I have blood-sugar issues," Jerry whined.

"I was hungry," Aidan said, nonplussed.

I shifted my gaze to Griffin.

"I waited for you," he said.

"And that's why you're my favorite," I said, channeling my father.

After shoveling an obscene amount of food into my mouth – and then cleaning up the mess I'd made under Jerry's watchful eye – Griffin and I returned to the living room.

"What are you guys watching?"

"*Sports Center*," Jerry said, making a face. "It's not very entertaining. No one is singing and no one is making snarky comments."

"I asked for five minutes to check scores," Aidan said, scowling. "I didn't ask you to watch any actual games."

"I don't want to watch ESPN," I said. "Put something else on."

"I have the remote," Aidan challenged. "I get to choose."

Griffin sighed. "Are you two going to fight again? I thought you'd made up."

"What made you think that?" I asked.

"He was sitting next to you and trying to make you feel better at the hospital," Griffin replied.

"That's family, not forgiveness," I said. "Not that I've done anything that I need to be forgiven for." My eyes were slits as I focused on Aidan.

"Do you know what we should do?" Jerry jumped to his feet and clapped his hands to garner everyone's attention.

We all waited.

"Let's play Monopoly."

"Absolutely not," I said. "I told you I would never play that game with you again."

"I have to agree with Aisling," Aidan said. "You can't be trusted to play Monopoly."

"Okay, I'll bite," Griffin said, blasé. "Why can't Jerry play Monopoly?"

"Because he's a poor loser," I said. "When someone beats him, he throws the board in the air and pitches a fit."

"I do not!"

"You're both addicted to the game and horrible when you play it," Aidan said.

"I'm wounded," Jerry said, clutching his heart. "I am as delightful in defeat as I am magnanimous in victory."

"You usually dance around the room calling yourself 'the king of the world' when you win," I reminded him.

"I do that when I watch *Titanic*," Jerry countered.

"You do it when you play Monopoly, too," I said.

"That is a vicious prevarication!"

Griffin sighed. "Do you have any other games?"

Jerry thought it over. "Risk."

"No," Aidan said, shaking his head vehemently. "We'll be picking up those little plastics pieces for weeks if we play that."

"Jerry can't lose at Risk either?" Griffin was confused.

"No, Aisling can't lose when we play Risk," Aidan explained.

Griffin looked to Jerry for explanation.

"She needs to dominate the world," Jerry said.

"I do not!"

"Don't you have Trivial Pursuit or something?" Griffin asked, rubbing his forehead. "We can separate into teams and it has fewer pieces."

I arched a challenging eyebrow in Jerry's direction. We're all poor losers when it comes to Trivial Pursuit.

"That's a great idea," he said. "A great idea."

"ANDRE AGASSI."

I lifted my eyes to Jerry, who had the card pressed to his chest, and waited. Our final question came from the sports category, so I'd deferred to Griffin. Jerry always picked sports questions when it came time for the win, mostly because he was convinced no one knew the answers. He didn't get that people had different knowledge bases.

Jerry groaned. "How could you possibly know that?"

"Sonovabitch." Aidan grabbed the edge of the board and tossed it into the air. He'd never been a good loser, but something about this game had driven him over the edge. He'd argued vociferously when Jerry insisted on asking a sports question when we'd finally landed in the center of the board. He knew sports was Griffin's strength, and he didn't want Griffin to be the one to answer the final question.

If it had been an entertainment question, and I'd supplied the final answer, Aidan would have pouted but retained his dignity. Griffin being the hero tipped him over the edge.

Colored plastic pie wedges flew around the living room.

"Oh, really?" I shot Aidan an exasperated look.

Griffin hadn't moved. He didn't even flinch when one of the pie containers – the blue one we'd been using – hit him in the cheek.

"We won," I said, fixing Aidan with a smug look.

"You cheated," Aidan hissed.

"How?"

"You … just did."

"Oh, it's going to take me hours to find all of those little wedges," Jerry complained.

"I'm going to bed," Griffin said, refusing to engage in our drama. He got to his feet. "He who throws the board picks up the pieces." He held his hand out to me. It was a direct challenge, and the look on Aidan's face gave me pause. He didn't just look angry, he looked hurt.

"You cheated," Aidan challenged.

"I'm not doing this with you," Griffin said. "It's … ridiculous."

"No one watches tennis," Aidan shot back.

"I happen to love tennis," Griffin said. "It's my favorite sport."

"Oh, come on! Tennis isn't anyone's favorite sport." Aidan was beside himself.

One look told me he was beyond reason tonight. I slipped my hand into Griffin's and let him lead me to the bedroom. I stopped long enough to lower my mouth close enough to Aidan's ear so only he could hear my parting shot: "I love you," I said. "You're just … breaking me. Please stop."

I couldn't see Aidan's face, but the slump of his shoulders told me my words had hit home.

We needed to talk … and soon.

16
SIXTEEN

"Aren't you going to carry me?"

Cillian was obviously feeling better. When Dad and I arrived the following morning to transport him back to Grimlock Manor he was nothing short of … sparkling. Of course, I had a feeling he was playing things up for someone else's benefit.

"Does your father often carry you?" Maya asked, smiling fondly at Cillian.

According to Braden's report, Maya had drummed him out before midnight, insisting Cillian needed a good night's sleep. Apparently, she'd checked in on my handsome brother no less than five times during the night. Something told me Griffin wasn't going to like this development.

"When Aisling was hurt, he wanted to carry her," Cillian pointed out.

"That's because I'm his favorite," I said, teasing.

"Not this week, you're not," Dad said, elbowing me out of the way so he could examine Cillian up close. "You look better."

"I look great," Cillian said, winking at Maya. "I always look great, by the way."

"You're definitely my hottest brother," I agreed.

Cillian pursed his lips. "I notice you're only saying that when the rest of our siblings happen to be absent. It would mean more if you said it in front of them."

"You've got it," I said.

Cillian grabbed my chin and tipped my head so he could stare into my eyes. "What's wrong with you?"

"Nothing."

"Something is wrong with you," he said. "Did you have a fight with Griffin?"

Maya furrowed her brow. "Did my brother upset you?"

"Griffin is fine," I said, jerking my chin away from Cillian's grasp. "He's been great. In fact, we teamed up and beat Jerry and Aidan in a rousing game of Trivial Pursuit last night."

Cillian smirked. "Did Jerry throw the board?"

"He only does that when we're playing Monopoly."

"I thought he did it when you played Risk," Dad said. "I seem to remember picking up those little plastic pieces for days after that board went flying."

"That was Aisling," Cillian said. "Once she lost Africa, it was all over."

"I did that once," I protested. "You people just won't let me forget it."

"We're all poor losers," Cillian explained to Maya.

"Aidan was the poor loser last night," I said. "It started when we finally landed in the center circle and Jerry insisted on asking a sports question."

"Aren't the sports questions easiest?" Maya asked.

Cillian snickered. "Jerry thinks because he doesn't care about sports that no one does."

"Well, Griffin loves sports," Maya said. "Did he answer the question?"

"He did," I said. "Then Aidan threw the board and accused him of cheating because it was a question about tennis."

"Oh, Griffin loves tennis," Maya said. "His dream is to be able to actually see a Wimbledon match some day."

That was interesting. I filed that tidbit away for future mulling. "Well, he got the question right and Aidan freaked."

"That doesn't sound like Aidan," Dad said. "He's usually a good sport."

"He's been a pain for days," I said. "It started the day we thought Griffin was cheating on me with Maya."

Dad scowled. "I need to have a talk with that boy."

"He wasn't cheating on me," I said. "I overreacted."

"Oh, you would never overreact," Cillian teased, tugging my hair. "I don't believe that for a second."

"Don't push me," I warned. "I'm only willing to play nursemaid for so long. Eventually, I'm going to go back to beating the crap out of you every chance I get."

"You're so loving," Cillian said, his eyes far away and wistful. "You make me want to cry."

I bumped my forehead against his softly. "Are you ready to go home?"

"I'm not sure," Cillian said. "I think I might need to stay here another night."

Was he serious? Because his eyes were locked on Maya I had a feeling he was flirting more than anything else. "I am not going to give you a sponge bath," I warned.

"Well, thank you for that nightmare," Cillian said, flicking my ear. "What are you going to do for me?"

"Anything you want," Dad said.

"Within reason," I cautioned.

"Are you going to bring me breakfast in bed?"

"Really? Are you saying you're too sick to sit at the table?"

"Hey, you spent an entire day in bed after you got hurt," Cillian reminded me.

"I was thrown through a plate-glass window," I countered.

Maya's forehead wrinkled. "You got thrown through a window?"

Crap. I'd forgotten we had an audience. "I have a really bad attitude," I said.

"She does," Cillian agreed.

"But … ."

"We should get going," Dad said.

"Well, it was really nice to meet you," Maya said, patting Cillian's hand. She seemed reluctant to see him go.

"I might need a private nurse," Cillian said. "Do you moonlight?"

Dad finally focused on the scene in front of him, realization dawning. "Oh," he muttered.

"You're quick on the uptake, Pa."

He shot me a look. "Do you think you need a home nurse, son?" Dad asked, his tone serious. He was trying to help.

"Yes," Cillian said. "Only if it's Maya, though."

"I already work here sixty hours a week," Maya replied, laughing.

"Oh." Cillian was disappointed.

"You two are pathetic," I said. "Instead of trying to trick her into the house why don't you just invite her for dinner?"

Cillian's face brightened at the prospect. "Hey, that's a good idea," he said. "You're smarter than you look."

"Why do you people keep saying that?"

"That is a good idea," Dad said. "Would you like to join us for dinner tonight? We're planning a big feast. It will feature all of Cillian's favorites."

"And what are his favorites?" Maya asked, her eyes twinkling.

"I think it's nurses," I said, my tone dry.

"We're having a nice prime rib, mashed potatoes, corn on the cob, red velvet cake and a lobster bisque," Dad said.

"Wow," Maya said, impressed. "Do you always eat like that?"

"And since when are you so up on the menu?" I asked. "Aren't you the guy who said, 'It's food, shut up and eat it?'"

"Since I wanted to make sure everything was perfect for your brother," Dad said.

"I don't want red velvet cake," I said. "Can't we have chocolate?"

Dad fixed me with a hard look. "Did you almost die?"

"No."

"Next time you almost die, you can pick the dessert."

"You're so mean to me," I grumbled.

"I'll ask the cook to make you cupcakes," Cillian said.

"You're sweet," Maya said.

"That's just the type of brother I am."

My eyes rolled so hard I almost tipped over. "You used to wrestle me down and rub my face in your armpit."

"That's also the type of brother I am," Cillian conceded.

"Don't worry. Griffin used to do that to me, too," Maya said. "I think that's a universal brother thing."

"I think it's a testosterone thing," I said.

"We should be going," Dad said. "Maya, you didn't answer. Would you like to come to dinner tonight?"

The hope on Cillian's face almost crushed me. He really seemed to like Maya. This was going to kill Griffin.

"I would love to," Maya said. "May I walk you out?"

"Absolutely," Cillian said, jumping to his feet.

"You have to go out in a wheelchair," Maya said.

"I'm fine," Cillian said, tapping his chest. "I'm young and virile."

"You were unconscious for hours yesterday," Maya countered.

Cillian tried again. "I'm fine today, though."

"It's hospital policy."

Cillian sighed. "Fine. I'm only doing this because I don't want you to get in trouble with your superiors," he said.

"That's just the kind of guy you are, right?"

"Right."

"CAN YOU CLIMB INTO THE ESCALADE YOURSELF, OR DO YOU NEED ME to lift you?"

Cillian stuck out his tongue.

We stood under the awning in front of the hospital waiting for Dad to pick us up.

"He should rest this afternoon," Maya said. "Don't let him do too much. I know he seems fine, but … ."

"Trust me. My father is going to shove him in his bed and make him stay there all day," I said. "He picked you up a bunch of books, by the way."

"What books?"

"Romances."

Cillian pinched my arm.

"I don't know," I said, rubbing the tender spot ruefully. "A bunch of that science fiction stuff you like."

"Those are classics."

"Do you read a lot?" Maya asked, interested.

"I like to read," Cillian said.

I took a step away so they could flirt. I scanned the parking lot for lack of anything better to do, and when my gaze fell on a familiar figure I swore under my breath.

"What is it?" Cillian asked, instantly alert. His ordeal the day before had made him hyper-vigilant, I realized.

"It's nothing," I said.

"Do you always swear like that when it's nothing?" Maya asked.

"Fine, it's something," I conceded. "Something really trashy."

"What?" Cillian peered around me. When he saw Angelina heading in our direction he frowned. "Why?"

"She wants to torture me," I grumbled.

"I think she's here for me," Cillian said.

"Do you really want to argue about which one of us has the worst luck?"

Cillian sighed. "No."

"I'll get rid of her." I stepped off the curb and put myself directly in Angelina's path.

"She's not going to kill her, right?" Maya sounded worried.

"Not unless losing one's hair at the root is a legitimate cause of death," Cillian said.

"Didn't you read the sign?" I asked. "No skanks allowed."

Angelina frowned. "What are you doing here?"

"I'm donating my time in the children's ward," I deadpanned.

"As what, a clown on weekends?"

"Oh, funny," I said. "You know tyrannical hell beasts are banned, right?"

"Shut up, Aisling," Angelina snapped. "I'm here to see your brother."

"He doesn't want to see you," I said.

"You don't know that." Angelina pasted a bright smile on her face as she regarded Cillian. "How are you?"

"I'm great," Cillian replied, his face drawn. "I'd be even better if you left."

Angelina's face fell. "But … I came to see you."

"Why?" Cillian asked. "Why would you possibly think I'd want to see you?"

"Oh, you're not still mad about our misunderstanding, are you?"

"Misunderstanding?" Cillian's voice jumped.

"I think she's referring to when she slept with half of the football team even though she really loved you," I said.

Cillian's eyes were dark when they landed on me. "You're not helping."

"Oh, I didn't know that was what I was supposed to be doing," I said. "I'm sorry. I was in bitch mode. I'll switch to supportive-sister mode now." I mock saluted in his direction.

Cillian blew out a frustrated sigh.

"Why don't you let me take you home?" Angelina suggested. "We could talk."

"I don't want to talk to you," Cillian said.

"Because Aisling doesn't want you to talk to me?"

"Because I have nothing to say to you," Cillian countered. "We don't have anything in common. We never had anything in common. I fooled myself into thinking you were a decent person despite all of the terrible things you did to Aisling and Jerry. I was an idiot."

"But … I could make it up to you," Angelina whined.

"I don't want you to make it up to me," Cillian said. "I don't want you to do anything to me, or for me, or with me. I just don't … want you."

Angelina's face crumbled. "But … ."

"Just go," Cillian said.

Dad pulled his Escalade to the front of the hospital and climbed out, fixing Angelina with a hateful look as he moved past her. "What is she doing here?"

"Realizing she's obsolete in Cillian's life," I said, smug.

Angelina whipped around. I saw her hand heading toward my face, but it was too late to duck. She slapped me. "This is your fault," she hissed.

"Hey," Dad snapped. "If you touch her again I'm going to forget that I don't hit women."

"And I'm going to help him," Cillian warned.

"You had no problem with her slapping me last night," Angelina protested.

"That was funny," Dad said. "And you had it coming. No one invited you here, Angelina. No one wants you here. Find someone else to chase, and find someone else to torture."

"But … ."

"No," Dad said. "Cillian, get in. Aisling, I assume you're coming back to the house in your own car?"

I nodded.

Dad smiled at Maya warmly. "We'll see you for dinner, right?"

"Um, yes," Maya said, her gaze bouncing between faces as the scene continued to unfold. "I'm looking forward to it."

"I'll make sure she has the address," I said.

Dad glanced at me. "You're not going to get in a brawl with Angelina once I leave, are you?"

"No," I said. "I've already beaten Angelina. There's no reason to dance on her grave."

Angelina scowled. "This isn't over."

"It's been over for a really long time, Angelina," I said. "You just refuse to accept it. It's sad and it's pathetic, but there it is."

"This isn't over," Angelina seethed, her fists clenched.

"Yes, it is."

17

SEVENTEEN

"So, do you like Maya?"

Cillian had been home only twenty minutes and was already going stir crazy. Dad had forced him upstairs and into bed the second he walked into the house, despite Cillian's unrelenting protests. It seemed his bouts of weakness were fleeting, and usually only when a sympathetic nurse was in the immediate vicinity.

"She's attractive," Cillian said, averting his eyes. "I cannot sit in this bed all day."

"You're going to have to," I said. "If you're good, Dad will let you out of bed for dinner."

"He's being oppressive," Cillian complained.

"He likes to hover," I said. "It's his way. I think he was worse with me."

"That's because you're his only daughter," Cillian said. "I have three replacements."

I smirked. "Do you really think you're replaceable?"

"No," Cillian said. "I just … I feel like an idiot."

I climbed onto the bed and settled next to him. "Why?"

"I didn't even see the wraith," Cillian said. "By the time I sensed it, it was already too late."

"That's not your fault," I said. "They're sneaky."

"You saved me," Cillian said. "If it hadn't been for you … ."

"You wouldn't have a nurse to hit on," I teased.

"Thank you," Cillian said, now serious. "You rushed headlong into danger to protect me."

"Haven't you done that for me since I was born?"

"I don't think fighting off horny football players in high school is quite the same thing," Cillian said.

"Oh, but it's more important," I said, resting my head against his shoulder. "You saved me from sleeping with someone who was incapable of giving a woman an orgasm. You saved my life."

Cillian snorted. "I'm being serious, Ais," he said. "You saved me."

"Well, I can't live without you – any of you – so I really saved myself," I said.

"You're a lot sweeter than you act sometimes," Cillian said.

"Oh, that's a vicious thing to say to the woman who saved your life."

"I saw the tears when I woke up," Cillian reminded me. "I saw the worry on your face. You only look that way when Jerry is trying out new recipes and you have to fit into your skinny jeans."

He knew me so well. "Are you going to ask Maya out?"

Despite his earlier bravado, Cillian's eyes were starting to droop. "I don't know," he said. "How would you feel about that?"

"She's not really my type," I said. "You can have her."

"That's not what I meant," Cillian said. "Would it cause problems between you and Griffin?"

"Would that stop you?"

"Yes," he said. "I want you to be happy. You seem to be happy with him, even when he reverts to Detective Dinglefritz mode from time to time."

"I think that Griffin doesn't want any of you to date his sister," I said after a moment.

"Then I won't date her."

"I don't think it's for the same reason you think it is," I said.

"I'm all ears."

"You're all hair," I countered. "Anyway, I don't think Griffin is against you guys dating Maya because he doesn't like you. Well, he really doesn't like Aidan right now, but there's no chance of a love connection there, so we're safe.

"I think Griffin wants to keep Maya away from us because we're reapers," I continued. "He doesn't want her in this life."

"Are you worried that he's going to walk away because our life is so … odd?"

"Not really," I said. "He seems okay with it. I've tried explaining that the past few weeks haven't exactly been normal, but every time something goes wrong I look like an idiot."

"He's not going to run, Ais," Cillian said. "It's written all over his face when he looks at you. I think that's the root of Aidan's problems right now."

"What do you mean?"

"Aidan, just like the rest of us, used to worry that you would fall for the wrong guy and get hurt," Cillian said. "Now, the opposite is true. Aidan is worried you've found the right guy."

"That should make him happy, shouldn't it? I'm happy for him and Jerry."

"Give him time," Cillian said. "You two have a special bond."

"You don't think we're bonded?"

"We're all bonded. You and Aidan have a different relationship, though."

"Because we're twins?"

"Because you're so tight," Cillian said, his voice tapering off. "It's going to work out."

"I hope so."

"It will. Try looking on the bright side for a change. You might be surprised how things work out for you."

"Are you saying I'm a pessimist?"

"Shh," Cillian whispered, his chin dropping onto his chest. He was out within seconds, and despite my best intentions, I followed him into slumber a few minutes later.

What? It had been a long couple of days.

"THEY'RE SO CUTE."

I forced my eyes open and focused on the open doorway of Cillian's room. A quick scan told me we'd drawn a crowd. Dad was sleeping in a nearby chair, a book on his lap, and Braden was snapping photographs with his phone.

Griffin stepped into the room and smiled down at me. "They are kind of cute."

I glanced over to find Cillian rousing next to me. "What time is it?"

"It's three, Sleeping Beauty," Braden said. "By the way, I'm putting these photos all over Facebook."

"Don't make me break that phone," I warned.

"I can't believe we slept all day," Cillian said.

"You needed your sleep," Braden said. "That doesn't explain Aisling and Dad, though."

"They needed their sleep, too," Griffin said. "Your father is downright adorable when he's asleep."

"You know I can hear you, right?" Dad wrenched his eyes open.

"I figured," Griffin said, shifting his attention to me. "Are you going to spend all day in bed with your brother?"

"I didn't mean to fall asleep," I said, rubbing my eyes. "I'm not sure how it happened. We were just sitting here talking … and then … I don't know."

"What were you talking about?" Braden asked.

"Life," Cillian said.

"Love," I teased.

"Dig it, man," Cillian poked me in the side.

"This family is so odd," Griffin said.

"What are you doing here?" I asked. "I thought you were working today."

"I was. You slept the whole day away."

"Oh."

"I have information, too," Griffin said. "I thought you'd all want to hear it."

"Is anyone else home?" Dad asked.

"Redmond is finishing a job in Hamtramck," Braden said. "Don't worry, Aisling. He's picking up your favorite doughnuts from that shop you like."

I smiled. My brothers take such good care of me sometimes.

"Where is Aidan?" Dad asked.

"Jerry probably has him searching the carpet to make sure none of the Trivial Pursuit pieces are missing," I said.

"This family really shouldn't be allowed to play board games," Griffin said.

"You should see us play Twister," I said.

Braden snorted and climbed onto the bed on the other side of me. "Your hair is a mess."

"Leave your sister alone," Dad ordered. He turned to Griffin. "What did you find out?"

"I have some information on Morgan Reid," Griffin said. "I'm sorry, am I the only one who thinks it's weird that the three of you are in bed together?"

"We're not naked, so why does it matter?" Cillian asked.

"It's just … weird."

"When we were kids, Aisling used to be afraid of thunderstorms," Braden said. "She used to climb into bed with us all the time."

"Aisling wasn't the only one afraid of thunderstorms," Cillian scoffed.

"Aidan was, too," Braden said.

"So were you," Cillian pointed out.

"That's a vicious lie."

Griffin rolled his eyes. "Okay, let's talk about real life now, shall we?"

"You're grumpy," I said.

Griffin ignored me. "Morgan Reid is not a good guy," he said.

"You could tell that just by looking at him," I said. "He's got evil hair."

Braden reached over and grabbed my hand to study my fingernails. "I like this color."

"Seriously?" Griffin placed his hands on his hips. "It's like this whole family has ADD."

"What?" Braden asked, nonplussed.

"Focus," Dad snapped. "You're irritating him."

"We're not doing anything," Braden said.

"You're irritating me, too."

"Oh, this family is just a laugh a minute," Braden grumbled. "Go on, detective."

Griffin scowled. "Reid has been arrested eight times, although he's never been charged with anything."

"How does that happen?" I asked.

"He has a very good lawyer," Griffin said. "Also, there's been a string of 'mistakes' in police procedure during his arrests."

"Does that mean there's a turncoat in the department?" Cillian asked.

"Ooh, intrigue," I said.

"What has Reid been arrested for?" Dad asked.

"Money laundering."

I frowned. "Who is he laundering money for?"

"The highest bidder."

"I'm not sure whether that helps us," Dad said. "It's interesting, but it opens up a really big suspect pool. I'm guessing every lowlife on the east side has a reason to want to kill Reid."

"It doesn't explain why the wraiths keep showing up, either," I said. "I don't think wraiths have much use for money."

"No, but the person in charge of the wraiths might," Griffin suggested.

"Oh, I hadn't thought of that."

"That's because you're too busy sleeping the day away with your brother," Griffin said.

"Oh, man, you're going to keep harping on this, aren't you? Have you considered that now I'm very well rested so I can focus my attention on you this evening?"

Griffin's cheeks colored.

"My baby sister, ladies and gentlemen," Braden said, flicking the side of my head. "Don't gross me out."

"Oh, grow up," I said. "I'm not grossing you out."

"No, but you're freaking me out," Cillian said.

"Dad," I complained.

"What? I'm on their side," Dad said. "You're royally ticking me off."

I glanced at Griffin for support. "You make me tired," he said.

Well, I do have a way with people. "I'm hungry," I said. "What time is Cillian's big feast?"

"I don't know," Dad said. "What time is Maya getting here?"

Griffin stilled. "Maya?"

Uh-oh. "Um, yeah, did I fail to mention that? We invited Maya to dinner and she accepted."

Griffin narrowed his eyes. "Why would you invite Maya?"

"Because she was hungry," I said.

"And?"

"And we're generally polite people," I added.

"And Cillian has the hots for her," Braden teased.

Griffin slapped his forehead. "Oh, no. I knew this was going to happen."

"What's the problem?" Dad asked. "It's just a family dinner."

"But … ."

"It will be fine," I said, climbing off the bed and patting Griffin's chest as I moved past him. "We'll be on our best behavior."

"Is that saying much?"

I shrugged. "Not really."

"I just … ."

"It's going to be fine," I said. "She's already seen us at our worst."

"That was nowhere near your worst," Griffin said. "Trust me."

"Well, we'll be better tonight," I said.

"You'd better be." Griffin followed me down the hallway. "Where are you going?"

"I need to change my clothes. I'm going to my room."

"Don't you think it's weird that you own a townhouse with Jerry and yet you still have a room here?"

"No."

"How did this dinner even come up?"

"Well, Cillian really wanted a sponge bath, but I thought you would frown upon that," I teased. "I came up with the dinner idea as a nice compromise."

"It was your idea?"

"No," I said. "Not if I'm going to be in trouble. Absolutely not."

Griffin grabbed me by my shoulders and shifted me around so he could press me against the wall. He gave me quick kiss, one promising fun later that night. "You're lucky I find you irresistible," he growled.

"That's what I'm counting on."

"Your whole family is going to be good tonight, right?"

"Of course," I said. "What could go wrong?"

That was probably the wrong question to ask.

❧ 18 ❧

EIGHTEEN

"So, I'm curious. How many rooms does this house have?"

Griffin and I sat in my favorite parlor – the house boasts five – waiting for Maya's arrival. Griffin sipped bourbon from a cut-crystal glass, which bordered on absurd, but I was trying to make him feel comfortable in my father's oppressive house.

"I don't know," I said, shifting closer to him on the couch. "I've never counted."

Griffin placed his glass on the coffee table and glanced around, nervous. "Should you be this close to me?"

"Are you worried I have cooties?"

"I'm worried one of your brothers – or worse, your father – is going to come in here and assume we're doing something," Griffin said.

"We are doing something," I replied. "We're sitting on the couch."

"Yes, but you're touching me."

"Three hours ago you shoved your tongue in my mouth in the hallway," I said. "You didn't have a problem with that."

"Shh." Griffin looked over his shoulder to ascertain if we were still alone.

"I thought you were a big, bad cop?"

"I am," Griffin said.

"You're afraid of my father!"

"Your father is terrifying when he wants to be."

"Oh, you're such a girl."

Griffin poked my stomach. "Is that the insult your brothers used to hurl at each other when you were a kid?"

"Why?"

"Because you use it a lot."

I shrugged. "I guess. I never really thought about it. You are acting like a girl, though."

Griffin grabbed me around the waist and tugged me down on the couch to roll on top of me and kiss me. We played tongue tag – and "what's under your shirt" – until the sound of voices stopped the fun.

"This is the parlor my late wife designed," Dad said, ushering Maya into the room. He didn't miss a beat when he saw what we were doing on the couch. "And you remember my daughter and your brother, of course. I think they're preparing their audition for *Monday Night Raw*."

Cillian walked into the room behind them and snorted. "I think Griffin is winning."

Griffin jerked away. "We were just … ."

I arched an eyebrow, mildly curious as to whether he would bother trying to come up with a lie.

"I know what you were doing," Dad said, his tone grim. "I raised five children. All of them have been caught doing … that … at one time or another."

Griffin smiled sheepishly.

"Of course, they were all teenagers when they were doing it," Dad said.

"At least they weren't naked this time," Aidan said, breezing into the room and heading straight for the bar. "That's much more traumatic."

I shot him a harsh look.

Dad's eyebrows knit together. "When did you see them naked?"

"Oh, don't worry, it wasn't here," Aidan said.

"No, it was at my house," I said. "My house! My house where you don't live so you have no right to get all … funky … about what I'm doing in the privacy of my own home."

"I don't want to hear this," Dad said.

Braden pushed his way into the room. "What's going on now?" he asked. "Hey, by the way, my photo of you and Cillian on the bed has gotten more than a hundred likes on Facebook."

I shot him a sarcastic thumbs-up.

"Apparently Aidan saw your sister and her friend naked on the couch," Dad said.

"Oh, I already heard about that," Braden said, unimpressed.

"Who told you?"

Braden pointed at Cillian.

"What? It's funny," Cillian said.

"It's not funny," Aidan said. "It's mentally scarring."

"And seeing you and Jerry rub each other like cats in heat is fun for me?" I shot back.

"Oh, man, the floor show has already started," Redmond said, shuffling into the room. He pulled up short when he saw Maya. "Hello, Nurse Maya." He grabbed her hand and kissed it. "I can't tell you how nice it is to see you again."

"Don't be fresh," Griffin warned.

"You were just groping my daughter on the couch," Dad said.

"We hadn't gotten to groping yet," I said. "Calm yourself. You'll give yourself a heart attack."

"Do you think that's funny?" Dad asked.

"That you interrupted us before we could start groping? Absolutely not."

"You're going in the dungeon tonight," Dad said. "That's final!"

"I do kind of want to see that dungeon," Griffin mused. "Don't worry. I'll sleep in there with you. Are there chains on the wall?"

"I'm going to kill you," Dad threatened.

"Wow," Maya said, her gaze bouncing around the room. "If this is the floor show, what happens when the main event arrives?"

"I CANNOT BELIEVE HOW BEAUTIFUL THIS ROOM IS," MAYA SAID, HER eyes trained on the over-the-top chandelier above the long, rectangular dining table.

"It's not creepy at all," I agreed, sliding into my usual seat.

"Creepy? I've dreamed about eating in a room like this," Maya said, scanning every nook and cranny. "I mean, look at the statues."

"Oh, Monty and Mort," Redmond said, following her gaze to the marble lions standing guard at either side of the door.

"I used to have nightmares that they were going to eat me," I said.

"Who named them Monty and Mort?" Maya asked.

Everyone pointed in my direction. "She names everything," Aidan said.

"Is that because you thought they were pets?" Maya asked, smiling as Cillian ushered her to a chair and held it out until she was seated.

"No. It's because I knew it drove my father crazy," I said. "I used to put collars on them, too."

I watched as Griffin purposely took the chair between Maya and me. He aimed for subtlety but he was drawing a non-too-inconspicuous line in the sand between Maya and my brothers. Cillian stepped right over the line as he sat down in the chair on the other side of his sister.

For her part, Maya appeared oblivious to the musical chairs power play. "Did you put ribbons on them?"

"No," I said. "Aidan did, though."

"I did not," Aidan protested.

"No, but I put rhinestone collars and tiaras on them," Jerry said, striding into the room. "Sorry I'm late. I had a big catering order come in and it took forever to get the lady to see that rainbows and leprechauns were too over-the-top for a gay wedding."

"What did you decide on?" I asked.

"Unicorns and elves," Jerry replied, guileless.

"Oh, are you a party planner?" Maya asked.

"I own a bakery in Royal Oak," Jerry explained.

"Get Baked," I supplied. "It's amazing. If you get the chance, you should stop in. Jerry is a culinary genius."

"He is," Griffin agreed.

"You've been there?" Maya asked.

"No, he cooks breakfast every morning," Griffin said.

Dad scowled from the head of the table.

"I know because I stop in to wish Aisling a 'good day' every morning before I go to work," Griffin said. "That's after I've spent the night at my own place."

What a wuss.

Redmond snorted. "Bravo, detective."

"Everyone sit down," Dad ordered. "You all know very well that the staff can't start serving until everyone is seated."

"Why is that?" Maya asked.

"Because it gives Dad indigestion," Braden said.

"Do you remember the time Jerry insisted on performing the entire death scene from *Romeo and Juliet* because he was practicing for the school play?" Redmond asked. "Dad drank an entire bottle of Pepto-Bismol watching him cry over Aisling's lifeless body, and the staff was freaking out because the roast was drying out because Jerry's death flop was so over-the-top."

"You were in a play?" Griffin asked, dubious. "You don't strike me as the acting sort."

"Oh, I fake stuff all the time," I teased.

Griffin's face clouded.

"I'm just joking," I said, patting his leg under the table.

"Keep your hands to yourself, Aisling," Dad ordered.

"How do you even know I'm doing anything?"

"You're always doing something," Dad said. "You can't help yourself."

"You're sleeping in the dungeon tonight," Aidan sang.

"I was not in the play," Aisling said. "I just helped Jerry practice his lines."

"We loved it," Redmond said. "Aisling was quiet for hours on end."

"Hey, you leave her alone," Jerry scolded. "Don't you listen to them, Bug. I'll have you know she came to every performance to cheer me on."

"Both of them," I confirmed.

Griffin smirked. "Don't Romeo and Juliet have to kiss?"

"We didn't play those scenes," I said.

"Aisling said my lips reminded her of a fish," Jerry said.

"I said they reminded me of Swedish Fish," I corrected. "You insisted on wearing lipstick."

"Why did you wear lipstick?" Maya asked.

"Because it was winter," Jerry replied.

Maya shifted her attention to me. "Did he just explain something?"

"He's pale in winter," I said. "He needs the extra color so people don't mistake him for a really pale straight guy."

"Oh," Maya said, running her eyes over Jerry's bright pink shirt. "Does that happen often?"

"Not since elementary school," I said. "He's never gotten over it."

"It was the worst day of my life," Jerry agreed.

Maya smiled. "You're all very close, aren't you?"

"We're a family," Dad said. "Aren't all families close?"

Maya and Griffin exchanged a brief look. "Not all," she said. "You're very lucky."

Something about the exchange bothered me. It wasn't something I wanted to explore now, but it occurred to me that Griffin rarely talked about his family. I hadn't even known his sister lived in the area until I thought he was dating her.

"We are lucky," Dad said.

"We should play the lottery," I said.

"You're definitely sleeping in the basement tonight, young lady," Dad said.

"I have my own house," I said. "That threat doesn't work on me anymore."

"Did it ever work on you?" Griffin asked. "Were you afraid of the basement?"

"I wasn't afraid of the basement," I said. "I was afraid of the snakes."

"There are snakes in the basement?" Griffin didn't look convinced. "Don't you have twenty maids cleaning this place?"

"We have three," Dad said. "There are no snakes. Redmond told her that to keep her out of the basement when he was doing his … experiments … down there."

"Experiments?"

"Oh, they're not the kind of experiments you think," Jerry said. "I was crushed when I found out what he was really doing. I had a huge crush on him when I was younger. When he said he was experimenting, I thought I had a shot."

Maya pressed her lips together to keep from laughing. "What kind of experiments?"

"I thought I was going to be a scientist at one time," Redmond said evasively.

"He bought three grow lights and tried to grow pot down there," I corrected.

"Hey, there's a cop here," Redmond said.

"He doesn't care that you thought you were growing pot when you were in high school," I scoffed.

"He was really growing pansies," Braden said.

"How did that happen?" Griffin asked.

"Stupid Tom Mulligan," Redmond growled.

"He sold him bogus product," Cillian said, smirking.

"So, don't leave me hanging," Maya said, clearly enjoying herself. "What happened?"

"There was a lot of yelling," Cillian said. "And Jerry and Aisling really helped matters when they suggested Redmond should have to smoke the pansies as penance."

"I forgot about that," Redmond said, rubbing his chin.

"Finally, Mom stepped in," Braden said. "She reminded Dad that he'd tried to do the same thing when he was in college, and Redmond got off with a simple grounding."

"Did your mother always take your side?" Maya asked.

A pall settled over the table.

"I'm sorry," Maya said, realizing her mistake. "I didn't mean to pry."

"It's fine," Dad said. "She did always take their side. That's why they got away with murder as children. And why they're such pain-in-the-ass adults."

"Well, they seemed to have turned out okay," Maya said.

"They did indeed," Dad said, gracing her with a small smile. "Now, where is my dinner?"

19

NINETEEN

"So, do you always have nightcaps as a family?"

Dad was going above and beyond in his efforts to seduce Maya for Cillian.

"No," I said. "Most of us storm out halfway through dinner."

Dad shot me a look. We were back in the parlor, and he was busily pouring drinks from behind the bar. "Aisling is exaggerating. We don't fight very often."

"What's your definition of often?"

Dad pointed at me. "You're on my last nerve."

"Oh, look, he just got another gray hair," Redmond said as he moved up beside me. "Isn't Aisling the one responsible for all of your gray hair?"

"She is this week," Dad said.

"Hey, Cillian was the one who almost died," I said.

"Because of you," Dad said.

Maya shifted her gaze. "How is it Aisling's fault that Cillian was mugged?"

Dad faltered. "Everything is always her fault," he said finally.

"Hey!"

Griffin rubbed my back. "Let it go," he said, his voice low. "You're going to tip her off that we're all lying if you're not careful."

He had a point. That was the last thing I wanted. "You can't possibly still be blaming this all on me," I exploded.

Dad shot me a look. "Who else am I supposed to blame?"

"Oh, I don't know," I said, snarky. "What about Morgan Reid?"

"Who is Morgan Reid?" Maya asked.

"No one," Griffin said.

"But … ."

"He's no one," Griffin pressed. "He's … ."

"Aisling's imaginary friend," Jerry supplied.

I glared at him.

"What? I'm trying to help."

"Well, stop helping," I said.

"Don't you yell at him," Aidan said.

"He's my best friend."

"He's my boyfriend."

"He was my friend first," I said. "I can speak to him however I want to speak to him."

"Is that a new rule?" Aidan asked. "It seems I can't speak to your boyfriend any way I want to speak to him."

"What's going on now?" Dad asked, pinching the bridge of his nose. "Is this about the Trivial Pursuit game?"

"He cheated," Aidan said.

"I did not cheat," Griffin said. "You're just a poor loser."

"We're all poor losers," Braden said. "You should see us play billiards. There are balls flying everywhere."

"And not in a fun way," Jerry said.

I couldn't swallow my snicker.

"Oh, so now you're friends again?" Aidan asked.

"We're always friends," I said. "Stop being a … girl."

"You're a girl," Aidan said.

"You take that back."

"All of you, shut up right now," Dad ordered. "You're giving me heartburn."

Braden pushed around to the back of the bar and rummaged for something out of sight. When he stood back up, he handed Dad a bottle of pink medicine without saying a word. Dad chugged it down straight from the bottle.

"Have you guys ever considered therapy?" Maya asked. "We have some nice family therapists on staff at the hospital."

Maya sucked all of the energy – including the electricity – out of the room with the suggestion, because the room went black.

"What just happened?" Maya asked, worried.

"The Earth tilted on its axis," Redmond said.

"Therapists everywhere just used their combined mental power to send us a very distinct message," Cillian said.

"Or Dad imploded and took the electricity with him," Braden suggested.

"You're the one sleeping in the dungeon tonight, Braden," Dad said.

I clapped my hands. "The snakes are going to get you."

"The rhythm is going to get him," Jerry corrected.

"Everyone shut up!"

"Jeez, Dad, lighten up," Aidan said.

We all cracked up at the joke.

"I hate you all," Dad said.

The room fell into silence for a few moments.

"Do you have an emergency generator?" Griffin asked.

"It's in the back," Dad said.

"Does it automatically come on?"

"No," Redmond said. "We have to start it manually."

"Don't you think we should?" Griffin pressed. "I'm starting to feel odd about just standing here in the dark together. Hey! Whose hand is that?"

"Mine," I said.

"Keep your hands to yourself, Aisling," Dad barked.

"I was touching his arm," I said.

"That wasn't my arm."

"I know," I replied. "You didn't need to tell my father that, though."

"Okay, that's enough of that," Dad said. I heard shuffling in the direction of the bar. "We need to get the generator up and running."

"I think we should check to make sure that someone isn't trying to get through the front gate," I said.

"Why?" Cillian asked.

"Why do you think?" I challenged.

The room was silent.

"All right," Dad said after a beat. "New plan. Griffin, you and I are going to start the generator. Redmond, Braden and Aidan, you're going to check the front gate – and walk the perimeter."

"Why are they walking the perimeter?" Maya asked.

"What should I do?" Cillian asked.

"You stay here and rest," Dad said.

"I'm not an invalid."

"Fine, you stay here and watch the women."

"Hey!" Jerry was incensed. "I am not a woman."

"Fine," Dad snapped. "Jerry, you come with Griffin and me."

"I'm not staying here like an idiot," Cillian said.

"Fine," Dad said. I could practically imagine him running his hand through his hair until it stood on end. "You come with us, too."

"I want to go with the other group."

"No!"

"Am I missing something?" Maya asked.

"Oh, this is just how they get along," Griffin said. I felt his hand on my back. "You're going to stay here, right?"

"This is where the bar is."

"Stay with my sister," he whispered. "I don't want her to wander away on her own in case … ."

"I know," I said. "It will be fine."

"It had better be," Griffin said, giving me a quick kiss. "You two stay together."

"I heard the lip smacking," Dad said.

"How do you know we weren't smacking something else?" I asked.

"You're going into the dungeon with your brother, young lady."

"Kinky," Braden deadpanned.

"That's your sister, you sicko!"

"THERE'S SOMETHING DIFFERENT ABOUT YOUR FAMILY, ISN'T THERE?"

I'd managed to find my way to Maya, and then to the couch, and we sat in the parlor uncomfortably waiting for the lights to come back on.

"What was your first clue?" I asked.

"I'm not talking about the way you interact with one another," Maya said. "That is interesting, though."

Uh-oh. "What are you talking about?"

"You're not antiquities dealers, are you?"

"Why would you think that? We have tons of antiques in this house."

"Yes, but you're something else," Maya said. "You're all hiding something."

"We're not hiding anything." I was so glad she couldn't see my face.

"Whatever it is, Griffin knows," Maya mused.

"I … ."

"It's okay," Maya said. "You don't have to tell me. It's really none of my business."

"Okay."

"You can tell me if you want to, though."

"Mmm … I'm good."

Maya shifted on the couch. "You're really not going to tell me?"

"Tell you what?"

"What's different about your family."

"We're incredibly childish," I said.

"I got that," Maya said. "I actually find that cute to watch."

"Your brother doesn't."

"Oh, you're wrong there," Maya said. "He was smiling all through dinner."

I'd missed that. "He acts as though he doesn't like it."

"It does get old after the tenth time someone tells someone to 'shut it,' but it's still cute," Maya said. "You're trying to distract me."

"Is it working?"

"Does it ever?"

"I once distracted my father so long he forgot I took his car without asking and wrecked it," I said.

"I doubt that."

"No, really."

"Okay," Maya said, inhaling heavily. "If you don't want to tell me, you don't have to."

"You already said that."

"I meant it."

"Then why did you continue to push?"

"I didn't," Maya protested.

I leaned back on the couch.

"So, are you guys like spies or something?" Maya asked.

I snorted, but the sound of distant shuffling caught my attention. "Did you hear that?"

"Is this going to be your new tactic?"

"No, I'm not joking," I said. "I heard something." I got to my feet.

"Are you just going to leave me here?" Maya asked, alarmed.

"I … ." Crap. I'd made Griffin a promise. I held out my hand and felt around.

"What are you doing?" Maya asked.

"Looking for your hand."

"That wasn't my hand."

"I know," I said. "They're very nice, though."

Maya laughed. "Thank you." I felt her hand slip into mine. "Are we really going to investigate the noise? Isn't that how everyone dies in horror movies?"

"It depends on the franchise," I said. "If we were in *Friday the 13th* or *Halloween*, yes."

"Oh, that makes sense," Maya said. "What movie are we in?"

"*Poltergeist*."

"Didn't the little girl get eaten by her television in that?"

"That was before flat screens," I said, jerking her hand. "Don't worry. It's probably just my brothers."

"Then why are we investigating?"

"Because I can't not look," I said. "It will drive me crazy."

"Fine," Maya said. "If we die, though, I'm going to tell my brother to break up with you."

"Duly noted."

We crept through the dark, me taking the lead and Maya shuffling uncertainly behind. I knew where every doorway and statue was located, so we made the trek relatively quickly. We found ourselves at the front of the house, the moonlight from outside giving us some ambient light to work with as it filtered through the glass panes on the door.

Maya released my hand. "I don't hear anything."

"Shh."

"But … ."

"Shh."

"You're really bossy."

"Don't you hear that?" I said, pressing my head to the large door.

"It sounds like a cat is trying to get in," Maya said. "Do you have a cat?"

"Just Monty and Mort," I said. "They're not very much fun to cuddle with."

"You have a really odd sense of humor."

I jumped back when the door handle started to turn. The movement was slow, as though someone was striving for quiet.

"Isn't that locked?"

"Not unless my brothers locked it after they walked out of it," I said.

"Shouldn't we run?"

"Not if it's my brothers."

"Do they always try to sneak in?" Maya was beside herself.

"It depends on the mood my father is in," I whispered.

I watched as the door pushed forward, curiosity mingling with dread in my stomach.

The head that poked through the door was about a foot and a half shorter than it should have been if a wraith was trying to sneak in. Even though it was dark, the moon provided enough light that I could clearly see it wasn't one of my brothers.

Without hesitation, I reached out and smacked the face. I'd recognized the slope of the nose and flat hair without even taxing myself.

"What the hell!" Angelina grabbed the side of her face.

"What are you doing?" I asked.

Angelina straightened and faced me, unsure. "I'm … here to see if you want to sell your house."

I smacked her again.

"Stop doing that," Angelina screeched.

"You broke into my house," I said. "I can legally kill you and get away with it."

"Not when there's a witness," Angelina said, gesturing to Maya. "What are you doing here?"

"She's on a date with Cillian," I said.

Maya's mouth dropped open. "I was invited to dinner with the family."

"Cillian is warm for her form," I said, enjoying the hurt look that washed over Angelina's face. What? I don't like hurting everyone. She is a special case.

"I think he's just naturally flirty," Maya said. I had no idea why she was trying to spare Angelina's feelings. If the roles were reversed, Angelina would walk over Maya's back as she gasped for breath on the floor.

"He wants to make sweet love to her while Shania Twain is singing in the background," I said.

"Are you trying to upset her?" Maya asked.

"She broke into my house!"

"I tried knocking," Angelina said. "All the lights were out."

"So, you naturally just let yourself in," I said. "I'm calling the police."

"Why?"

"You're breaking and entering," I said. "That's a crime."

"You broke into my house when we were in high school and stole all of my underwear," Angelina countered. "You then wrote my phone number on them and handed them out at truck stops."

"I handed them out at one truck stop," I countered. I turned to Maya. "They were very slutty underwear. The truckers kept sniffing them."

"One of them called me!" Angelina was incensed.

"And I handed out twenty pairs," I said. "That should tell you a little something about the way you smell."

"I hate you," Angelina growled.

"Right back at you."

"Okay," Maya said, holding up her hands. "Can't you two call a ceasefire?"

"Only if someone actually shoots and kills her," I said.

"I hope you get herpes," Angelina said.

"I hope you get leprosy."

"I hope you get Ebola."

"I hope you get ... shh ... did you hear that?"

"Oh, you're not going to do that again, are you?" Maya had gone from irritated to irate in two seconds flat. "It's probably your brothers coming back."

"Why is it so dark in here?" Angelina complained.

"I ... ." I didn't get a chance to finish my sentence, because Angelina's body flew in my direction as another form filled the door frame.

I recognized this one, too, and it wasn't one of my brothers. "Run!"

20
TWENTY

"What is that?"

I shoved Angelina off of me. Her weight had been enough to knock me over and we'd both tumbled to the ground during the confusion. The wraith stood above us, its cloak billowing, but it was clearly unsure what to do. The element of surprise was gone and there were more of us than it probably had banked on.

"It's our neighbor," I lied. "He's addicted to Halloween."

"Your neighbor is seven feet tall?" Maya's voice was shrill.

"He likes to walk on stilts." I slapped Angelina for good measure. "Stop grabbing at my arm like that."

"Stop slapping me."

"Get out of my house."

"You don't even live here."

"What is wrong with you two?" Maya asked. "There's a … monster … in your house."

"Only when I have PMS," I said. I had no idea what I was doing. I was at a loss. The proverbial cat was out of the bag, and this was going to be really hard to explain. Maybe I could hit Maya hard enough to knock her out and tell her she'd imagined the whole thing, but I knew Griffin would frown on me doing that to his sister. That also didn't solve the other problem in the room.

"Aisling Grimlock."

Crap.

"It knows your name," Angelina said. "You probably gave it herpes and it wants payback."

"Why don't you look in his underwear and see," I suggested. "We'll wait here."

"I can't believe you two are arguing like this," Maya said. "It's just … unbelievable."

I rolled over and fixed her with a look. "You need to run now."

"What are you going to do?"

"I'm going to feed Angelina to our friend, and then I'll be right behind you."

"Aisling," the wraith hissed, extending its fingers.

I pointed at it harshly. "You stand right there," I said. "I have a few other things to handle. I'll be with you in a second."

"I am not leaving you," Maya said. I had to give her credit. She was terrified, but she refused to abandon me to certain death. Unfortunately, she made things harder rather than helping.

"You need to find my father and brothers," I said. "Tell them our neighbor is off his meds again. They'll know what to do."

Maya pushed herself to her feet, uncertain. "But … ."

"It will be fine," I said. "Go now!"

Maya didn't argue further. She turned on her heel and disappeared into the house. I only hoped the wraith was alone. If she came upon one while looking for help she wouldn't survive. I didn't know what else to do, though.

"Why didn't you give me the option of going to get help?" Angelina sniffed.

"Because you'll steal stuff," I said, hoisting myself to a standing position.

"I am not a thief," Angelina said, getting to her feet. I couldn't help but notice she purposely kept me in front of her in case the wraith attacked. "You must have me confused with you."

"You stole every boyfriend I had in high school."

"You can't steal a person," Angelina said. "They came willingly."

"You suck balls."

"Who told you that?"

I wrinkled my nose and turned my attention back to the wraith. "So, are you selling Girl Scout cookies? I like the samoas, but I'll settle for the thin mints."

"Aisling Grimlock must not be hurt."

"Awesome," I said. "That is great news." I pointed at Angelina. "What about her? Can you hurt her?"

The wraith shifted his attention to Angelina, confused.

"I know she looks all gristly, but I'm betting she tastes just like chicken," I offered.

"You shut your hole," Angelina said. "If that thing is going to eat someone, it should definitely be you. You're much fatter. You'll get a lot more meat off of her," she told the wraith.

"I am not fat!"

"You're a tub."

I smacked her again, simply because I could.

"If you do that one more time … ."

"You'll what, pull my hair until I die?"

Angelina squared her shoulders. "Excuse me, sir. If you could just move to the side a little bit, I'll be going."

The wraith cocked its head.

If Angelina had easy access to a door – whether it led inside or outside – she would have already fled. Unfortunately for her, she was trapped behind me. Every time she tried to edge around my back and move toward the door that led inside the house I cut her off. What? If I'm dying, I'm taking her with me.

"Mine," the wraith hissed.

"Why do you guys keep saying stuff like that?" I asked. "Are you bored all day and have nothing to do but watch *Lord of the Rings*?"

"Oh, is that your new plan, you're going to geek it to death?" Angelina snapped.

I smacked her again.

"I am going to kill you," Angelina seethed, rubbing her cheek. "I'm going to have a bruise tomorrow. How am I going to explain that?"

"Tell people you read *Fifty Shades of Grey* and wanted to explore your inner whore," I suggested. "Trust me. They'll believe you."

"Mine," the wraith repeated.

I took a step to the side. "You can have her."

"Aisling!" Angelina squeaked.

The wraith moved toward Angelina, its gaze shifting to me to see whether I would attack.

"Go ahead," I prodded.

Once the wraith's attention was fully on Angelina, I grabbed the marble statue off the nearby table. It was incredibly heavy, but if I could beat a wraith to death with a brick I was sure I could do it with Dad's ugly statue.

Angelina retreated, her face flushed with fear. "I … oh … I don't want to die."

"Then you shouldn't have broken into my house," I said, moving behind the wraith. I didn't hesitate. I slammed the statue down on the back of its head three times before it dissolved into a pile of ash.

Once it exploded all over her, Angelina started screaming. It truly was loud enough to wake the dead.

"I'M SUING YOU."

Redmond handed Angelina an ice pack so she could press it to her cheek. "You broke into our house."

"And I was attacked," Angelina said. "First, that fat cow slapped me."

I raised my hand to hit her again, but Aidan snatched it back. "Don't make things worse."

"I don't think that's possible," I said, pointing to the couch where Griffin was sitting with his arm around Maya. I couldn't hear what he was saying, but he was obviously trying to soothe her. I sensed a very uncomfortable conversation in my immediate future. "At least let me have my fun."

"She has slapped me like five times since I walked into this house," Angelina said.

"You mean broke into this house," Dad corrected, fixing Angelina with a scornful look. "I could have you arrested."

"Oh, you're not going to do that," Angelina said. "Then you'd have to explain how Aisling killed a monster in the foyer."

"What monster?" Braden asked. "We didn't see a monster."

"That's because it poofed into dust when she hit it with that incredibly ugly statue."

Dad made a face. "That is an antique."

"Well, it's ugly," Angelina said.

"So is your face," I said.

Dad held up his hand to still me as he hunkered down so he was at Angelina's eye level. "You and I are going to come to an understanding," he said. "I'm not going to press charges for you breaking into this house, and you're going to keep your mouth shut about what happened here tonight."

"And if I don't?" Angelina challenged.

"Then I'm going to take Aisling's leash off and let her do every horrible thing to you that she's ever wanted to do," Dad said.

"There's something worse than what she's already done?"

"You have no idea," Dad said.

Angelina glanced around the room, finally focusing on Cillian. "Aren't you going to say something?"

Cillian shrugged. "Goodbye."

Angelina took the opportunity to leave, but I could see her mind working. She was trying to figure out how to use the situation to her advantage, but she knew she would sound like a crazy person if she told anyone what happened. Once she was gone, Maya became our primary concern.

"So, you guys aren't really antiquities dealers, are you?" Her voice was even, but her eyes were watery.

"No," Dad said.

"Are you … monsters, too?"

"Only when Aisling has PMS," Aidan said.

"And DMS," Jerry added.

"What's DMS?" Braden asked, confused.

"During Menstrual Syndrome."

"Oh, fun."

"Speaking of that, I picked up tampons for you for next week," Jerry said, patting me on the shoulder. "I knew you'd forget."

I glanced at Griffin, mortified.

"Thanks for the heads up," he said, nonplussed. He was rubbing Maya's shoulder, his eyes distant. "Are we sure it was just the one wraith?"

"You know what that thing was?" Maya asked, incredulous.

"It's not the first one I've had the pleasure of dealing with," he said.

"Is that how you met Aisling?"

"Yes."

"And what are you?" Maya asked, shifting her eyes to me. "Are you … vampires?"

"No, but that would be totally cool," I said.

"Aisling, let me do the talking," Dad said. "You'll just make things worse."

"Thank you for having faith in me," I said.

He ignored me and focused on Maya. "How much do you want to know?"

"I want to know all of it."

"All of it?"

Maya crossed her arms over her chest. "All of it."

Dad sighed. "Okay, someone make drinks," he said. "This is going to be a long night."

"THAT IS ... ." MAYA WAS HARD TO READ. SHE'D LISTENED TO MY father's story quietly, interjecting only a handful of questions over the duration of what felt like a weeklong dissertation, and now that it was over she seemed to be processing.

"Freaky?" Jerry supplied. "Don't worry. I thought that, too. You'll get used to it. Now I think it's cool."

"Cool?"

"My boyfriend is a super hero," Jerry said, his eyes sparkling.

Aidan puffed out his chest.

"Yeah, he's Poutyman," I said.

Braden cuffed the back of my head. "Not now."

"Hey, in case you didn't notice, I took out another wraith today," I said. "I did it all by myself. That's two in the same week. You should all be bowing down and thanking me for being awesome."

"Fine, you're awesome," Dad said. "You're still sleeping in the dungeon tonight."

"Oh, I'm not staying here," I said.

"All of you are staying here," Dad said, straightening.

"Even me?" Maya was confused.

"Even you," Dad said. "The security system is back up and running, and no one is leaving this house until dawn."

I opened my mouth to argue.

"No one," Dad said.

"Fine," I grumbled. "I'm not sleeping in the dungeon, though. I don't want to see a snake."

"How many times do I have to tell you?" Dad asked. "Your brother made that story up."

"I'm still terrified of snakes."

"That's probably why your sex life was so dismal before Griffin," Jerry said.

I shot him the finger.

"I happen to love snakes," Jerry said.

"We know, Jerry," Dad said, rubbing his forehead, exhaustion rolling over him.

"I'm not sure what to think about all of this," Maya admitted.

"I know that, too," Dad said. "Why don't you sleep on it? I have a feeling you're going to have more questions tomorrow. They'll be easier to ask on a full stomach."

"And I might need some nursing tonight," Cillian said. "I feel a relapse coming on. I think a sponge bath will help."

Griffin scowled, but the hint of the smile playing at the corner of Maya's lips told me she was as enamored with Cillian as he was with her.

"It's settled then," Dad said, getting to his feet. "I'll have the maid make up guest rooms for Griffin and Maya."

I balked. "Griffin is sleeping in my room – with me."

"Don't even think about it," Dad said.

"Why does it matter?" I asked.

"You're not married," Dad said. "You can only share a bed under my roof if you're married."

"Is Jerry going to have to sleep in a guest room, too?"

"Oh, thanks," Aidan muttered.

Dad faltered. "Yes."

I narrowed my eyes. "I know what you're doing," I said.

"Good," Dad said. "I wasn't trying to be subtle."

"It will be fine," Griffin said, weary. "I think we all should just get some sleep. It doesn't matter where everyone does it."

"See, he's thinking," Dad said.

I pursed my lips. This wasn't over. Dad just didn't need to know that.

21

TWENTY-ONE

I expected Griffin to sneak into my room once he was sure everyone was asleep. Once midnight rolled around, however, I realized he was too much of a coward to challenge my father's wrath. Luckily, I didn't have that problem. If he started to yell, I wasn't above crying to get my way. He hates it when I cry, and I've taught myself to do it on cue. I just think about E.T. dying and I'm golden.

I climbed out of my bed and into my slippers. It was one of those huge sleigh beds, and it was too big to sleep in alone. My mother had insisted on buying it as soon as she saw it, the strong lines of the bed calling to her for some reason. When we were kids, Jerry and I used to pretend we were on the high seas and surrounded by sharks, using the boat as home base while we treaded water in dangerous seas. My father had even bought a whole cadre of stuffed sharks for us to play with, enjoying the game enough to mimic Quint from *Jaws* on rare occasions.

While my father was immovable on his bed assignments, he had relented and put Maya and Griffin in the same wing of the house where my old room was located. That was going to make my stealthy sex bid all the easier.

When I opened my door, someone was already standing on the other side. For a second, I thought it was Griffin. One look at Jerry's *My Pretty Pony* pajamas told me otherwise.

"What are you doing here?"

"I'm mad at you," Jerry said, placing his hands on his hips as he glared at me. "I'm really mad at you."

"What did I do?"

"You threw me under the bus when your father refused to let you fornicate with Griffin under his roof," Jerry sniffed. "Now I can't sleep. My room is too big, and I feel lonely."

"So?"

"So, you're going to have to sleep with me," Jerry said. "I'll have nightmares if you don't."

"Just sneak into Aidan's room," I said. "He's probably already naked and greased up."

"You're a sick, sick woman."

"Jerry, it doesn't matter," I said. "Just go in there."

"What if Cormack finds out?"

"Then cry," I said. "That's what I plan to do."

"You're going to cry?"

"He can't keep yelling when I cry," I said. "He always buckles under the pressure."

"He doesn't like it when I cry," Jerry pointed out. "He thinks it's pathetic."

"So?"

"I don't want your father to think I'm pathetic," Jerry said. "I want him to respect me."

"He does respect you," I said, pushing Jerry out of the archway and shutting the bedroom door. "He thinks it's great you started your own business. He loves you like you're his own son."

"That's really sweet."

"So … suck it up," I said, slapping his arm. "You're getting in the way of my fun."

"Where are you going?" Jerry asked.

"Where do you think?"

"Griffin's funeral? That's what's going to happen if you climb into his bed and seduce him," Jerry said.

"Do you have to say it like that? I'm not seducing him. We're just going to … cuddle."

"Oh, whatever," Jerry scoffed. "You're going to rub yourself all over him until he can't stop himself from engaging in the act that shall not be named."

"Have you been watching Mexican soap operas again?"

"They're very good."

"They make you act crazy," I said.

"I think we should just go in your room and sleep," Jerry said. "You can survive one night without Detective Delicious."

I snorted. "Is that what you're calling him now?"

"Until he screws up again. Then he's right back to Detective Dinglefritz."

"Well, I don't want to survive without him," I said. "You don't want to sleep with me any more than I want to sleep with you."

"We don't have to sleep," Jerry offered.

I narrowed my eyes. "What did you have in mind?"

"HURRY UP AND SWIM TO THE BOAT," JERRY ORDERED. HE WAS standing in the middle of my bed and pointing. "The tiger shark looks hungry."

I had no idea where he'd found my old stuffed sharks (I'd long since thought them packed away or discarded), but he'd been prepared for our *Jaws* reenactment. "That shark is like a mile away," I said, focusing my attention on the floor. "It would have to swim really fast to get to me."

"It's a shark," Jerry said. "That's what they do."

I rolled my eyes.

"Oh, look, the shark is about to eat that guy in the lagoon," Jerry said, pointing toward the television on the dresser. "I've never understood why he ate the older guy and left the kids alone. You'd think they'd be more tender and taste better."

"That's assuming the shark knows the difference between a child and an adult," I said. "You know very well most sharks only attack people because they mistake them for seals or turtles."

Jerry straightened. "*Shark Week*?"

"You know it."

"Come on," Jerry prodded. "Swim."

I started moving toward the bed, but the sound of my bedroom door swinging open stopped me mid-stroke. I slammed my arms down to my sides as I focused on Aidan and Griffin. "What's up?"

"What are you two doing?" Griffin asked, scanning my bedroom curiously.

I noticed another face poking around Griffin's shoulder, and waved to Maya. "Hey. Are you feeling okay?"

Maya smiled. "I am."

"What are you two doing?" Griffin repeated.

"They're playing shark," Aidan said, moving into the room and jumping onto the bed. He understood the rules of the game. He'd played it a time or two with us. "You have to get out of the ocean or you'll be eaten."

Griffin studied my blue carpet. "We're in the ocean?"

"The Atlantic."

Griffin reached down and snagged one of the sharks. "These look old."

"Dad bought them for me when I was in elementary school," I said.

"So you guys could play shark?"

"It's more difficult than it looks," Jerry said, fixing Griffin with a harsh look. "Only the fittest survive."

Maya giggled as she pushed her way into the room. "Wow. This is a great bed." She climbed up on it.

"I never liked it," I admitted. "It was too big. It gave me nightmares."

"So you turned it into a boat so you could survive a shark attack?" Griffin obviously was missing the appeal of the game.

"It's not just a boat," I said. "It's a fishing boat."

"Yeah," Jerry said. "We don't just run from sharks. You have to do a hard day's work fishing first."

"Oh, well, now it all makes sense," Griffin said.

I studied him for a moment. I should be embarrassed, but his eyes were actually glittering with amusement. "Just so you know, I was on my way to your room when Jerry distracted me."

"Your father said he wouldn't put up with any funny business."

"Oh, don't worry about that," I said, tapping his chin. "If he catches us, I'll just cry."

"Does that really work?"

"Oh, yeah," Jerry, Aidan and I answered in unison.

Aidan studied the assembled sharks. "Where's the hammerhead? That was always my favorite."

I pointed to the other side of the bed.

"Awesome," Aidan said.

Maya shifted her attention to the television. "Wait. Are you watching *Jaws* while playing shark attack? Isn't that a little too on the nose?"

"We wanted to use the Wii fishing game, but it's in Aidan's room," I said.

Aidan brightened. "I'll get it."

"YOU HAVE TO YANK HARDER," I INSTRUCTED, SLAPPING GRIFFIN'S ARM for emphasis. "You can't just flick your wrist. The sensor knows when you're not trying."

"I'm sorry. I've never fake fished before," a scowling Griffin said, focusing on the television as the game ramped up.

"Aidan is totally kicking your ass," I said. "He's already caught three fish. You haven't even reeled in one."

"You're very … competitive," Griffin said.

"You're only saying that because I want to win."

We'd divided into teams: Jerry and Aidan on one side, and Griffin and I on the other. Maya was happy to serve as judge. My bed was big enough for all of us to settle in – and comfortably.

"I don't like this side of you," Griffin said, mime casting with the Wii game controller again. "You're ugly when it comes to games."

"He just doesn't understand us," Aidan said, crowing as he hooked another fish. "I am awesome."

Jerry and I inadvertently broke into *The Lego Movie* theme song in unison.

Griffin jolted when he heard it. "What was that?"

"It's a great movie," I said. "Come on. Work harder. If you don't, I'm taking that controller away from you."

"Just … back off," Griffin said. "I don't like backseat fisherwomen."

Cillian appeared in the open doorway. "What are you guys doing?"

I noticed that Maya sat up a little straighter when he entered.

"We're fishing," I said.

Cillian glanced around at the floor, his face conflicted until realization dawned. "Oh, you guys are playing shark attack. You have to catch the fish before you run from the sharks."

"I'm not playing shark attack," Griffin said. "I'm just trying to catch fish. I'm an adult."

I ignored him. "Do you want to play? If you join, we can have even teams."

Cillian considered the offer. "Fine," he said. "I don't want to be on Aidan's team, though."

"Maya will have to be," I said. "We need you anyway. Griffin can't fish."

"If you think it's so easy, you try it," Griffin said, handing the controller over to me.

I took it wordlessly and flicked my wrist. After a few seconds, the controller buzzed. "I've got one."

"What?" Griffin was bubbling with disbelief.

I started reeling it in. "It's a big one. It's three times the size of anything Aidan has caught."

"How many times do I have to tell you that size doesn't matter?" Aidan asked.

"Only men say that," I said. "And we're on the board," I crowed when I finished reeling in the fish.

Cillian climbed on the bed behind me. "Give me that. I want to try."

"I just got it."

"I almost died," Cillian shot back.

"Fine," I grumbled. "You only get five chances, though. We're behind because Griffin is afraid to bait the hook."

Griffin scowled. "I am not afraid to bait the hook," he said. "I just didn't realize you had to do it in a pretend game."

"It's not a pretend game," I explained, relinquishing the controller to Cillian. "It's a game based on real-life events. Can you catch a fish in the real world without bait?"

Griffin leaned forward and knocked me off the bed.

"What the hell?"

"I'm throwing you off the boat," he said. "You're going to have to fight off the sharks if you want me to pull you back in this boat."

Well, at least he was finally playing right.

22

TWENTY-TWO

"What the hell?"

I lifted my head from Griffin's chest, confused, and focused on my father. He stood in the doorway of my bedroom, and for a moment I thought I was back in high school. I glanced around the bed and frowned. I had no idea how all six of us had managed to fit – and fall asleep – but we had. Sometime around dawn we'd wrapped up shark attack and everyone had conked out.

"Good morning."

"There are no words," Dad said, stepping into the room. He glanced down at the floor. "Where did the sharks come from?"

"They were in that storage room at the end of the hall," Jerry said, shifting on his side as he wiped the drool from his face. "I found them around Christmas when I was looking for ornaments."

Dad's face was unreadable. "I need someone to explain what is going on here."

"Well, I was sneaking out of my room because I wanted to go to Griffin's when I ran into Jerry," I said.

Griffin stiffened beside me. "Really?"

I ignored him. "Jerry was angry because I ruined his night with Aidan, and he was too afraid to stay alone."

"I wanted to play shark attack," Jerry said.

"So, we put *Jaws* in and started to play," I said. "We were making so much noise we woke Griffin, Maya and Aidan. They wanted to play, too."

Griffin raised his hand. "Just for the record, I did not want to play. They forced me."

Dad scowled.

"To make it really authentic, Aidan got the Wii so we could get our fishing in before running from the sharks," I said. "Then we divided into teams."

"When did Cillian decide to join the game?" Dad asked.

"I have no idea," I said. "I think he was just checking up on Maya. It's a good thing he came here, though. We didn't have even teams without him."

"I see," Dad said, rubbing his chin. "Who won?"

"We did," Cillian said, running his hand through his hair. "It came down to the wire, but Aisling and I cannot be denied."

We high-fived.

"You cheated," Aidan grumbled.

"I still don't understand how you all ended up sleeping together," Dad pressed.

"We were tired," I replied.

"I thought I said you couldn't sleep together if you weren't married," Dad said.

I immediately worked up some tears. "I didn't think it would be a problem if we were all together," I said, sniffling. "Are you going to yell at me?"

Dad's face softened. "Well … I guess no harm was done," he said. "It's not as though anyone is naked." He turned to leave. "Breakfast is served in twenty minutes. If you're late, you're not getting fed."

I snapped back to reality the second he was gone. "Okay, let's split up and shower," I said. "I'm betting we're getting an omelet bar this morning, and I'm not missing that."

Griffin studied me. "Did you just actually fake cry and snow your father?"

"He's not snowed," Cillian said, pushing past Griffin. "He knows he's being manipulated. He still can't take it when she cries."

"How often have you done that to him?"

"As many times as I had to," I said. "I was working at a disadvantage because I was a girl."

Griffin smirked and leaned in to give me a kiss. "You are … a constant wonder."

"THIS IS AMAZING," MAYA SAID, DIGGING INTO HER OMELET enthusiastically. "I can't believe the food you have here."

"Despite your lack of sleep, you look better this morning," Dad said. "How are you feeling?"

"Well … I feel surprisingly relaxed," Maya said. "I thought I would feel weird waking up in your house, but a night of fishing and shark attacks was kind of fun."

Dad smiled. "They used to do that all the time."

"They told me," Maya said. "Jerry said you used to play with them."

Dad shifted his gaze in my direction. "They were very enthusiastic."

"It's great that you played with them," Maya said. "It proves you're a great father."

"He was a great father even without the sharks," I said. "They were just a bonus."

Dad grinned. "You're just a manipulation machine this morning, aren't you?"

"The love is gone," I said, forcing a big bite of tomato into my mouth.

"So, do you have any questions?" Dad asked, turning his attention back to Maya.

"Actually, Aisling and Cillian explained quite a bit while we were fishing last night," Maya said. "I think they've got me all caught up."

"Really?" Dad seemed surprised.

"Really," Maya said.

"Why didn't you wake us up?" Redmond asked. "I love that fishing game."

"There wasn't enough room in the boat for two more people," I said. "You guys needed your beauty sleep."

"You're mean," Redmond said. "If I was on your team, we would've crushed them."

"We won without you," I said. "That's all that matters."

"We're having a tournament," Redmond countered. "We'll do it in the parlor."

"The parlor has wood floors," I pointed out.

"So?"

"Sharks can't swim on wood," Jerry supplied.

"We're not playing shark attack," Braden said. "We just want to fish."

"That's an entirely different game," I said. "We were playing shark. The fishing was incidental."

"You didn't say that when we were losing," Griffin said.

"That's because you fish like a woman," I said.

Griffin smirked. "You're kind of cute when you're competitive."

"She's always cute," Jerry said.

Dad cleared his throat. "So, down to business," he said. "We have a limited load today. I only need two of you to work. Volunteers?"

No one raised a hand.

"Cillian is out," Dad said. "He needs time to rest. The rest of you are going to have to draw straws."

I groaned. I was too tired to work. Sure, it was my own fault, but I would never admit that in front of my brothers. "I think Redmond and Braden should do it," I said. "They got a good night's sleep last night."

"Whose fault is that?" Dad asked.

Yeah, that wasn't going to work. I wondered briefly if I should start crying again, but then another thought entered my mind. "I fought off and killed a wraith last night. I think I should be exempt."

Dad sighed. "Fine."

"What?" Aidan was angry.

"She needs her rest, too," Dad said. "That leaves the three of you."

"I'm exhausted," Aidan said. "I think it should be Braden and Redmond."

"Playing shark attack is not an acceptable reason to get out of work," Dad said.

"It was for Aisling."

I stuck my tongue out. "I got out of work because I'm awesome and brave," I said. "I fought off a wraith and saved the universe. You lost at shark attack. This should be your penance."

"I agree," Dad said. "It's you and Braden."

"Oh, man," Braden complained.

Aidan narrowed his eyes as he regarded me from across the table. "You're going to get your ass kicked later."

"Bring it on."

BECAUSE Griffin had to put in an appearance at his office, I was left to my own devices for the bulk of the afternoon. Jerry had an important wedding to start planning and Maya had a shift at the hospital. I was a lonely little orphan.

Therefore it made perfect sense to go to Eternal Sunshine Cemetery. I told myself I was going because I wanted to visit my mother's grave. I even stopped to pick up a bouquet of lilies to place near her marker in the mausoleum.

I had other things on my mind, though.

My mother's marker was in our family mausoleum, so that was my first stop. The fire that had taken my mother's life had raged so ferociously we had only remnants of bone to inter. Of course, we found out later she'd survived thanks to Genevieve Toth – only to die later without her family – but I still considered this her final resting place. My father had been so ravaged in the wake of her death Redmond had to pick out her marker. It was simple, the only adornment a lily on the corner.

I placed the bouquet in the holder next to the marker after pulling a dead bouquet of flowers out and tossing it into the trash. I ran my hand over the lifted letters, tracing the name "Lily Grimlock" as I went. People say you can find solace talking to the dead. I found only sadness.

I sat on the bench in the middle of the mausoleum and studied the plaques around me. Grimlocks had been laid to rest here for almost a century. Some I knew, like my grandparents; others were merely names from family lore.

After a few moments, I got to my feet. "I'll come back when I can, Mom."

I never talked to her. I had no idea what to say. My mother had never appeared on our list when it was time. It was a neighboring family, one that worked out of Ann Arbor, who we assumed collected her. That's the way it works in our business. The higher-ups always worried that reapers would try to save their own, so whenever possible, the soul-gathering task was handed off to others.

We'd never questioned her collection. Now, though, I had to wonder who collected her when she died that second time. Of course, in the grand scheme of things, it didn't really matter. She was gone either way.

I was still slightly bitter. The opportunity to say goodbye to my mother would have meant a lot. I felt robbed on that front, even though I understood why it was necessary. I kissed my fingertips and pressed them to her marker briefly. "I'll talk more next time. I promise."

It took me a few minutes to collect myself once I left the mausoleum. It wasn't that I didn't like to think about my mother. In fact, she was a headliner in some of my favorite memories. It was just too hard sometimes. It was easier to lock her away in a box, one that I opened only when I felt especially depressed – or had PMS. Speaking of PMS, I was about due to stock up on chocolate.

I turned my attention to the mausoleum two doors down. It belonged to the Olivets, descendants of Genevieve Toth. When the big wraith confrontation had occurred weeks ago, it was in that mausoleum. That was why I'd really come. I was curious about whether the wraiths were gathering here again. I just wanted to be sure.

I scanned the cemetery to make sure no one was watching me, and then made my way to the door. Most people don't lock their mausoleums because the cemetery is closed at night. I wasn't surprised to find the door unlocked. I pushed it open and readied myself in case I had to make a hasty retreat. Part of me expected danger. The other part knew I was readying myself for nothing.

The mausoleum was empty.

I blew out a sigh as I shuffled inside. I searched every corner, taking special care not to miss anything, and then turned back to the door. That's when a hint of color caught my attention – a lone flower in one of the vases.

I stepped toward it, curious. It wasn't fresh. It had been here several days, and had wilted, but it hadn't been here during the big fight. That meant someone had been here.

That doesn't mean it was a wraith, I chided myself. It's not as if they can walk into flower shops and buy blooms. It must have been a family member. I moved up to study the four markers surrounding the flower. None of them offered hints. All of the occupants had been gone more than twenty years, and in two cases, they'd died more than fifty years before.

I exhaled heavily. There was nothing here. It wasn't as though I was expecting easy answers. Some answers would have been welcome, though. With a final glance over my shoulder, I left the mausoleum and closed the door behind me.

If I wanted to solve this, I was going to have to broaden my horizons. I needed to think.

23

TWENTY-THREE

When I returned to the townhouse, a huge bag of chocolate in hand – the beast is ready to rage, people – I found someone waiting for me on the front stoop. The figure wasn't large and dressed in a cloak, so I wasn't particularly worried.

That changed when I realized who was standing there.

"I … what are you doing here?"

Morgan Reid lifted his head when he heard my approach and blessed me with a flirtatious smile. "Is that any way to greet a gentleman caller, Aisling Grimlock?"

I froze. I'd never told Reid my real name. How had he figured it out? "Mr. Reid," I said, shuffling on the sidewalk instead of closing the remaining few feet separating us. "How did you find me?"

"I looked you up on the Internet." Reid didn't appear ruffled by my standoffish nature.

"How?"

"I typed your name in that little window on the Google home page."

I narrowed my eyes. "How did you know my name?"

Reid shrugged. "You told me."

"No, I didn't," I said.

"Yes, you did."

"No, I didn't."

"I think you did." Reid wasn't backing down.

I pursed my lips. "Okay, maybe I did tell you my real name," I conceded. I totally didn't. "That doesn't explain why you're here."

Reid produced a bouquet of flowers from behind his back. It didn't escape my attention that they looked as though he'd bought them from a grocery store – and the day-old bin, at that.

"You're here to scare me with wilting flowers?"

Reid frowned. "They're not wilting."

"That one is brown."

"It's depressed because you're rejecting it," Reid said, trying for something approximating charm.

Whatever. "So, what are you doing here?" I clutched my bag of chocolate to my chest.

"I'm asking you to dinner," Reid said.

Oh, well, Hell had frozen over. "I'm flattered … but … I'm going to say no."

Reid wasn't about to be deterred. "Can I ask why?"

"I have a boyfriend."

"I thought you were married."

I scowled.

"Are you saying you and your brother have divorced and you're now dating?"

He was really starting to bug me. "I was never married to my brother," I said. "That doesn't mean I'm not involved. I believe you met him the other day." Before you disappeared like a sneaky rat, I silently added.

"Are you engaged?" Reid studied my hand for a ring.

"No."

"Then you're still open for offers as far as I'm concerned," he said.

I had a feeling Griffin would feel differently. "Well, I'm not."

"You could be."

"Nope."

"You should be."

"Nope."

"Are you really going to turn me down?" Reid faltered for the first time.

I considered my options. We'd been trying to find more information on Reid since he escaped death the first time. Now that he'd done it twice, things were starting to get out of control. Oh, hell, what could it hurt to have dinner with him?

"Nope," I said. "Let's go to dinner."

Reid arched an eyebrow, surprised. "Really?"

"I have to put this bag inside, and you're going to stand right over there while I do it," I said, pointing to a spot on the lawn. "If you move from there, I'm calling the cops."

Reid grinned. "Don't you trust me?"

"No."

"You're still going to have dinner with me, right?"

"Sure," I said. "You're buying, and I'm picking the restaurant."

"I can live with that."

We'd have to see about that.

"REALLY, THIS IS YOUR FAVORITE RESTAURANT?"

I glanced around the Coney Island dubiously. On short notice, it was the brightest and most populated place I could think of within walking distance of my townhouse. There was no way I was getting into a money launderer's car – especially when people kept trying to kill him. "I love hot dogs."

Whoops. That was probably the wrong thing to say to a guy who I was sure was a demented pervert.

"Fine," Reid said, reaching for a menu. "What's good here?"

I made a face. "It's a National Coney Island."

Reid waited.

"Everything is good here," I said.

Reid pressed his lips together. "Okay. What do you recommend?"

"Whatever you want," I said, ignoring the menu. Seriously, who looks at a menu at a coney restaurant?

"What are you going to get?" Reid asked.

"Two coneys and chili fries."

"That's a lot of onions," Reid pointed out.

"I'm getting them on the fries, too."

Reid frowned. "That's going to make getting close to you … uncomfortable."

That's what I was betting on. "You'll live."

Reid's face was conflicted. "If you don't trust me, and you don't want to kiss me – and you're missing out there, let me tell you – why did you agree to go to dinner with me?"

"I'm all kinds of odd," I said.

"That's why I like you."

I leaned back in the booth. "How did you really find out who I was?"

"You told me," Reid said.

Why did he keep saying that? I'd lied when I first met him, and then I'd lied poorly when I met him the second time. I'd never told him my name, though. "Okay," I said, my tone even, "why don't you tell me about yourself?"

"What do you want to know?"

"What do you do for a living?"

"I'm an investment banker."

"That sounds boring," I said.

"It's quite lucrative."

"That's different from being boring," I pointed out.

"I happen to like numbers," Reid said. "What do you do for a living?"

"I'm an antiquities dealer," I said.

"What does that entail?"

"I go to estate sales and buy antiques," I said. "Then I take them to my father and he sells them."

"That sounds boring," Reid said.

"Only if you don't like garage sales," I countered.

Reid furrowed his brow. "Do you like garage sales?"

"I love them," I said. I hate garage sales. Used stuff freaks me out. I keep imagining naked people rubbing items up and down their bodies. Yes, I know it's not reasonable or feasible. I still can't stop myself. "I love looking at used stuff."

"Aren't antiques valuable used stuff?"

He had a point. "Yes."

"And that's not boring?" Reid pressed.

"Not in the least," I said. "Let's talk about you. What kind of banking do you invest?"

Reid looked confused. I'm not going to lie. Numbers confuse me. I have no idea what an investment banker does. My idea of investing is buying new Converse.

"I take money from my clients and invest in various things," Reid said.

"Why?"

"To make them more money."

"If they're already rich, why do they need more money?" I asked. Yes, I know, that's rich coming from a woman who grew up in a castle. I'm a hypocrite. Don't judge me.

"Well, if you look at it that way, I guess it does seem absurd," Reid said.

"How do you look at it?"

"I'm helping my clients increase their wealth," Reid replied. "The richer I make them, the richer I make myself."

"Oh, fun."

"I take it you're not a capitalist," Reid said, laughing.

"I'm an Aquarius."

Reid scanned my face. "Are you joking?"

"Nope. I'm a free spirit and thinker. I'm definitely an Aquarius."

"Okay," Reid said, glancing around the restaurant. "Where is that waitress?"

I internally smirked. "She'll be along," I said. "So, tell me about your clients."

"What do you want to know?"

"Who are they?"

"I'm fenced in by certain rules," Reid said. "My clients expect anonymity."

"Why?"

"Because … people might try to rob them."

"Is that really the reason?" I asked.

"I … yes."

He was lying. "Do you do anything else on the side?" That was such a stupid question. The incoming PMS was making me irrational – and stupid.

"Like what?" Reid asked, shifting nervously.

"Oh, I don't know," I hedged, wracking my brain. "Do you ever take money from criminals and funnel it into legal avenues to wash it?" I am a moron.

Reid was taken aback. "Are you asking me if I'm a money launderer?"

Part of me wanted him to know I was on to him. He thought he was snowing me, and power is important in a relationship. Of course, I'd ceded my power now because Reid knew I was smarter than I looked. That's always my mistake. "Of course not," I said. "I just wondered if you had mobsters for clients."

"Mobsters?"

I thought quickly. "Sonny on *General Hospital* is a mobster who owns a coffee business," I explained. "He also does work at a bank all the time. He's hot, too."

"You know I don't really work at a bank, right?"

No. I didn't know that. I need to start reading the business pages of the newspaper. "Of course. I'm not stupid."

"No," Reid agreed. "You are hot, though."

I didn't like the predatory look on his face. "You should see me in the morning," I said. "I look like a wildebeest."

"Is that an invitation?"

Definitely not. "Where is that waitress?"

Reid smiled. He was back in control of our date. "Tell me about your family."

I wrinkled my nose. "We're like the Osmonds."

Reid's face was conflicted. "That singing family from the eighties?"

"Seventies," I corrected.

"Is that better?"

"It depends on how much you value singing," I replied.

"Uh-huh."

I was back in control. "Is something wrong?"

"I feel like I'm on a dating show," Reid admitted. "Have you been checked to see whether you have a chemical imbalance?"

"I have PMS." What? Men are scared of women stuff – and their parts.

"I see."

"Yeah," I said, sinking into my role. "I'm a bloated and hormonal mess. I could snap you like a twig right now."

It was a warning, and it wasn't lost on Reid. "Good to know."

"Do you know PMS has been a legitimate defense in murder cases?" I was on a roll now.

"I hadn't heard that." Reid shifted uncomfortably.

"I'm also licensed to carry a concealed weapon." Technically, pepper spray is a weapon. Unfortunately, Jerry used the last of my stash when he was convinced the neighbor was stalking him because he was "hot for his bod" – and also a homophobe. No, I can't explain it.

Reid straightened. "Check, please."

I'm an awesome date.

24

TWENTY-FOUR

"You didn't have to walk me home," I said, casting a sidelong look at Reid as he trudged along the sidewalk with me.

"You're a woman and you're vulnerable," Reid said. "You shouldn't walk home alone after dark. It's not safe."

The short trek had been tense. My stomach wouldn't stop growling – we never did order – and I was anxious to raid the refrigerator when I got home. The one good thing about living with a baker is that there's always something to munch on.

"It was three blocks," I pointed out.

"You're still vulnerable."

"I'm fine."

"Why are you being so difficult?" Reid asked.

"I'm not difficult," I said. "I'm honest."

"You're difficult."

"I'm awesome."

"You're deranged."

"I'm still awesome."

"I don't understand eighty percent of what comes out of your mouth," Reid said.

"And yet you still stalked me." I stepped onto the sidewalk leading to the front door of my townhouse.

"I didn't stalk you."

"Don't be … obnoxious," I said. "We both know you stalked me."

"I did not stalk you!"

Griffin stepped out of the shadows, his keys in his hand. He'd obviously just arrived from the adjacent parking lot. "Is someone stalking someone?"

I was relieved to see him. "You remember Morgan Reid, right?"

"Yes."

"Well, he's stalking me," I said.

"I am not stalking her," Reid protested. "I showed up to ask her out on a date. I had flowers, for crying out loud."

"From the grocery store."

"They were still flowers," Reid said. "You agreed to go out on a date with me."

Griffin's face was grim. "You went on a date with him?"

"I went to dinner with him," I said. "We walked three blocks, we engaged in inane chatter, and then he ran like a little girl. We didn't even order, and I'm starving."

"I see," Griffin said.

"She says she has a boyfriend, but I don't believe her," Reid said. "She also told me she was married to her brother. She keeps flirting with me."

"You need to look up the word 'flirting' in a dictionary," I said. "That doesn't change the fact that you stalked me."

"I'm a handsome guy," Reid said. "I don't need to stalk anyone. You're just a … slut."

Griffin growled.

"She is," Reid continued. "She wants me. She just won't admit it."

"If Jerry hadn't used all of my pepper spray, I'd totally spray the crap out of you right now," I said. "You're a freak."

"You're a freak," Reid countered.

"You're both freaks," Griffin said. He studied us for a moment. "Mr. Reid, I can assure you that Aisling has a boyfriend."

"Oh, really, how is that? Last time I checked, she was dating her own brother. That's illegal. You know that, right?"

"I know that because I'm her boyfriend," Griffin said, tapping his chest. "I'm her boyfriend."

"Well, then you need to tell her that dating other men isn't allowed," Reid said. "She clearly doesn't understand basic rules. She told me you were her boyfriend the same day she said her brother was."

I stomped my foot. "I still told you I was dating someone."

"And then you went out to dinner with me," Reid countered.

"Because you wouldn't leave."

Griffin stepped between us, his hands raised. "Okay, here's what's going to happen," he said. "Mr. Reid, I don't believe your services are required any longer. Aisling is in a relationship, and I don't like to share my toys."

"You should tell her that," Reid grumbled.

"You can go now," Griffin said, gritting his teeth.

Reid's glance bounced between us a moment, and then he stalked away without a parting shot. Once he was gone, Griffin fixed me with a look. He didn't speak immediately, and after a full minute, I was starting to feel uncomfortable.

"What?"

"You went on a date with another guy," Griffin said, clearly trying to control his temper.

"It wasn't a date," I argued. "He took me by surprise. I was perfectly happy to curl up on the couch with my big bag of chocolate and wait for you."

"You really do have PMS, don't you? I thought Jerry was … being Jerry … but he was right, wasn't he?"

I shrugged. "So?"

"It's just weird," Griffin said.

"Technically, I won't have PMS until tomorrow," I clarified. "I was just getting prepared."

Griffin furrowed his brow. "How did he find you?"

"He claims I told him my name," I said. "I didn't."

"So, you agreed to go out on a date with him?"

"I agreed to walk down to the National Coney Island with him," I corrected. "I never got anything to eat. I'm starving, by the way."

His sigh was dramatic, and his face showed he was conflicted, but when Griffin finally focused on me, it was hurt I saw reflected back from the depths of his eyes. "We're together, right?"

I faltered. "I … yes."

"Last time I checked, people in a relationship don't date other people," Griffin said.

"It wasn't really a date." This was somehow snowballing, and I needed to stop it. "I was just trying to get information."

"You're not an investigator," Griffin said.

"But … ."

He held up his hand. "I need to be able to trust you."

My lower lip started quivering. Hormones bite. "Don't you?"

"I did until I found you coming back from a date with another man," Griffin replied. "I thought … I thought we were together."

I ran my hands through my hair, confused. "Okay, I don't want to start a big fight here, but we've never really defined our relationship. That doesn't mean I was going to touch him or let him touch me."

Griffin cleared his throat as he scanned the night sky. "That's a fair point," he said after a moment. "Let's define our relationship."

This was new … and scary. "Okay."

"When I look at you, I see my girlfriend," he said. "What do you see when you look at me?"

Fear was the most obvious answer. "I don't know," I said. "I … we haven't had as much time together as I would like. We had a week together – and it was the best week of my life – and then you left."

Griffin nodded, waiting.

"I know you have a job to do," I continued. "I still felt like an afterthought." Now was the time to tell the truth.

"I guess that's fair," Griffin said, crossing his arms over his chest. "I didn't expect to be called away on an assignment. I think you need to know that. I usually have some lead-up when that happens."

"I'm not blaming you," I said, my voice low.

"I don't expect to be called away on a lot of undercover assignments," he said. "They do happen, though. I don't volunteer for them, and I don't plan on volunteering for them. If they happen, though, I need to know you can handle that."

It was a pointed statement. "I didn't complain about you being gone."

"No, you just freaked out when you saw me in a restaurant the day I got back," he reminded me.

"I saw a woman touching you in a restaurant," I corrected. "I didn't even know you had family in the area. Why would I think she was your sister? You never talk about your family."

Griffin ran his hand through his hair. "Not all families are like yours."

"I … ."

"I don't want to talk about that right now," Griffin said, firm.

I nodded.

"That doesn't mean I won't talk about it eventually," Griffin said. "I just … not now."

"Okay."

"I want to talk about tonight," he said. "I don't want you to go on dates with other guys."

"Because I'm your girlfriend?"

Griffin smirked. "Yes."

"Fine," I said. "I'm assuming that means you won't be sleeping with women for information while you're undercover, right?"

Griffin snorted. "It's not like the movies, baby." He held out his hand. "I don't want to sleep with anyone else and I don't want to date anyone else."

I took his hand tentatively. "I don't either."

"Good," Griffin said. "Now we need to talk about your sense of self-preservation."

I shifted. "What?"

"We know Reid is a criminal," Griffin said. "We know he has dangerous associates and that he's marked for murder. Knowing all of that, why would you go to dinner with him?"

"I wanted to see if he would let anything slip," I admitted.

"Did he?"

"No," I said. "His whole goal was to knock me off my game."

"Did he?"

"No."

"So, how did things end?" Griffin was working hard to appear calm.

"I told him I was licensed to carry a concealed weapon and then he yelled for the check before we'd even ordered," I said.

Griffin smiled. "You do have a way about you."

"I didn't mean to upset you," I said after a moment. "I … I just had to make a quick decision. He took me by surprise."

"Yeah, we have to figure out how he knew who you were," Griffin said, rubbing the back of my hand with his thumb. "I just … we're clear here, right?"

I nodded. "Yes. I'm your girlfriend."

"And I'm your boyfriend," Griffin said. "It's okay to call me that. I know you've been … conflicted. It's okay, though. I'm not going anywhere, Aisling. You don't have to be afraid all of the time."

His words were warm when they washed over me. "What if Aidan doesn't let up?"

Griffin sighed. "Aidan is having issues," he said. "I'm not sure what they are, but he'll let us know when he wants to remedy them. His issues are not my issues."

"What are your issues?"

"I don't want my girlfriend dating other men," he said. "I want you all to myself."

I snickered. "You know I have PMS, right?"

"Jerry told me."

"Jerry told everyone."

"He's my walking mood calendar," Griffin said. "I think he'll probably come in handy in that department."

"He's a handy guy."

"He's your … best friend," Griffin said, smiling. "He has a certain charm that just can't be denied."

"He always did."

"I like Jerry," Griffin said. "The shark thing was weird, and yet I get it. You guys managed to make my sister feel safe when she should have been having nightmares. I appreciate that."

We hadn't talked about Maya's new reality yet. "Are you angry about all of that?"

"Am I angry that you risked yourself to save my sister? Is that what you're asking?"

I shrugged.

"Aisling, I don't want you to ever put yourself in danger," he said. "The thing is, I'm a cop. I'm in danger whether I like it or not. You don't complain about it, your meltdown at the restaurant notwithstanding.

"I don't feel I can complain about your job," he continued. "That would make me a hypocrite, and I try really hard not to be a hypocrite. I don't always succeed, but I try. I know that you put yourself in danger to keep Maya safe. I want to be angry, but she's my sister. I know you didn't have a lot of options, and you did an outstanding job."

"I always do an outstanding job."

Griffin drew me to him, wrapping his arms around my waist as he rested his forehead against mine. "I need you to keep safe," he said. "I'd be … sad … without you."

"I didn't know what else to do."

"I know that. I'm not angry."

"Even though I had dinner with the dirty money launderer?"

"Oh, you're going to pay for that," Griffin teased. "I'm going to make you give me a massage and then do something dirty."

I smirked.

"You have PMS, though, right? How long do I have?"

"Four days."

"I guess I'd better make them count." He pressed a sweet kiss to my lips and then pushed me toward the door of the townhouse. "Start moving. You're going to have a busy four days."

Somehow, that didn't sound too bad.

25

TWENTY-FIVE

"Get up."

"Go back to sleep."

I poked Griffin's bare chest. "Get up. I'm hungry."

"Go back to sleep. We were up half the night." Griffin's eyes remained shut. "Not that I'm complaining, mind you."

"That's because you insisted on the world's longest massage," I said. "I did all the work, and I'm starving."

"Shh. If you close your eyes, you'll naturally fall back to sleep."

I was quiet for a moment. "It's not working."

"You're not trying hard enough."

I rolled on top of him, resting my weight on his chest so he had no choice but to open his eyes. His hair was tousled from heavy sleep and his smile was lazy as he finally focused on me.

"I'm really hungry."

He reached over and pressed my head down to his chest. "Go back to sleep. Jerry will feed you in an hour."

"But … ."

Griffin growled as he grabbed me around the waist and flipped me over, pinning me beneath him playfully. "Were you always this much of a pain in the ass?"

"I am sunshine and light," I argued. "You should bow down and worship me every day because I'm the best thing that ever happened to you."

Griffin grinned. "You're in a good mood this morning."

"I'm in a good mood every morning," I countered.

"You realize I've met you before, right?"

"Are you insinuating I'm not fun to be around in the morning?"

"I'm flat out saying you're usually a morose pouter in the morning," Griffin replied. "You're smiling this morning."

"That's because I'm … happy."

Griffin gave me a kiss. "You'd be happier if you slept another hour."

"Feed me now!"

"And we're back to being a pain in the ass," Griffin said. "How about we work up more of an appetite first?"

"What did you have in mind?"

I wasn't the only one starting the morning with a smile today.

A VERY ENTHUSIASTIC AND ENERGETIC HOUR LATER, WE EMERGED from my bedroom. Jerry and Aidan were already up, and Jerry was banging around the kitchen when we walked into the room.

"Hello, naughty ones," Jerry said, not bothering to turn from the stove. "Are you hungry this morning?"

"Aisling is," Griffin said, settling at the table and grabbing the front section of the newspaper so he had a reason to ignore Aidan. "I just want coffee."

"I'm making homemade cinnamon rolls," Jerry teased.

"Oh, yum," I said, rolling up on the balls of my feet so I could kiss Jerry's cheek. "Did you put nuts on them?"

"I know you love nuts," Jerry teased, flicking my nose. "They just went into the oven. It will be a few minutes. Here's some coffee."

"Thanks." I took the two mugs and moved to the table, slipping one in front of Griffin before grabbing part of the newspaper. "Is there anything good in there?"

"Rape. Murder. Corruption."

"I'm confused. Do you think that's good or are you just commenting on the state of the world today?"

Griffin smirked. "My world is fine today," he said.

"Oh, you two are just so cute," Jerry cooed.

Aidan muttered something under his breath I couldn't quite make out. "What's your problem now?"

"I didn't say anything," Aidan said.

"No, you purposely mumbled because you're obviously feeling the need for negative attention this morning," I shot back.

"I think you're hearing things."

"I think you're being a butthead."

"I think you're being a PMS monster."

"Okay," Griffin said, shaking the newspaper. "You all talk far too much about … that."

"It's a natural part of life for women," Jerry chided. "You should get used to it. Aisling is a bear when the monster possesses her."

Griffin slid a look in my direction. "The monster?"

"You've seen *The Exorcist*, right?" Jerry asked.

Griffin chuckled, but his eyes reflected doubt.

"Don't worry, she's vacillates wildly between monster and baby," Jerry said. "We just lock her in her bedroom."

"I'll keep that in mind," Griffin said. "I'm sure I can handle her."

"I'm sure I can handle her," Aidan mimicked.

Griffin cocked his head to the side. "Do you have something you want to say to me?"

"No, he doesn't," Jerry said. "We talked about this," he warned Aidan. "You said you were going to try to be nicer to him."

"I did try," Aidan said. "I failed. Failure is a part of life."

"Oh, just stop it," I snapped. "I can't take much more of your crap."

"My crap? My crap?"

"Do you see anyone else here being a big baby?"

"I am not being a baby!" Aidan pounded the table to prove his point. "I'm the one getting the shaft here."

Jerry opened his mouth and I knew he was about to say something filthy. "Don't!" Jerry frowned, but he pressed his lips together. "How are you getting the shaft?"

Griffin focused on Aidan, interested in the response.

"Because he's … taking you away from me."

I froze. What the … ?

"I'm taking her away from you?" Griffin asked, nonplussed. "Don't you think that's a little crazy?"

Jerry flapped his hands nervously. "I don't think we should finish this discussion."

Everyone ignored him.

"Yes, of course it's crazy," Aidan said. "I know it's crazy. I can't help it. You're trying to push me out of her life. You think I don't know, but I know."

"I think someone has sympathetic PMS," I said.

Aidan stuck out his tongue. "That wasn't funny the first time you said it in middle school. It's not any funnier now."

"You're being irrational," I said. I glanced at Griffin for support, but he was busy studying Aidan with a thoughtful expression.

"I am not being irrational," Aidan said. "Every time I turn around this … guy … is in my face. When we watch *The Golden Girls*, he has to watch it with us. When you laugh now, it's always with him. I told an outstanding joke the other day and you didn't even crack a smile."

"That was a good joke, honey," Jerry said, trying to bolster him.

"And worse, when you're upset, you don't come to me," Aidan said. "You go to him. He's the one who makes you feel better. Do you have any idea how that makes me feel?"

"Like you're inappropriately attached to me?" I was completely thrown. I couldn't believe he would think this, let alone say it out loud. Griffin already thought there was something wrong with my relationship with my brothers. This was going to send him over the edge.

"Wait a second," Griffin said, holding up his hand. "I think we should hear him out."

What? Did I wake up in an alternate dimension where everyone is crazy today? Maybe I'm still asleep? I reached over and pinched Jerry.

"Ow! Why did you do that?" Jerry jerked his arm out of my reach.

"I wanted to make sure I wasn't dreaming," I said.

"Then you should have asked me to pinch you."

"You really dig in when you pinch," I said. "You leave little half-moon marks on my skin. I don't like it."

Griffin and Aidan stared at one another.

"Are you saying you don't like me because you think I'm stealing your sister from you?" Griffin asked.

"I don't dislike you," Aidan said. "I just don't like how Aisling always goes to you. I'm the one she used to go to when she was upset. It was a big job, but it was my job."

"Hey, what about me?" Jerry protested.

"She still goes to you," Aidan said. "You're her best friend."

Realization washed over Griffin's face. "And she's your best friend."

Aidan faltered. "She's my sister."

"She's also your best friend," Griffin said. "I didn't … I should have taken that into consideration."

"What?" Everyone was definitely going crazy. "He's been awful to you."

"He's just been marking his territory," Griffin said. "That's a man thing. I'm fairly certain I did the same thing last night when you came back from your date with Morgan Reid."

Aidan shifted. "You went on a date with Morgan Reid last night?"

"Can we get back to the conversation at hand? We can talk about that later. How can you possibly think I would let anyone replace you?"

"He already has," Aidan said, crossing his arms over his chest. "You haven't spent any time with me since he came back."

"We played shark attack."

"We all played shark attack, and he was on your team. We're always on the same team. That's how we win."

"Oh."

"He was on your team for Trivial Pursuit, too. That's our game. We dominate at that game."

"I'm sorry," I said. "It just made sense to break up into couples."

"Right. Couples."

I wrinkled my nose. "Have you ever considered that I felt the same way when you started dating Jerry and stole my best friend?"

"I did not steal your best friend," Aidan said.

"I'm no longer the most important person in his life," I countered. "You are."

"Oh, please. He still takes your side instead of mine."

"That's because I'm always right."

"She is," Jerry agreed.

"Life is about changing and evolving," I said. "Because I'm dating Griffin doesn't mean I don't need you. I'll always need you. We shared a womb."

"And you totally kicked me for nine months. Now you're just kicking me in a different way."

"She didn't have feet for nine months," said Jerry, ever pragmatic in tense situations. "She looked like a tadpole for a lot of that time."

"Jerry, butt out," Griffin said. "Let them talk."

"For crying out loud, Aidan, you're being a … ."

"If you call me a girl, I'm going to beat the snot out of you," Aidan warned.

I sucked in a breath to calm myself. "Griffin isn't here to take your spot," I said. "He has his own spot. You still have your spot."

"I don't feel like I do."

"I don't understand why this is just coming up now," I said. "You were the one taking his side in the restaurant the other day. You were standing up for him. You didn't feel this way then."

"That was when I thought there was a chance he was going to break up with you," Aidan said. "I thought that was why he hadn't called. I figured I would get to put the pieces of your life back together, be the big hero and curse his name for weeks when you realized what was going on. I didn't think he was really working."

"You said you did," I pointed out.

"I was trying to make you feel better," he said. "Once he showed up that night, I knew it was all over for me. I was the forgotten person in your life."

"I can't forget about you, dumbass," I said. "I also want to have my own life. I think it's harder for you because you've managed to get your own life, and it still overlaps with mine."

Aidan considered for a moment. "That makes sense," he said.

I was surprised.

"I still don't want Griffin to watch *The Golden Girls* with us. That's our thing."

I scowled.

"I think that's fair," Griffin interjected.

"What? You can't miss out on *The Golden Girls*. They're comedic perfection."

"I think it's fair for you and Aidan to have one night a week where it's just the two of you," Griffin said. "I'm okay with it. We'll set up a schedule."

"A schedule?"

"You know what I mean," Griffin said. "No one needs to feel displaced here." He turned to Aidan. "You and I need to come to an understanding, though. I don't appreciate your attitude. I admit I was wrong. I should have called her while I was undercover.

"It was a new situation for us, and I was worried about waking her up. I had no idea I would be gone as long as I was," he continued. "That doesn't mean I'm going anywhere, though. You need to accept that I have a spot in her life, just like I accept you have a spot in her life."

Aidan grudgingly nodded.

"It's not easy for me to share her with you and Jerry, either," Griffin said. "I find this whole arrangement … odd. It is who she is, though, and I happen to like who she is. I'm not asking for us to be best friends. I don't expect us to have guys' nights and shoot pool. I do think I deserve a modicum of respect."

"Fine," Aidan said. "I'm sorry."

Griffin arched an eyebrow.

"I am sorry," Aidan said. "I didn't mean to hurt Aisling. I didn't really care about hurting you, but I didn't want to hurt her, and that's what I was doing."

"I think you should shake on it," I prodded.

Aidan and Griffin exchanged a stiff handshake.

"Yay!" Jerry clapped excitedly. "Now, let's talk about having guys' nights. I know you were joking, but I think they're a great idea. Instead of shooting pool, though, we should go to a spa. I don't like getting that blue chalk on my fingers. It stains."

"Yeah, that's not going to happen, Jerry," Griffin said.

"Besides, spa days are what we do together," I reminded him. "I don't want Griffin to displace me in your life."

Jerry beamed.

"So, everyone is okay here, right?" Griffin pressed.

Aidan nodded.

"Good," he said. "Now someone feed Aisling. She's been whining about breakfast for an hour."

Aidan lifted his eyes up to me. "Are you happy now?"

"We'll see," I said. "I'm happier, if that helps."

"Good. Now, tell me what possessed you to go on a date with Morgan Reid. If I don't like your answer, I'm still going to beat the snot out of you."

And things were back to normal.

26

TWENTY-SIX

"Is there a reason we couldn't have done this over the phone?" Griffin parked in front of Grimlock Manor later that afternoon, his morning smile replaced with a grim frown. "I thought we were going to spend quality time together."

"We did that last night," I said. "We did it this morning, too. We also did it after you and Aidan made up."

"That's not quality time together," Griffin said. "Not everything is a euphemism for sex."

Huh. You learn something new every day. "Dad wants everyone together for a meeting. He's technically our boss. I had to come. You didn't."

"Yes, but I wanted to make sure he didn't hijack you again and try to make you stay here," Griffin said.

"He only did that because of the wraiths."

"He did it because he's a control freak." Griffin pocketed his keys once he got out of the car. "You're all control freaks."

"I am not a control freak. I'm easygoing."

"Has anyone … other than yourself, I mean … ever accused you of being easygoing?"

I searched my brain. Someone must have. I snapped my fingers. "My fifth-grade teacher, Mrs. Lucifer, did."

"Mrs. Lucifer? That can't have been her real name."

"No, but she looked like a female devil. Her real name was Mrs. Lumen."

"And she said you were easygoing?"

"When my parents went in for parent-teacher conferences, she told them that compared to my brothers I was the easiest one," I said. "That's the same as being easygoing."

"No, it's not."

"Yes, it is."

"Get in the house," Griffin ordered.

"You're awfully bossy," I grumbled. "No one ever accused you of being easygoing, did they?"

"I'll have you know most people think I'm very easygoing," he said. "It's just when I get around you and your family that my demeanor shifts."

"Are you saying you have multiple personalities?"

"Have you been watching soap operas again?"

"Hey, soap operas are wondrous things," I argued. "They take the everyday and make it surreal."

"You really are a lot of work," Griffin said.

"Again, I did all the work last night … and this morning."

"Stop saying things like that in your father's house," Griffin warned. "He already thinks I'm a sexual deviant."

"Just wait until he really gets to know you," I said. "Then he'll know you're a sexual deviant."

"Work. Work. Work."

"OKAY, WE HAVE SOME NEW INFORMATION," DAD SAID, LEANING forward in his desk chair and steepling his fingers in front of him. He always did that. He thinks it makes him look scholarly. "Why is he here again?"

I glanced at Griffin. "Because he's part of this, and he was at my place when you called."

"Why was he at your place?"

"Because he spent the night."

"Are you trying to give me a heart attack?"

"Are you trying to give me an ulcer?"

"Are you … ?"

"Let it go," Redmond said. "That townhouse is a den of sex and debauchery."

I shot him a look.

"I wasn't talking about only you," Redmond soothed. "I was talking about Aidan and Jerry, too."

"Thanks, man," Aidan said.

Redmond clapped him on the back. "Don't mention it."

"Oh, I'm going to mention it," Aidan said. "I'm just going to wait until Dad isn't watching."

"I'm going to help him mention it," I threatened.

"I think you have your hands full already," Redmond said.

"No, she had her hands full this morning," Aidan said, waggling his eyebrows.

"You shut your filthy mouth," Dad exploded.

Aidan had the grace to look abashed. While things weren't perfect between us again the tension had noticeably eased.

"Oh, it's all fun and games until Dad's aorta blows," I teased.

Griffin pinched the back of my neck. "I'm starting to feel uncomfortable."

"I am, too," Dad said. "Aisling, you can't sit there."

I had settled on the arm of Griffin's wingback chair when I entered the room. "Why?"

"Because I don't want to be constantly wondering where Griffin's hands are," Dad said.

"They're in his lap."

"Go and sit with your brothers," he ordered.

I rolled my eyes, but did as I was told. I pushed between Braden and Cillian, forcing them to make room for me on the leather couch. "Move over."

"Sit over there."

"I want to sit here."

"We don't want you to sit here," Braden said.

"I want her to sit here," Cillian said, slinging an arm over my shoulders. "I'm a good brother."

"That's why you're my favorite," Dad said.

Cillian shot a smug look in Braden's direction.

"Enjoy it while you can," Braden said. "I'm going to be back on top in a few days."

"All of you shut up," Dad snapped. "We have serious business to attend to."

"Yeah, stop being immature," I said. "You're going to give Dad a heart attack."

Braden poked me in the ribs.

"I will never understand why your mother insisted on procreating," Dad said.

"I think you should've just had one child," Redmond said. "You had perfection with me. You mucked everything up by adding the rest of them."

"I see we all have the attention span of gnats today," Dad said. "I'll make this brief."

"That's what Redmond does on all of his dates," Aidan said, smirking.

Dad extended his finger. "Not one more word."

We all snapped our mouths shut. We'd pushed him about as far as we could safely manage for one afternoon.

"As I said, we have some new information," Dad said.

"Where did this new information come from?" I asked.

"I've been working on the computer," Cillian supplied. "Dad won't let me do anything else."

"That's because you're recovering," I said. "You need your rest."

"Listen to your sister," Dad said.

"Oh, man, can you say that again?"

Dad furrowed his brow. "What?"

"I need you to repeat the 'listen to your sister' thing, but I need you to wait until I have my phone out so I can record you," I said.

"I will gag you if you don't shut your mouth," Dad said.

I mimed zipping my lips.

"Anyway, I've been going through Reid's finances," Cillian said.

Griffin leaned forward. "How did you get his financial information?"

"Let's just say it wasn't legal," Cillian said.

I watched Griffin to see how he would react. Instead of flying off the handle, he merely shrugged. "Continue."

"His clients are interesting," Cillian said. "All of them have a rap sheet."

"Do we have a short list?" Braden asked.

"Well, not exactly," Cillian said. "There was one name that looked fairly innocuous until I delved a little deeper."

"Well, don't keep us in suspense," Redmond said. "What's the name?"

"Sylvia Dobbs."

"Is she that woman who won the lottery last week?" I asked.

"No."

"You need to learn how to tell a story faster," I said, snapping my fingers. "I'm feeling the urge to nap coming on."

Aidan rolled his eyes. "That's because you were up all night … ." Dad cleared his throat. "Watching *The Golden Girls*," he finished.

"Sylvia Dobbs appears to be a normal woman," Cillian said, trying to alleviate the snowballing tension. "That's why she stood out."

"No one is normal," I said.

"Especially not you," Aidan said.

"Oh, and you're the poster boy for normal," I scoffed.

"I will kill you both," Dad threatened. "Cillian, please finish. If your sister opens her mouth again, shove something in there to shut her up."

"I think that's Griffin's job," Aidan said.

Dad's clenched jaw muscles tremored.

Cillian was trying hard not to laugh. "Sylvia Dobbs has financial ties to someone else we know," he said.

"Who?" Now I was genuinely curious.

"Duke Fontaine."

The joking attitude that filled the room seconds earlier dissipated quickly.

"Who is Duke Fontaine?" Griffin asked. "The name sounds familiar, but I can't remember why."

"Duke Fontaine is Dad's nemesis," I said.

Griffin racked his memory. "Is he the freelancer who keeps trying to steal souls for the highest bidder?"

I nodded.

"He's the one who fought with you and Cillian a few weeks ago, right?"

"He is," I said. "He's a horrible asshat. I won that fight, by the way."

"I won that fight," Cillian corrected. "You slipped in and stole the scepter while I used my impressive muscles to protect your honor."

I patted his shoulder. "Your muscles are impressive. Griffin's are better, though."

"So, how is Sylvia Dobbs tied to Duke Fontaine?" Griffin asked.

"We're not completely sure," Cillian said. "There are financial ties. She has made a series of payments to Fontaine."

"How much?"

"Three payments," Cillian said. "Fifty-thousand each."

"Well, not that I don't find that suspicious, but how can we be sure she's a person of interest? It could be just a coincidence," Griffin pressed. "I'm not sure why this is so important."

"The first payment was made the day before the first attempt on Morgan Reid's life," Cillian said. "The second payment was made the day before the second attempt on Reid's life."

If Griffin's face was any indication, things were starting to fall into place for him. I still needed further explanation. "When was the third payment?"

"Yesterday."

"Are you insinuating that Reid is supposed to die today?"

Cillian shrugged. "It could be a coincidence."

"Well, I'm not going to shed any tears if Reid dies," I said. "Is he on our list today?"

Dad shook his head. "Our list is light. Part of our workload has been shifted to other groups until this Reid situation remedies itself. If he does show up on a list, though, I've been promised that it will come to us."

"Where do you guys get these lists?" Griffin asked. "Do they come from … God?"

Redmond snickered. "They come from the main office."

"There's a main reaping office?"

"There is."

"Huh. That's … just so weird."

"You'll get used to it," I said. "If Reid isn't on any lists, that means he's safe for the day. If I understand what you're hinting at, though, you're suggesting that Sylvia Dobbs hired Fontaine to kill Reid. You're forgetting that someone else was supposed to kill Reid that first day. His name showed up in the files, and he was the one killed by the wraith. Plus, he was killed with a knife. We've seen wraiths use weapons before, but usually only as a last resort."

"Maybe Spencer was on Fontaine's payroll," Redmond suggested.

"Do we have any proof of that?" Griffin asked.

Cillian shook his head. "Just a theory."

"That still doesn't explain why the wraiths keep showing up," I said. "We also don't know who was supposed to kill Reid the second time. It wasn't in the file."

"Is that normal?" Griffin asked.

"Reaping is like any bureaucracy," Dad said. "Sometimes the paperwork isn't complete."

"That's a freaky thought," Griffin mused. "So, what we need to find out is how Sylvia Dobbs and Duke Fontaine play into all of this."

"Essentially," Dad said.

"Well, I can go into the office and look through our files," Griffin offered. "I won't be able to do it until tomorrow, but I'm willing to try. I'm not sure I'll find anything, but it can't hurt to look."

"Will that put you in a bad spot?" Dad asked. I was surprised he even cared about Griffin's professional well-being.

"It shouldn't be an issue," Griffin said. "No one will question what I'm doing."

"Well, that's a start then," Dad said. "I'm going to talk to a few contacts as well. To my knowledge, no one has seen Fontaine since I ran him out of town a month ago. He could be back, though. Just because we haven't seen him doesn't mean he's not here."

"Great," I said. "What do you want us to do?"

Dad smiled. "You and Aidan are going to work today."

Bummer. "Why?"

"It's your turn," Dad said. "Don't worry. It's only one job, and it came up at the last minute."

"Where is it?"

Dad smiled. "Presbyterian Hospital."

Crap. I hate hospital jobs. "Fine. I want a raise, though."

27

TWENTY-SEVEN

"I'm so excited." Jerry's eyes sparkled from the front seat of Aidan's car.

"You're staying here," I said. "We only brought you because we all agreed to go to dinner together tonight as part of Aidan and Griffin's new truce. You're here only because we didn't want to have to drive back to Royal Oak to pick you up."

"You're such a killjoy," Jerry said. "Why can't I come?"

"Because, this isn't a movie for your enjoyment."

Jerry crossed his arms over his chest. "Does Griffin get to go inside?"

"I'm a cop," Griffin said. "I'm used to danger."

"It's not going to be dangerous," I said. "It's a guy who has been in a coma for ten years. He's dying today. We'll be in and out. Griffin is staying here with you."

"I'm coming with you," Griffin argued.

"If he's going, I'm going," Jerry said, determined.

Aidan met Griffin's gaze in the mirror, something silent passing between them. I think it was a challenge.

Griffin sighed, resigned. "We're going to stay here, Jerry," he said.

"We are?"

"Aisling and Aidan have a job to do, and we're going to let them do it."

"Since when are you so eager to let Aisling walk into danger?"

Griffin chafed at the question. "I am not letting her walk into danger."

He grabbed my hand and squeezed it momentarily. "I'm trusting her to do her job. I'm not her boss."

"Oh, well, great," Jerry complained. "I can't believe you picked now to play the role of supportive boyfriend."

"I'm not playing," Griffin said, shifting his shoulders to face me. "If he whines the whole time I'm in this car with him, I can't guarantee he'll be alive when you get back."

I gave him a quick kiss. "We'll be fast."

"That means you're not going to talk to him, right?" Aidan pressed. "We're just going to go in, suck, and then leave."

"You have such a way with words," I teased.

"I'm not joking," Aidan said. "I don't want any of your nonsense. I'm hungry, and I'm totally looking forward to going to Greektown tonight. I want some chicken and rice and … other stuff."

"You're also a culinary genius."

Aidan shot me a look.

"I won't talk to him," I said. "I'm done with that."

"No, you're not," Aidan scoffed. "You can't help yourself. You feel bad for them. Sometimes I find it funny. You can't do it today, though. Promise me."

"I promise."

"Really promise me," Aidan said.

"I really promise."

"Maybe you should pinky swear," Jerry suggested.

"Just sit here," Aidan said, kissing Jerry before climbing out of the car. "We'll be right back."

"WHICH WAY?"

Aidan scanned the numbers on the wall. "This way."

I followed him down the hall, fighting the urge to be a woman and hound him at an inopportune time. "We're okay, right?"

"I'm fine."

"I know you're fine. That's not what I was asking," I said.

"What were you saying?"

"We're okay, right? You and me?"

Aidan paused long enough to give me a brief hug. "We're okay. I'm sorry I've been such a tool."

"I'm used to it."

He flicked my ear. "I'll be nicer to Griffin. I just … ."

"I'll try not to ignore you."

Aidan smiled. "You're going to buy dinner tonight, too. I think you owe me."

I scowled. "Fine. I'm not picking up your drink tab, though."

"Agreed."

We returned to our task and continued down the hall. After two turns – only one of them was wrong – we found ourselves outside the right room.

"What time is it?" I asked.

"Two minutes until show time," Aidan said, peering into the room. "Did you bring your ring?"

I nodded. Grim reapers are outfitted with special rings that make them invisible. We only use them in specific situations – most of the time we don't need them – but reaping in busy hospitals and senior living centers are examples of occasions when they come in handy.

"I guess we should get ready," I said, rummaging in my pocket. "I'm kind of hungry, too."

"I'm always hungry," Aidan said. "Dating Jerry has been detrimental to my waistline."

I snickered. "Is that why you're in the gym five days a week?"

"I like to look good for my man."

That was interesting. "Maybe I should start going to the gym."

"I think Griffin is fine with the way you look," Aidan said. "You forget, we can hear you in the next room."

"I can hear you, too."

Aidan's face slipped. "Do I sound like I'm impressing him?"

I smacked his arm. "You're totally grossing me out."

"I just got here and I'm totally grossed out, too." The voice took me by surprise, and Aidan's face was awash with worry as he glanced over my shoulder. When I turned , and my gaze fell on the recognizable wall of muscle and shining bald head, I wished we'd put on our rings before we decided to talk about our feelings.

"Fontaine," Aidan said, his voice cool.

"Grimlock."

"Dickhead," I said.

"Prettier Grimlock," Fontaine said, flirting. He's so nasty.

"What do you think you're doing here?"

"Unfortunately, I think I'm doing the same thing you're doing," Fontaine said. "I was hoping this one would slip by you because it popped up out of nowhere. I guess I'm not that lucky."

"And yet you still approached, even though you saw we were already here," Aidan said. "That's … ."

"Ballsy?"

"Stupid."

Fontaine's face was unreadable. "Well, I need to get past you if I'm going to claim that soul."

I shared an incredulous look with Aidan. "I'm sorry, you think you're getting that soul?"

Fontaine's smile was wolfish. "Yes."

"And how are you going to magically accomplish that?"

"I'm going to walk past the two of you, wish you a nice evening, and then I'm going to collect my soul," Fontaine said. "If you want to wait for me, Aisling, I'd be happy to take you out to dinner when I'm done. I'm going to be looking for a way to … relax … after a hard day's work."

I had a way for him to relax. It involved a ball peen hammer and the back of his skull.

"Don't you dare say things like that to my sister," Aidan said. "In fact, don't you even look at her."

"She's too pretty not to look at."

"And you're too ugly and gross to stand a chance," I shot back sweetly.

"Honey, you couldn't handle a man like me."

I narrowed my eyes. "I've handled bigger and better men than you."

"I was under the impression your brothers kept you under lock and key," Fontaine said. "You're the Grimlock princess, right? I think it's about time you found someone to rebel with."

I'd rather set him ablaze with a can of hairspray and a cigarette lighter. In the back of my mind, an idea started to form. "Do you think you can handle me?" I purposely moved around Fontaine, forcing his attention to remain on me as I circled around him. I didn't stop until his back was to Aidan – and the hospital room door.

"I'd love to handle you," Fontaine replied, looking me up and down. "Why don't you give me a little preview?"

"Sure," I said, reaching for the hem of my shirt.

Aidan's face was flushed. I sent him a silent message, willing him to understand what he was supposed to do. After a moment, his eyes cleared and he moved closer to the door, although he never entirely took his wary gaze off of me.

"Now, you understand I'm just showing you the goods, right?" I purposely played with my shirt, as though I really was going to lift it.

Fontaine was frustrated. "Yeah. I get it."

"If you touch me … ."

"I promise not to touch you until we're alone."

"Okay," I said, lifting my shirt higher and giving him a glimpse of my bare midriff.

Fontaine was so distracted he didn't notice Aidan slip into the hospital room at his back. Fred Robertson had passed moments before, and Aidan was discreet as he collected the soul before it had a chance to fully materialize. The only hint anything had occurred was a brief flash of light, and since Fontaine's back was to the action he didn't notice.

I lifted my shirt a tad higher.

"Come on, whip them out," Fontaine prodded.

I scowled and let my shirt drop once Aidan was back in his previous position, the scepter in his pocket and an innocent look on his face. "I changed my mind."

"What?" Fontaine sputtered. "You can't change your mind."

"Well, I did."

Fontaine reached a hand out, but Aidan grabbed his wrist before he could touch me. "Don't even think about it," Aidan growled.

Fontaine jerked his arm away. "You're a stupid little tease."

"You're a big, dumb tool."

"I think he probably has a small tool," Aidan interjected.

"You're right," I said. "That's why he's overcompensating."

"I don't have to overcompensate for anything," Fontaine said, reaching for his belt. "I'll show you right now."

Oh, gross. I couldn't see that. I'd have nightmares. "Look, we have a job to do. You need to go. We're already running late."

Fontaine straightened. "I'm taking that soul," he said. "I've already got a buyer lined up. I need that money."

"Well, it's ours," I said. "We were here first."

"I'm taking it." Fontaine shoved Aidan out of the way and strode toward the door. "There's nothing you can do to stop me. I don't care how high you lift that shirt."

I pursed my lips. "Fine. Take it. Be a jackass."

"I will." Fontaine disappeared inside the room.

I grabbed Aidan's arm. "We have to run now."

Aidan pushed me. "You should already be running."

We scampered down the hall just as the buzzers on the machines that were keeping the husk of a patient alive started razzing in Robertson's hospital room to alert the nursing staff that he had passed.

"There must have been a delay," Aidan said, directing me toward the stairwell. "Go."

"Can't we take the elevator?"

"We need to get a head start."

"Sonovabitch!" I could hear Fontaine swear from around the corner.

I plunged down the stairs. By the time we made it to the main floor I was gasping. I really should start working out. Aidan didn't look any different.

"Move faster, Ais," Aidan pushed me in front of him. "Stop panting like a dog."

"I hate you," I mumbled.

We both hit the parking lot at the same time. It was only at that moment we remembered we'd parked on the south side of the hospital, not the north.

"Crap," Aidan said.

"This is your fault," I said.

"Fine. I'll buy dinner. Start moving."

"I'm done running," I said. "There's no way I can run another step."

"I'm going to kill both of you!" Fontaine had caught up to us, and he looked pissed. His chest heaved as he moved down the sidewalk. "I'm going to rip your head off of your shoulders and send it to your father in a box."

I broke into a run I didn't think I had in me and headed toward the far side of the hospital, knowing I was out of options. I couldn't let Fontaine get his hands on me. It would be all over if he did.

"Run, Ais!" Aidan was right behind me. By the time we made it to the south parking lot, my lungs burned and I was convinced I was going to die. My eyes landed on Griffin and Jerry, who were standing beside the car talking. Griffin lifted his head, as if sensing my presence, and met my gaze from a hundred feet away. He broke into a smile, but it was fleeting when he saw the look on my face.

"Aisling?" He stepped away from the car. "What's wrong?"

The sound of pounding footsteps behind me came nearer. Since Aidan was at my side, there was no mistaking the runner.

"There's nowhere left to run, girlie," Fontaine yelled. "I'm going to take you and use you up."

Aidan stepped between us, handing me the scepter. "Run."

"I'm not leaving you."

"You have to," Aidan said. "Get in the car and go."

"I'm not leaving you!"

Fontaine's hands were on Aidan, and he was such a behemoth he lifted my brother off of the ground without strain. He threw him … hard … against a nearby car. Aidan groaned as he bounced off of it, hitting the pavement with a sickening thud.

"Aidan!"

Griffin was moving in my direction.

Fontaine grabbed my arm, his fingers digging into the flesh as I twisted. Fontaine used his other hand to grab a fistful of hair and pull my face flush with his. "I'm going to get what you teased me with earlier."

"Let me go." I struggled, but it was like fighting a giant.

That's when things shifted. A figure moved into my line of sight from the side, slinking out from behind a clump of trees, and I recognized it as a wraith before my mind could process what I saw. What the hell?

"Let her go," Griffin ordered. He was still too far away to help me, his pace slowing uncertainly when he saw the wraith shambling toward us.

"Aisling!" Aidan rolled to his knees.

"You're going to give me that soul," Fontaine said, shaking me as the toes of my shoes barely touched the ground. He didn't seem too worried about our new guest. "You're going to give it to me … and so much more."

The wraith reached out, red talons flashing in the waning sun, and I cringed when I saw the white fingers reaching for me. To my surprise, the wraith didn't touch me, though. Instead it grabbed Fontaine's arm.

Fontaine groaned as the wraith started to drain him.

"Aisling Grimlock must not be touched," the wraith hissed. "She's not for you. She's not for us."

"Let me go," Fontaine screeched. "Let me go."

"Aisling Grimlock must not be touched," the wraith repeated.

Fontaine shrugged off the wraith, his face ashen as he regarded me. "Fine." He mustered whatever remnants of strength he had, and then he threw me. I shot out of his arms and slammed into a nearby car, my head snapping back as bright light flashed behind my eyes. The pain was overwhelming.

Uh-oh. This wasn't good.

28
TWENTY-EIGHT

"Baby, look at me."

I shook my head, forcing the sparkly cobwebs to recede. I hadn't lost consciousness, which was a nice change from some of my previous interactions with wraiths. My back was on fire, though, and I knew it was going to be a mess for days.

Griffin kneeled in front of me, his hands on my shoulders. "Look at me."

"Is she all right?"

"I think she's coming back to me," Griffin said, his eyes dark as he studied me. "Aisling, please look at me."

"I'm okay," I murmured.

I felt gentle hands moving across my hair. "Did you hit your head?"

"No."

"Did you break any bones?"

"No."

"What hurts?"

I finally focused all of my attention on Griffin. "Does my pride count?"

"Sure," Griffin said, forcing a thin smile onto his handsome face. "What else hurts?"

"My back."

"It's not broken, is it?" Jerry asked, appearing behind Griffin and wringing his hands. "Don't worry if it is. I can totally trick out a wheelchair."

"It's not broken," I growled. "It's just … hot."

"Hot?" Aidan was holding his shoulder, but my injuries were affecting him more than his own. "Can you lean forward and let me look?"

"Sure." I started to move. "Ow. Ow. Ow!"

Griffin pressed his forehead to mine as he waited for Aidan to run his hands over my back.

"I think she's okay," he said, eliciting a relieved sigh from Griffin. "She's probably not going to be able to walk tomorrow."

"I'll be fine," I said. "I just need to walk it off now."

Griffin arched an eyebrow. "You're going to walk it off? Do you know how far he threw you?"

Memories flooded in. "Wait. Where is Fontaine?"

"He ran," Aidan said.

"What about the wraith?"

"Is that what that was?" Jerry asked. "I couldn't figure it out."

"What did you think it was?" Griffin asked, annoyed.

"I don't know," Jerry said. "People wear odd things. Grief can do horrible things to a person. I figured it was someone in mourning."

"You need to be quiet for a few minutes," Griffin ordered.

"Hey, I'm traumatized here." Jerry's voice was shrill.

"I will beat you," Griffin said.

Aidan motioned for Jerry to take a step back. "You're not helping," he said. "I know you're upset. I'll make you feel better later. We need to get Aisling up and out of here. We got lucky no one saw us fighting. We can't press our luck."

Griffin reached down, shifting a hand under my rear and lifting with his legs. "I've got her."

Aidan was impressed. "Do you work out?"

Griffin chuckled, the sound hoarse. "Yeah."

"We should go to the gym together sometime. I mean … if you want to."

"I … okay." Griffin seemed surprised, but also relieved. "That sounds like something we can do without killing each other."

"It's a start," Aidan agreed.

I rested my head against Griffin's shoulder. "I'm going to start going to the gym. I'm in terrible shape."

"You're going to bed," Griffin said. "In fact, I think maybe we should take you to the hospital just to have you checked out."

Jerry pointed to the building behind us. "We're at the hospital."

"I'm fine," I said. "I just need a hot bath."

"With bubbles," Jerry said.

"With bubbles," I agreed.

"And ice cream," Jerry added.

"Definitely ice cream."

"I will buy you a whole truck of ice cream," Griffin said, kissing my cheek. "In fact, if you want anything extravagant, now would be the time to put in your request."

"Ask for a pony," Jerry prodded.

"I just want a bath and ice cream," I said.

"I want a pony," Jerry said.

"I think the bath and ice cream is all I can handle tonight."

"You've got it," Griffin said. "Let's get out of here."

"ARE YOU SURE YOU'RE OKAY?" AIDAN WAS GENTLE AS HE SETTLED ON the couch next to me.

"Yeah. I'm just going to be sore. I'm betting you will be, too. He threw you with more force than he threw me."

"Yeah, that whole wraith thing was a surprise," Aidan agreed, putting his arm around my shoulders. "It was saying something, but I couldn't hear it. My ears were ringing."

"It kept saying that I couldn't be touched."

"I don't know if that's a good or bad thing," Aidan said. "On one hand, I'm glad they don't want to touch you. On the other, that means they have something else in mind for you."

"Fontaine didn't seem surprised to see it," I said, resting my head against Aidan's shoulder. "He seemed surprised it dared touch him, but not to see it."

"They have to be working together," Aidan said.

"That means all of our assumptions were wrong."

"I know," Aidan said. "I'm going to have to call Dad. You know that, right?"

"Yeah. He's expecting us to deliver the soul."

"Do you still have it? I figured Fontaine took it from you."

"It's in my pocket. I'll get it out when I take my bath. I can't stand right now."

Aidan pressed his cheek to my forehead. "You should have given it to him."

"No way."

"It's like when a mugger tries to steal your purse, Ais," he said. "You don't fight. You just give it to him. Nothing is worth losing you."

"I am not purposely losing to Fontaine," I said. "It's just not going to happen."

"You're a stubborn fool."

"I know."

"I need to call someone to come and pick up the soul," Aidan said. "If I don't, one of them is going to show up. I'd rather have Redmond or Braden here than Dad."

"Dad won't come here," I said. "The last time he did, there was a bunch of underwear hanging over the shower door in the bathroom and he freaked out because he thought it was mine."

"Was it Jerry's?" I could feel Aidan's smile against my temple.

"You know how he is about his delicates."

"I do indeed."

"When I explained that to Dad, it only made things worse."

Aidan chuckled. "I'm sorry I missed it."

Griffin stood in the door between my bedroom and the living room watching us when I glanced up. "Hey."

"Hey," he said, his eyes soft.

I felt Aidan shift next to me. "I suppose I should relinquish my spot."

"You don't have to," Griffin said. "She looks … comfortable."

"She is," Aidan said. "I think she'll be more comfortable with you." It was hard for him to say, but he seemed earnest.

"You don't have to … ."

"I know," Aidan said. "It's your … spot, though. You should probably take it. I need to make sure the pizza is taken care of and I have a call to make."

"To your father?"

"To Redmond," Aidan said. "I don't think anyone needs to deal with Dad tonight."

Aidan kept me upright until Griffin slid into the spot next to me. Once he was settled, he brushed my hair out of my face so he could study me, finally deciding I wasn't going to die – or cry – in the next few minutes. "I would rather not deal with your father," Griffin agreed. "He's going to yell and I'm going to have to listen, because I deserve it."

"How do you figure that?" Aidan asked, pulling his cellphone from his pocket.

"I shouldn't have left her."

"We had no way of knowing Fontaine would be there," I protested.

"She's right. It was a fluke," Aidan said.

"No offense, but you guys seem to have a lot of flukes lately," Griffin said. "I've known you for two months and she's almost died three times."

"Oh, let's not get dramatic," I said. "I didn't almost die today."

"It was close enough to scare me," Griffin said. "That's not even counting the time Aidan fought off the wraith to save you and you fought off the wraith to save Cillian."

"We have been having a bad run," Aidan acknowledged. "This honestly isn't how it usually is."

"You don't have to apologize or make excuses," Griffin said. "I'm not happy with what happened today, but I have no control over her job. We just have to come up with a better way to keep her protected."

"Yeah ... well, I'm a little worried about why the wraiths won't touch her."

"You guys know I'm in the room with you, right?"

"I do," Griffin said, brushing his fingers against my cheek. "I also know we're probably lucky you are. Something has to give here, and I'm guessing that's Duke Fontaine."

"I'll call Redmond," Aidan said. "We could use another mind to work through this. You're not used to this and I'm not at my best."

Jerry poked his head into the room. "That's why you have me."

Aidan smiled. "And Jerry is going to be too smart for all of us to keep up with."

"When you call him, have him bring some Epsom salt," Griffin said. "She's going to need it for her bath."

"I want a bubble bath," I whined.

"We'll talk about it later," Griffin said, sighing. "Just ... sit there and rest."

"I still want a bubble bath."

"You're going to be the death of me. You know that, right?"

"I want a bubble bath." What? If I'm ever going to get my own way, it's today.

"Fine. You can have a bubble bath," Griffin conceded.

I love winning.

"After you take a bath in the Epsom salt."

Life just isn't fair.

"HOW ARE YOU FEELING, KID?" REDMOND'S FACE WAS CONCERNED AS he floated into the living room.

"I've had pizza and PMS meds," I said. "I'm … great."

"PMS meds?"

"They help with pain," Aidan said. "Did you bring the Epsom salt?"

Redmond shook the bag in his hand. "Has she eaten anything?"

"She ate two slices of pizza," Griffin said. "Then we gave her the meds. Now I'm going to get her into a bath and put her to bed. She's going to be sore as hell tomorrow."

"That's going to make work a delight," I said.

"You're not working for the next few days," Redmond said.

"Dad won't like that."

"I don't care," Redmond said. "I'll handle Dad."

"How are you going to handle him without telling him what happened?"

"I have to tell him what happened, Ais," Redmond said. "He has to know. Fontaine is his … ."

"Arch enemy," I finished, resigned.

"He's the Joker to his Batman," Redmond agreed. "I'll take care of telling him. I just need to get the particulars straight."

Griffin glanced at Aidan. "You can do that, right? She's about to conk out."

"I've got it," Aidan said. "Just … take care of her."

"You might want to take a bath, too," Griffin said. "You took a hard jolt. The only thing that saved you is that you were lower down on the car. You didn't absorb the same impact she did."

"And I weigh fifty pounds more than she does," Aidan said.

"Fifty?" I think I've just been insulted.

"Sixty," Aidan conceded.

I narrowed my eyes.

"Fine. Seventy. You're pushing your luck, though."

Redmond chuckled. "Well, I brought you another treat," he said, digging into the bag. "Do you want this now or later?"

The pint of ice cream in his hand piqued my interest. "Is that Phish Food?"

"It's still your favorite, isn't it?"

"Oh, you're the best brother ever," I said, leaning forward to snatch the ice cream. The movement inadvertently caused me to whimper.

"Let me do that for you," Griffin ordered, grabbing the ice cream from Redmond. He studied the container for a moment. "This is your favorite ice cream?"

"Other than Blue Moon," Jerry said. "That's the real way to her heart."

"They didn't have any of that," Redmond said. "I looked. I figured this was just as good."

"That is awesome," I said.

"Well, how about this," Griffin said. "I'll get you in the bath, and when you're done you can eat the ice cream in bed."

"I'm fine," I said. "I want the ice cream now."

"You need to get in the bath," Griffin said. "You have no idea how much pain you're going to be in tomorrow."

"You have no idea how much pain I'm in now," I countered. "I want that ice cream."

"If I give you this ice cream now are you going to give me crap about the Epsom salt?"

"No." That was a lie. I wanted bubbles.

"Are you lying to me?"

"Yes."

Griffin rubbed his forehead with the heel of his hand. "Fine. Have your ice cream. I can't argue with you. It's too hard when you look like that. I can't say no to you."

Aidan smirked. "Welcome to the family."

29

TWENTY-NINE

"What's on the agenda today?"

I found Aidan and Griffin sitting at the kitchen table, their heads bent together as they discussed something in low voices. It had been three days since our confrontation with Fontaine, and after a tense visit from my father – during which he insisted I come home so he could take care of me, a suggestion I quickly shot down, mind you – I felt markedly better this morning. I wasn't a hundred percent, but I was well on my way to recovery.

Other than going to work, Griffin hadn't left my side. He'd even insisted on Maya visiting me, and about a half hour after her arrival Cillian had conveniently shown up for a visit. One look at Jerry's guilty face told me he placed the call. I'd expected Griffin to balk at the overt flirting, but he'd been friendly … and silent.

As far as Aidan and Griffin were concerned, they'd been pleasant and amiable with one another. After a long nap the previous afternoon, I'd found them watching baseball on the couch and arguing about whether or not the Detroit Tigers were going to make it to the playoffs. The swing between them had been sudden, but I welcomed it.

Jerry was having a harder time. He didn't get sports and he certainly didn't understand how Aidan and Griffin could waste an entire hour watching grown men run around bases. It baffled him, especially the unflattering socks, and I was worried his nose was going to be out of joint before long. For now, I couldn't dwell on it.

"Good morning, sweetie," Griffin said, looking me over. "You look a lot better today."

"She showered," Aidan said.

I shot him a look. "I showered every day this week."

"And then you slept on your hair when it was wet and woke up looking like Medusa."

"I thought she looked cute," Griffin said.

"Good. I took a few photos and posted them on Facebook," Aidan said. "Between her sleeping with Cillian and her hair during the past few days, you're her last chance to snag a man."

"Oh, you two are just so funny," I said. I stalked to the counter and poured a cup of coffee. "What's on our list today?"

Aidan shifted in his chair. "There's nothing on our list. I have two names on my list. You're staying here."

"I'm not staying here," I argued. "I'm ready to work."

"No, you're not," Griffin said. "Your range of motion is still limited, and since you're a target you're not wandering around and into danger."

"Aidan hasn't had one problem since I've been out of commission," I protested.

Griffin raised an eyebrow. "Have you considered that's because you weren't with him?"

I faltered, the truth of his words leaving me cold. "Oh."

"Don't do that," Griffin chided. "I can't take that sad face you make."

"Why do you think she's so spoiled?" Aidan asked. "My father can't take it either."

"I can't not work," I said. "It's not fair to you guys."

"It's fine," Aidan said. "Right now, keeping you out of danger is our primary job. You're safe here."

"But … what am I supposed to do?"

"What have you been doing?"

"Sleeping and watching soap operas."

Aidan sipped from his coffee and shrugged. "Do that."

"I can't do that again. I've peaked in the Soap Opera Olympics. It's time for something new."

"So, do something … girly."

I narrowed my eyes. "Define girly."

Aidan shifted his gaze to Griffin, silently pleading for help. He'd stepped into the middle of a minefield with no safe way to extricate himself with all of his limbs intact.

"Oh, you're on your own," Griffin said. "She looks angry."

"I thought you found that cute?" Aidan challenged.

"I think everything she does is cute," Griffin said. "I still don't want her angry with me."

"And here I thought we had an understanding," Aidan grumbled.

"We do," Griffin said, nonplussed. "I understand that I'm not in the mood to piss her off."

Aidan rubbed the back of his neck. "I forgot what we were talking about."

That wasn't going to work on me. "You were about to tell me what 'girly' things I should be doing."

"You just won't let things go," Aidan said. "Fine. Why don't you go to a spa? Wasn't Jerry talking about a spa day the other day? You could go and do whatever it is you do at a spa."

That actually sounded fun. "Where is Jerry?"

"He's at work, but I'll give him a call," Aidan said.

"He can't leave work to hang out with me," I said. "That's not fair."

"I'm betting he'll be all for it when I tell him I'm going to pay," Aidan said.

"You're going to pay?"

"I am," Aidan said, sensing he had an out. "I'm thrilled to pay."

"For everything?"

"What's everything?"

"Oh, you'll see when you get the bill," I said.

"THIS IS GREAT," JERRY ENTHUSED, GLANCING AROUND THE DAY SPA excitedly. "We haven't had a spa day in months."

"It's going to be fun," I agreed. "What do you want to do first?"

"I need to get my chest waxed," Jerry announced, guileless.

I made a face. I've never understood why men do that. I don't like a hairy beast, but there's nothing wrong with a little hair. It makes me know I'm cuddling with a man and not a prepubescent boy. "You want to do that first?"

"It hurts," Jerry said. "I'd rather get it out of the way."

"Okay. Go nuts. I'm going to get a massage."

"Oh, you have to wait for me to get a massage," Jerry complained. "That's when we gossip."

"I thought we gossiped when we were getting facials?"

"Then, too."

"And during pedicures?"

"There's no limit to the gossip I have," Jerry said, hands on hips, pout in place.

"Fine," I said, blowing out an exasperated sigh. "Go get your chest waxed. I'll wait for you here, and then we'll do the rest of it together."

"Great," Jerry said, excited. "This is going to be the best day ever."

I settled in one of the leather chairs and flipped through a well-worn magazine as I waited. I was lost amongst the beauty secrets of the stars when I heard the door that led to the inner sanctum open. I glanced up, my eyes landing on a middle-aged woman with perfectly highlighted hair and a very expensive suit as she moved to the counter, purse clutched in her hand.

"How was your massage, Ms. Dobbs?" The receptionist was pleasant and happy. I had a feeling she was medicated. What? No one is that happy. It's impossible.

"Call me Sylvia," the woman said, smiling back at the receptionist. "It was wonderful. I really needed it."

The receptionist scanned the computer in front of her as I tried to keep my breathing even and my interest hidden. Sylvia Dobbs? That's the name of the woman working with Duke Fontaine. What are the odds? Oh, who am I kidding, I wouldn't have luck if it wasn't bad.

"Okay, your total comes to a hundred and fifty," the receptionist said. "Is that credit or debit?"

"Debit."

"Okay, slide the card."

I considered my options. The smart thing to do would be to call Aidan and tell him what I'd discovered. I'm not smart and I didn't want to be sidelined. I was going to do the stupid thing. I was going to follow her when she left.

After checking out, Sylvia waved at the receptionist and exited. I followed her to the door, making sure to see what direction she left in before turning to the girl behind the counter. "Tell my friend I forgot something in the car and I'll be right back," I instructed.

The receptionist nodded.

"And if it takes a few minutes, tell him to wax something else until I get back," I said.

"Of course," the receptionist said. "We can have him hairless by the time you return."

That was truly frightening.

I left the spa and turned in the direction I'd seen Sylvia disappear. I kept my pace even as I scanned the sidewalk. It took me a few seconds, but I saw her weaving in and out of the foot traffic on Main Street. Downtown Royal Oak is kitschy and cool, but it's always busy in the summer. Parking is also an issue, and I couldn't help but wonder if Sylvia had another destination ahead of her or whether she was walking to her car.

I followed her for three blocks, every step reminding me that Jerry was going to have an absolute fit when I got back to the spa. I tamped my worry down as I continued to follow. Sylvia was a lead and we needed information. I could at least find out what kind of vehicle she drove.

Sylvia turned onto a side street, so I slowed to give her time to increase the distance between us. Main Street was busy enough to hide me. Side streets were an iffy proposition.

When I rounded the corner I pulled up short. There was no sign of Sylvia. Where had she gone? I moved down the sidewalk, scanning every store I passed to see whether she had made a stop. At the third store I stopped when I heard voices. I recognized one of them. It didn't belong to Sylvia.

"What are you doing down here?" Fontaine asked.

I pressed my back against the brick wall and listened. I knew better than to poke my head around the corner of the entryway and betray my position.

"I needed a massage," Sylvia said. "What does it matter?"

"I told you the Grimlock girl lives here," Fontaine said. "It's too dangerous to walk around. Her gay roommate owns a bakery right on Main Street."

"How would they possibly recognize me?"

"She's smarter than she looks."

"Well, I don't really care," Sylvia sniffed. "I wanted a massage. That spa has the best ratings on Yelp."

"Women," Fontaine growled. "From now on, you need to keep a low profile. We're nearing the end here. We can't make mistakes now."

"I don't make mistakes," Sylvia said. "You make mistakes."

"How have I made a mistake?"

"Really? We've been close enough to grab the girl three times and we've come up empty-handed each time. That's failure."

"She's never alone," Fontaine said. "She always has backup. They don't trust her to go on jobs by herself."

"Well, you're going to have to find a way around that," Sylvia said. "She's the key and we need her to unlock everything."

"I know," Fontaine said. "I'm not stupid."

"You were threatening to kill her in a hospital parking lot," Sylvia pointed out. "If that's not stupid, what is? They'll never let her out of their sight now."

"So, what do you suggest?" Fontaine asked.

"That's not my problem," Sylvia said. "You need to fix this and you need to fix it now. Don't you dare let me down one more time. You won't like what happens if you do."

"Are you threatening me?"

"I'm making you a promise," Sylvia said. "I'm not the one you need to fear. You know that. Don't make me turn you into the sacrificial lamb."

"I'll figure something out," Fontaine grumbled.

"Do it soon," Sylvia said. "I won't wait for you to handle this situation much longer. I'm ready to look elsewhere if you can't get results."

30

THIRTY

I was debating whether I should duck into a store to wait out Fontaine and Sylvia until I was sure they were gone or just amble down the street as though I didn't have a care in the world when Fontaine appeared in front of me. His face exploded, myriad emotions taking hold before anger finally settled in.

"You have got to be kidding me," he growled.

I took a step back. "I will scream bloody murder if you take one step in my direction."

Fontaine moved closer, taunting me.

I opened my mouth, the word "rapist" on the tip of my tongue.

"Fine." He took a step back. "You're the world's biggest pain in the ass."

"You're not the first person to tell me that."

"I'm stunned."

I scowled. "What are you doing here?"

"What are you doing here?"

I had no idea what to tell him. Lying seemed the best option. "I'm looking for some new shoes."

Fontaine glanced at the wine shop to my left. "In there?"

"I need wine to drink when I'm wearing the shoes," I said. "I'm not comfortable in heels. I have trouble balancing."

"And you think wine will help?"

He had a point. "It couldn't hurt."

Fontaine snorted and shook his head. "Do you want to know what I think?"

Not really. "Sure."

"I think you saw me somehow – maybe you were in the parking lot across the way or something – and you came over to eavesdrop," he said.

"Were you doing something worth eavesdropping on?"

"No," Fontaine said. "I was … buying shoes."

I glanced down at his combat boots. They were old and scuffed. They looked authentic, which made them ugly. "You should try wearing heels," I said. "They would make your legs look longer."

"You're fast with the one-liners," he said. "Do you think, if I put my mind to it, you're fast enough to get away from me?"

"I'm not trying to get away from you," I said. "If you try anything I'm going to start screaming that you're a rapist and that you tried to touch me. I just want to ask you a few questions."

"And you think I'll answer?"

"I don't know," I said. "Let's see."

Fontaine crossed his arms over his chest. "Shoot."

"What are you doing in town?"

"I have a few jobs," Fontaine said.

"Are they normal jobs?"

"Define normal."

"Well, you usually steal souls so you can sell them to the highest bidder without any concern about their wishes," I said. "Is that what you're doing?"

"Mostly."

I narrowed my eyes. He wasn't going to simply volunteer information. I had to find a way to trick him. "So, what were you and Sylvia Dobbs talking about?"

What? There's no way he's going to tell her I'm on to them. She's clearly the boss, and he defers to her. He'll hide it. I know how a coward thinks.

"So you were eavesdropping," Fontaine said, his face grim. "What did you hear?"

"I heard you want me. I want to know why."

"Why do you think?"

"I think the wraiths have been told not to touch me, but that admonishment doesn't go for my brothers," I said. "There has to be a reason and I want to know what it is. I also want to know who's giving the wraiths orders. Genevieve Toth is dead. Who took over her operation?"

"Maybe you're important," Fontaine suggested, ignoring the second question.

"I'm divine," I said. "Everyone loves me. That still doesn't explain why you want me."

Fontaine's smile was predatory. "I want you for a number of reasons."

"You just want to mess with me because you know it will piss off my father," I said. "I'm not buying for a second that you're interested in me personally for any other reason."

"Your father is a trip," Fontaine said, grinning. "How is he?"

"Good."

"How did he react when he found out what happened at the hospital?"

He vowed bloody revenge. "I was fine, so he was fine."

"You were fine? Is that why you're standing funny?"

I extended my middle finger in his face. "I'm the one who survived and held onto the soul," I reminded him. "I won."

"Is that what's important to you?"

"Beating you is important to me," I said.

"What about survival, Aisling? Is that important to you?"

"It depends," I said. "What do you and Sylvia have planned?"

"Okay, here's the situation," Fontaine said, hunkering down so he could meet my gaze levelly. "You need to watch your back. You are in a very precarious situation."

"Are you honestly trying to scare me?"

"I don't personally have anything against you," Fontaine said. "As much as I love messing with your father, I don't carry that grudge over to you and your brothers. I was genuinely fond of your mother, whatever you may think. She wouldn't want you hurt."

"Why are you working for Sylvia then?"

"Money."

"So, you don't personally want to hurt us but you're willing to do it for money?"

"Yes."

"Tell me about Morgan Reid," I said.

"What about him?"

"Why has he survived twice when he was supposed to be murdered?"

"How would I know?"

"Because Sylvia has paid you three times, and twice it was before attempts were made on Reid's life," I said. "You were either paid to take him out or …

." An idea formed. "Or you were hired to stop his death. That's it, isn't it? That's why you have the wraiths."

"You need to be very careful where Reid is concerned," Fontaine said. "Don't go near him. He's not some innocent little twerp you can play games with."

"We went out on a date about a week ago and I was totally playing games with him that night," I said. "I managed to survive."

Fontaine furrowed his brow. "You went out on a date with him?"

"Kind of."

"How did your cop feel about that?"

"Because it wasn't a real date he was fine with it." That was kind of true. Okay, it was a total lie. Fontaine didn't need to know that, though.

"I'm going to give you a freebie here," Fontaine said. "I'm going to let you walk away, mostly because I can't risk trying to grab you when there are hundreds of people within screaming distance.

"You need to stay away from Morgan Reid," he continued. "You need to stay away from Sylvia Dobbs. Put another set of reapers on Reid. I'm not joking. There's a bigger plan here and people want you for things you're not going to want to be a part of."

"How do you know that?"

"Because it's not in your nature to do evil," Fontaine said. "Just … stay out of trouble."

"I'll take it under consideration."

"You do that," Fontaine said. He turned to walk away, stopping long enough to give me one more look. "Watch your back. I will kill you if I have to. Never underestimate my reticence for fondness. I was fond of your mother. You're a pain in the ass."

"What are you guys up to?" What? It's worth a shot.

"Have a nice day, Aisling Grimlock."

WHEN I RETURNED TO THE SPA I FOUND JERRY PACING THE LOBBY. "Where were you?"

"I needed some air," I said. "I lost track of time." I knew I'd tell him the truth eventually, but I also knew now wasn't the time. "I thought it would take them longer to buff you up."

Jerry studied me, unsure. "Are you lying to me?"

"Yes. I can't tell you the truth until we're alone, though. It can wait until we're done here."

"Fine," Jerry said, throwing up his hands. "It's time for our massages. Are you ready to get rubbed?"

"I'm always ready to get rubbed."

"Let's go," he said, beckoning to the back. "When I'm done with you today you're going to feel like a new person."

"Cool. Do you think I can feel like Jennifer Lawrence?"

"Why do you want to feel like her?"

"She's pretty."

Jerry smiled. "She's got nothing on you, Bug."

"And that's why you're my best friend," I said. "You're a walking ego boost in a really pretty package."

"And that's why you're my best friend," Jerry said, following me behind the curtain. "So, just for curiosity's sake, do you think I look more like Peeta or Gale?"

Jerry was obsessed with *The Hunger Games*. He'd watched it once a week since the Blu-ray arrived on our doorstep. He also had the sequel, but he wasn't as thrilled with the outfits in that one.

"You're Gale all the way," I said. There was no other way to answer that question. Peeta was the hero, but Gale was the heartthrob.

"Good answer."

"I'm smarter than I look," I said.

"You're a genius."

31

THIRTY-ONE

"How was your day today?" Griffin dropped a kiss on my forehead and settled next to me on the couch in the parlor at Grimlock Manor.

"I spent the afternoon at the spa with Jerry," I said evasively. I knew there was a moment of truth in my future, but I was holding off so everyone could attack me at the same time.

"What did you do there?" Griffin asked.

"Spa stuff."

"Do you want to be more specific?"

I shrugged. "Spa stuff. Don't you know what happens at a spa?"

"Do you soak your feet in boiling water?"

"I did get a pedicure," I said. "You can see my freshly painted toenails later when you're giving me a foot rub." If you're still talking to me, I silently added.

Griffin smirked. "What else did you do?"

"Do you seriously not know what goes on at a spa?"

"I seriously don't," Griffin said. "They didn't go to the spa on *The Golden Girls*," he teased.

"Well, we started with a chest waxing for Jerry," I said.

Griffin made a face. "Seriously?"

"Oh, honey, his chest is smoother than a baby's bottom. You can't find a hair on his chest."

"Does Aidan wax his chest, too? Is that a … ."

I arched an eyebrow. "Were you going to say 'gay thing?'"

"Unfortunately, yes. I caught myself, though."

"I don't think all gay men do it," I said. "Jerry waxes his chest, but Aidan shaves his. To be fair, I think all my brothers shave their chests."

"Really?"

"They say it makes their muscles stand out," I said. "Apparently women drool over it."

"Do you drool over it?"

"I prefer a little hair," I said. "If it starts growing on your back, though, it has to go."

Griffin tickled my ribs. "Duly noted. How are you feeling?"

"I told you that I'm fine."

"Well, forgive me," Griffin said. "I can't help but worry."

"Oh, good, you told him," Jerry said, sliding into the room. The marble floors had always entertained us, and socks on marble can keep rambunctious kids busy for hours over long winter afternoons.

I shot Jerry a look, and mimed closing a zipper across my lips. The gesture wasn't lost on Griffin. "Told me what?"

Crap. "I got a facial," I said. "Feel my skin. It's soft."

"I talked her into getting a purifying mask," Jerry said. "She looks like a dream now."

"Then why do I feel like I'm about to step into a nightmare?" Griffin asked. "What else did you two do today?"

"I didn't do anything," Jerry said. "She disappeared while I was getting my chest waxed. It's all her fault."

I'm going to kill him.

"I'm sorry, Bug," Jerry said. "I'm too pretty to have a black eye."

The burning sensation climbing my cheeks was intense as I tried to avoid Griffin's accusatory gaze.

"Where did you disappear to?"

"Did I tell you I got massage, too?"

Griffin waited.

"The guy was really hot, but I didn't even look at him," I said. "I kept thinking about you all day."

"He was really hot," Jerry said. "Aisling moaned like … well … let's just say I've heard it before. You're a gifted lover."

"You're not helping, Jerry," I snapped.

"Men love hearing how good they are in bed," Jerry said. "It can't hurt to flatter him."

"You already threw me under the bus!"

"We are going to sit right here until you tell me what you did," Griffin threatened. "You're not getting a thing to eat – I don't care how much you beg – until you tell me the truth."

"What's going on now?" Cillian asked, stepping into the room with a wide smile on his face. He wasn't alone; a beaming Maya was at his side. I didn't know she was even invited. This was good for me. If we had a guest, my father would be less likely to burn the house down to get to me.

"Aisling and I went to the spa today," Jerry said. "Feel her face. She had a purifying mask. It feels like silk."

"I'll take your word for it," Cillian said. "She doesn't look like she wants to be touched right now, and I think Griffin has dibs."

"I think Griffin looks like he's going to strangle her," Braden said, joining the crowd. "What did you do, Ais?"

"What makes you think I did anything?"

"Your track record," Braden said.

I crossed my arms over my chest. "I'm feeling persecuted."

"You shouldn't all jump on her," Maya said. "She's recovering from being thrown into a car. This doesn't seem fair."

"Butt out, Maya," Griffin warned. "I want to know what you two did today."

"Uh-oh. Did the spa get out of control?" Redmond asked, stepping into the parlor. Aidan was a few steps behind him. "Aidan said the credit card company called because you guys went nuts."

"Eight hundred dollars," Aidan sputtered. "What could you two have possibly done that cost eight hundred dollars?"

"Pedicures. Manicures. I got my chest waxed. Aisling got her butt buffed. We got hot rock massages and purifying masks. Oh, and Aisling got a deep condition. Her hair looks like she should be walking down runway." Now that Jerry had listed everything, it did sound a little … extravagant.

"That sounds like a great day," Maya said. "Did the massage help you? I know your back has been giving you problems."

She was trying to help me by shifting the focus of the conversation. I admired the effort, but I knew Griffin and my brothers well enough to know that it wasn't going to work. That wasn't going to stop me from delaying the inevitable. "I do feel much looser."

"Aisling … ." Griffin clasped his hands together, fighting to retain control of his temper. "What happened today?"

I cleared my throat. "Well, while I was waiting for Jerry to get his chest waxed, a woman came out of the back of the spa. While she paid her bill, I heard her name."

"I'm practically salivating," Braden deadpanned. "Was it a celebrity?"

"Her name was Sylvia Dobbs."

The room fell silent. Maya was the only one who seemed oblivious to the chill. "Who is that?"

"She's a … person of interest … in the case I'm working on," Griffin said.

"What case are you working on?"

"It's kind of a case we're all working on," Cillian hedged.

Maya was confused. "But … ."

Griffin held up his hand. "Did you talk to her?"

"No," I said. "I knew that would be a mistake."

"Well, that's good news," Redmond said. "You could've done something really stupid."

"Wait for it," Griffin grumbled.

"I didn't speak to her," I said. "I did follow her out onto the street. I wanted to see where she was going."

"Yeah, Dad is going to kill you," Braden said.

"I'm going to help," Aidan said. "What were you thinking?"

"I was thinking that it was the best chance we had to get some answers," I said.

"Why didn't you call me?" Aidan asked.

"Or me?" Redmond asked.

"Why didn't you call me?" Griffin was beside himself.

"Because I knew all of you would have forced me onto the sidelines," I said. "Plus, by the time any of you got there, she would've been gone."

"So, you followed her?" Cillian asked.

"I did."

"Where did she go?" Braden asked.

"She went to a parking lot on one of the side streets off Main," I said.

"And she left without seeing you?" Aidan was hopeful.

"She never saw me," I said.

"See, I don't like the way you're answering questions," Redmond said. "You used to do this when you were a kid. You would lead with minor stuff that didn't make you look too bad and then ease into the really terrible stuff."

"Like the time she admitted to knocking the mirror off Dad's car,"

Braden supplied. "She came into the house holding the mirror, and then it took her an hour to admit she'd wrecked the rest of the car, too."

"That was an accident," I said.

"And what you did today was on purpose," Aidan said. "So, what happened next?"

I pressed the heel of my hand to my forehead, trying to stall for time.

"I just know this is going to be bad," Cillian said. "I'm almost afraid to hear it."

"Before she left, she had a visitor in the parking lot," I said carefully. "They had a conversation."

"Oh, just rip the bandage off, Bug," Jerry said. "You're making things worse now."

I made an exasperated sound in the back of my throat. "It was Fontaine, and they had a long discussion about the 'Grimlock girl' and how they needed to get me because I was the key to their plans."

"Sonovabitch!" Dad stormed into the room. Had he been eavesdropping? Now I know where I get it. "What exactly did they say?"

I recounted their conversation, and when it came time to address my interaction with Fontaine, I balked momentarily and then plunged in. The incredulous faces – even Maya's – were almost murderous by the time I was done.

"I'm going to kill you," Dad said, taking a step forward. "I … how can you be my child? There's just no way. No child of mine would be that stupid. I think someone had to switch you in the hospital. There can be no other explanation."

"Don't you dare yell at me!"

"You make me yell at you," Dad countered. "You almost died four days ago."

"I didn't almost die."

"Yes, you did." Dad was just starting. I'd been in this situation numerous times. "You and your brother had your asses handed to you by Fontaine, and he was partnering with a wraith. You were thrown into a car. You could barely walk.

"Then, the very day you start to feel better, you chase crazy people on the street and pick a confrontation with the guy who threw you into a car," he raged on. "You taunted him. You questioned him. You stood next to him five minutes after he admitted he wanted to kidnap you.

"I want a DNA test!"

"We all look exactly like you," Cillian said. "You need to … calm down. She's obviously okay."

I shot him a grateful look.

"You're still stupid," Cillian said.

"She's beyond stupid," Dad said. "She aspires to be stupid."

"Are you done? Can we talk about what we're going to do about this?" I was starting to get aggravated.

"You're not doing anything," Dad said. "You're grounded."

"You can't ground me. I'm an adult."

Dad ignored me. "She's going to have to stay here for the duration," he said. "They know she lives in Royal Oak, and that townhouse is too exposed. We can protect her here."

"I think that's the best option," Redmond said. "I'll go back to Madame Maxine to see if she has any updates."

"That's a good idea."

"I think we should move Jerry in here, too," Aidan said. "If they can't get to Aisling, they might try to grab him as leverage."

"I agree," Dad said. "Plus, with Jerry here, she'll be less likely to go stir crazy."

"You realize I'm in the room with you, right?" They were talking about me as though they were in charge.

"You need to make sure the staff understands the importance of keeping the doors and gates locked," Griffin said. "I think you should cut off all guests until we can form a plan of action."

"Does that include you?" Braden asked.

Griffin shifted. "If you think that's best."

"No way!" I jumped to my feet.

"Shut up, Aisling," Dad said. "You're the reason we have to go to these measures. You need to sit your behind back down and shut up."

That wasn't going to happen. "I am an adult!"

"Start acting like one."

I narrowed my eyes, my gaze bouncing between the serious faces in the room. I knew I was about to do something immature, but since they were already treating me as a small child, it seemed to be the right move.

"Fine." I pushed past Redmond and Braden and flounced toward the door.

"Where are you going?" Griffin asked, weary.

"I'm going to my room to think about what a rotten child I am. Then I'm going to mull over how stupid I am. Then I'm going to lock the door and hide in the closet and think about how I've ruined all your lives."

"So, you're going upstairs to pout?" Aidan asked.

"Yes." I had no intention of going to my room. They needed to think that's where I would be hiding out. I was making my escape, and there was no better time than when they were all congregated in the same room talking about me.

I'd show them.

32

THIRTY-TWO

Car theft is an interesting thing. Most people never get a chance to experience the heady highs of doing something you know is wrong, and the unfortunate lows of getting caught. When I stole my father's Bentley from the garage I knew I was taking a chance.

I didn't care. I needed out of that house and away from the Testosterone Mafia. Because Jerry had driven us to Grimlock Manor, I had to steal someone's car to make my escape. I knew where my father kept his keys, so it was the easiest option.

After wheeling around the upscale neighborhoods of Grosse Pointe for a few minutes, I decided to go to the one place I knew would make me feel better.

When I entered Woody's Bar, the owner greeted me with a warm smile and a hearty hug. "Aisling Grimlock, as I live and breathe. I haven't seen you in … a long time."

"I don't live in the neighborhood anymore, Woody," I said. "I drink closer to home."

"You're living in Royal Oak now, right?"

"Right."

"And how is Jerry? I miss that boy. For a while there, when you guys were coming in with fake licenses every Friday I didn't even have to hire a band for entertainment. He kept people coming back just because he was so darned entertaining."

Woody Thompson had owned the neighborhood bar for as long as I could remember. People had offered him millions for his piece of land, thinking the congenial bachelor would jump at the money and abandon his little dive without a backward glance. Whether from doubt, or sheer stubbornness, Woody refused to sell. The bar was the lone bastion of alcohol and debauchery in the area, and I loved it.

"Jerry is good," I said. "He's over at my Dad's place right now."

"How come you're not over there?"

"I'm mad at them."

Woody smirked. "Well, their loss is my gain." He sidled behind the bar. "What will it be? You can even drink legally this time."

"I don't know. Just give me a Jack and diet with a lime. Thanks."

"Oh, you're going for the hard stuff," Woody said. "You must have had a rough day. Do you want to tell your old friend Woody about it?"

There's nothing better than a sympathetic ear, even when you have to tell little white lies to get the sympathy. "I hate my family."

"Which one of them pissed you off?"

"All of them."

"Oh, little one, you simply have to realize you're always going to be the baby in your family," Woody said. I have no idea how he knew what I was stewing about. "You're not only the baby, you're the only girl. They can't help themselves."

Deep down, I knew that was true. Still … . "Do you think if I was the oldest, or even in the middle, they would treat me differently?"

"I don't know," Woody said. "I think they would still be overprotective where you're concerned. Men can't help it. They think of women as the fairer sex. I know you can take care of yourself, but it's still in their nature to want to protect you. You should feel lucky you're so loved."

"Yeah, you should feel lucky."

I cringed when I heard the voice, and shifted so I could meet Angelina's challenging gaze as she hauled herself onto the open stool next to me. "What are you doing here? You know they have a 'no-skank' policy, right?"

"Then how come they let you in?"

"Oh, good one."

Woody pressed his lips together. "Angelina. What can I get you?"

"A glass of red wine."

"Make sure it comes from a box," I said. "And then put the box over her head so I don't have to look at her face."

Woody rolled his eyes. "I see you two are still going at each other like rabid raccoons in a cage."

"That's because she's evil," I said.

"No, it's because you're mean and … stinky."

I stuck my tongue out. "Why are you even here? I thought you lived up in Macomb Township. You shouldn't be down here."

"For your information, I was over at my mother's house," Angelina said. "She's been having a rough time."

Angelina got her sweet disposition from her mother. They were both pains. "Oh, did the neighborhood finally rally and try to burn her at the stake?"

"Hey! Her dog is dying. She's very upset." Angelina's face was grim. "She's had that dog for like twenty years. It needs to be put down, but she can't bring herself to do it. I have to take it in tomorrow."

That was sad … for the dog. "I'm sorry," I said. "Is that the same little rat she used to dress up in sweaters?"

"Yes. Pixie."

"I hated that dog," I said. "Whenever I was walking on the sidewalk it tried to attack me through the fence."

"Pixie is horrible," Angelina agreed. "You have no idea how many times that dog has bitten me."

I was starting to like Pixie. "Well … ."

"Just don't," Angelina said, nodding in thanks to Woody as he placed the glass of wine in front of her. "I'm not in the mood for your nonsense."

"You sat down next to me."

"I figured your life is so sad you can't help but make me feel better," Angelina shot back.

"Girls," Woody warned. "If you're going to fight, you need to hold off long enough for me to get the mud pit going."

I scowled. "That's not funny."

"It's a little funny," Woody prodded.

"My brothers aren't going to think it's funny," I said.

"Speaking of your brothers, how is Cillian feeling?" Angelina asked.

I narrowed my eyes. I hate to kick people when they're down, but this is Angelina. She deserves it. "He's fine," I said. "He's got his new girlfriend up at the house having dinner right now."

Angelina stilled. "Maya?"

"Yup."

"Are you telling me they're really dating?"

"I'm telling you they're really on their way to dating," I said. "He's all aflutter when she's around. She's a definite step up from some of his other choices."

"But … they just met," Angelina complained.

"It was lust at first sight," I said.

"She's your boyfriend's sister."

"I noticed."

"Doesn't that bother him?"

I thought it over. "I think it would bother him if it was Braden or Redmond." I had no idea why I was telling her the truth. "Cillian is different. He's the sensitive one."

"That's why he's the only member of your family I can stand," Angelina said. "He's the love of my life."

Good grief. "Let's not romanticize things, okay? You guys dated for six months, and you only went after him because it bugged me. I'm not stupid."

"That might have been how it started," Angelina conceded. "I really did fall in love with him, though."

"And then you cheated on him."

"That was the biggest mistake of my life. I'm trying to make amends."

"You can't," I said. "It's not possible."

"It's possible," Angelina said. "You just need to tell him to give me a chance. He'll listen to you. You're the reason he keeps shutting me out, after all."

"First of all, I'd rather have sex with an inbred hill freak than tell Cillian to take you back," I said. "It doesn't matter, though. Cillian and you would've never worked out. It was only a matter of time before you imploded. You're not good enough for him."

"I am, too!"

"No, you're not," I countered. "You aren't the type of woman who can enjoy the lifestyle he wants to live. He doesn't want to spend the weekends shopping and having brunch. He doesn't want to live in a cookie-cutter subdivision and go to dinner parties. He likes to lounge around and watch sports. He wants to play golf. He wants to just … chill … with the rest of our family. You're not built for that."

"He could change," Angelina said. "He could change for me."

"You're missing the point," I said. "He shouldn't have to change. He's better off away from you. Quite frankly, you're better off away from him. You've convinced yourself that you two had some great love story, but it was just a blip on his radar screen. You need someone as shallow as you are. You're not going to be happy with Cillian, no matter what you tell yourself."

"But … I love him." Her ferret face was pitiful.

"I don't think so," I said. "I think you're in love with the idea of him. I also think you cling to him because you still want to beat me."

"I've already beaten you," Angelina said. "I'm more successful than you. I have a better house than you. I'm … prettier than you."

"You are not prettier than me."

"Yes, I am."

"You wish."

"I know."

"Woody, who is prettier?"

Woody glanced up from the glass he was polishing. He'd acted disinterested in our conversation, but I knew he'd been listening. "Oh, I'm not answering that. You're both gorgeous."

"She looks like road kill after it's been driven over a hundred times," I said.

"She looks like a skunk," Angelina shot back. "Who told you those highlights looked good?"

"Everyone who sees them."

"They're lying."

"You're a whore," I said, my temper flaring. Even a middling conversation with Angelina sends me over the edge. "You're a ferret-faced whore."

"You take that back!"

"No."

"Take it back or I'm going to rip your skunky hair out of your head," Angelina threatened.

"You can try." Angelina reached for my hair, but I spun away from her. "You have the agility of a dead ninja."

"Hey, if you two are going to fight, take it out to the parking lot," Woody said. "I'm too old for this nonsense."

I met Angelina's challenging gaze. "We'll be right back. It won't take me long to beat her down and make her cry."

"Oh, you're going to be the one crying," Angelina said, hopping off her stool.

Immaturity is one of the few skills I can exploit when I'm on the lam and pouting because my family is treating me like a child. There was no way I was going to let this opportunity pass. I needed to get my aggression out, and Angelina was an easy target. "Don't you dare throw my drink away," I said. "I'm not done with it."

Woody waved me off. "Don't kill each other."

Angelina moved outside of the bar ahead of me, her shoulders squared. I knew why I wanted to fight. I had no idea why she wanted to sink to my level. Yes, I know I've completely lost my mind. I'm just so … frustrated.

"We need to set some ground rules," Angelina said, swiveling to face me.

"Ground rules? You can't make ground rules for a street fight."

"No hitting in the face," Angelina said, ignoring me. "I have an open house tomorrow."

"Fine. No scratching with those acrylic talons of yours."

"Fine. No kicking. I'm wearing heels, and it gives you an unnatural advantage because you're wearing Converse. You should try buying adult shoes, by the way. Those make you look short and squat." Angelina's hands were clenched.

"So, what are you saying? We can hit each other in the chest?"

"Yes."

Well, it was better than nothing. "Fine. I don't want to hear you whine, though, when I beat your ass."

"That goes double for you."

"Great."

"Awesome."

I readied myself. "Wait. Where do we stand on hair pulling?"

"No hair pulling," Angelina said. "This weave cost me a fortune."

I knew she had fake hair. "Fine. Let's go."

"I'm ready."

"Well … hit me."

Angelina narrowed her eyes. "Why do you want me to hit you first?"

"Because, if I hit you first I'm going to look bad when I tell this story later," I said.

"You look bad regardless."

"You have all the appeal of a dirty toilet," I replied.

"You … ." Angelina flew to the side, crashing against the Dumpster as a flurry of black filled the spot she'd just been standing in.

"Oh, you've got to be kidding me," I howled as the wraith focused on me. "You couldn't wait five minutes? I've been waiting to beat her ass for fifteen years. You have the worst timing ever."

"Aisling Grimlock."

"You're like a broken record," I grumbled. "I know you can't touch me, so you'd better just … step off."

"Come," the wraith ordered. "Follow."

"No."

"What is that thing?" Angelina was sitting on the ground, her hand moving through her long hair as she regarded the wraith. "I thought you killed it?"

"There's more than one, moron."

"You're a freak. I always knew it. You just keep proving it."

"You're a freak."

"Come," the wraith repeated.

I ignored it and moved over to Angelina's side, watching the shadow out of the corner of my eye as I bent down. "Did you hit your head?"

"Yes."

"Did you lose consciousness?"

"No."

"You'll be fine." I felt along the ground behind Angelina.

"What are you doing? Are you trying to feel me up?"

"Yes. I want to grab your ass. That's what I'm doing." There's a reason I hate her. "I'm looking for … ." My fingers wrapped around a metal bar. I stood back up and studied the pipe. I had no idea what it was for, but it was the best option I had.

"Oh," Angelina said.

"You're such an idiot," I grumbled. I turned back to face the wraith, brandishing the pipe for emphasis. "I've had a really rough day. I'm not above beating you to death with this, though. I was ready for a fight, and you're as good an opponent as any.

"I can't beat up Angelina now," I continued. "You've ruined that. If I hit her now, I'll be the bully because she's already injured."

"Suck it," Angelina snapped.

"Now, you have a choice," I told the wraith. "You can attack me and let me kill you, or you can live to creep around dirty parking lots another day. It's up to you."

"No, it's not."

I recognized Aidan's voice, but I had no idea where it came from. The wraith started to turn, but it was too late. The blade of a knife appeared in the middle of its chest, and the wraith exploded into a pile of ash, leaving Aidan standing there covered with wraith ash and drowning in a pit of fury.

As the dust started to settle, I saw another set of murderous eyes regarding me from the spot next to Aidan. Griffin didn't look happy.

"You're in so much trouble they're going to have to think of a new word for trouble," Aidan said.

And I was right back where I started.

33

THIRTY-THREE

"I can't believe you brought me back here," I muttered.

Aidan pushed me through the garage door and into the back foyer of Grimlock Manor. He'd driven Dad's Bentley back, and I'd opted to ride with him because I feared Griffin would spontaneously combust if I climbed into his car. He hadn't spoken one word to me yet, and I was terrified the first word to escape his mouth was going to be "goodbye."

"Aisling, I know you think we're being unfair to you, but you are just … out of control," Aidan said.

"I know."

Aidan's face softened. "What possessed you to leave? You knew they were looking for you. You're almost too stupid to live. If this were a horror movie, you'd be the first one to die."

"I just … I'm sick of being treated like a child. You have no idea what it's like."

"You're sick of being treated like a child, so you decided to steal Dad's car and walk straight into danger to prove you're an adult?"

"It seemed like a good idea at the time. How did you even know I was there?"

"Woody called."

"Of course."

"What was Angelina doing there?" Aidan asked. He ushered me ahead of him and into the dining room. Everyone was seated around the rectangular table, their faces masks of bubbling anger as they awaited my arrival. Only Maya had the grace – or pity – to shoot a smile in my direction.

"Angelina was there?" Redmond asked.

"Yes. She and Aisling were going to fight in the parking lot for Queen of the Pointe honors," Aidan said. He nudged me forward. "Sit down."

The spot next to Griffin was open, but my body rebelled against the notion of heading in his direction.

"He can't kill you," Aidan said. "There are too many witnesses."

I blew out a sigh and sat down, placing the cloth napkin on my lap and focusing on my empty plate. "What's for dinner?"

"An ass chewing," Redmond said.

"I don't need to be talked down to again," I said. "I know I'm stupid. You've all drilled it into my head."

"You are stupid," Dad said. "We probably shouldn't call you stupid, though."

I lifted my eyes. "Excuse me?"

"You're not stupid," Dad said. "You're impulsive and annoying."

"Use your words," Maya prodded.

Oh, I saw what was going on here. In my absence, Maya had given all the men in my life a talking to about the proper way to speak to a woman.

Dad bit the inside of his cheek. "It has been brought to my attention that we might – and I stress might – have treated you poorly."

"We apologize," Braden said.

"I don't," Griffin said, reaching for a bread stick and ripping it in two.

"Griffin," Maya warned.

"I'm not apologizing," Griffin said. "I'm angry. I'm so angry I could just . . . ." He squeezed the breadstick until it was a mangled mess.

"I agree with Griffin," Dad said. "I know I shouldn't do this, but I don't know what else to do."

"Do what?" I challenged.

"You're banned from this family. I have no other options."

My brothers burst into simultaneous snickers.

"Well, great," I said. "I'm happy to be out of the family. Maybe now I can go through a day without being referred to as stupid."

"I'm sorry I called you stupid," Dad said. "You're stupid, though."

"Oh, I know."

"Stop rolling your eyes like that, young lady," Dad said, pointing. "I hate it when you do that."

"I hate it when you point at me and tell me what to do," I shot back.

"I hate it when everyone fights," Jerry said. "Can't we all just get along?"

"Shut up, Jerry," Dad said. "You're as much to blame in this whole mess as she is."

"Excuse me?" Jerry was shrill. "How is this my fault? I didn't steal your car."

"You knew she was antsy and you left her alone at the spa," Dad said. "You know she can't keep her nose out of trouble. You should have watched her more closely."

"Oh, now Jerry is my babysitter?"

"I know, it boggles the mind," Dad said. "I couldn't leave the two of you alone in a room together until you were teenagers because I couldn't decide which of you was the greater menace. You've edged him out, Aisling. Congratulations."

I scowled.

"Cormack, I think you're confused by your emotions," Maya said.

"I'm not confused."

"Are you really angry with Aisling?" Maya pressed.

"I'm furious."

"Could it be that you're not angry and that you're really fearful because an enemy has targeted her?"

"Nope. I'm angry."

"I think you're all afraid," Maya said, not backing down. "You're obviously all attached to each other, and I think losing any member of this family would be devastating for everyone. I also think you channel your fear in unhealthy ways.

"Aisling is the one in danger, and yet Cillian almost died last week," she continued. "You're all in danger. You're focusing on Aisling as a way to deal with the danger. While that's understandable, I'm not sure it's fair to her."

"I don't care about what's fair," Dad said. "I care about keeping her safe."

"We all do," Redmond said.

"There's an interesting family dynamic here," Maya said. "You all dote on Aisling, and she's spoiled rotten as a result. She's used to getting her own way, and you don't have a problem making sure she gets her own way.

"However, when things shift, you all smother her in an attempt to protect her," she said. "Now, instead of getting her own way, you all exert your wants and needs on her and demand she fall into line. You're sending mixed messages."

"I knew that year of psychology you took in college was going to come back to bite me," Griffin said.

"Your issues with Aisling are different," Maya said, ignoring the jab. "You're a cop, and you're used to people doing what you say. You're trying really hard to treat her like an individual and respect her job and decisions, but you're out of your depth because you're still getting used to this family's reality."

"Thank you, Dr. Phil," Griffin said, his eyes dark.

"Your other problem is that you fear if you unload on her, and I mean really unload, you're going to scare her away," Maya said.

"That is just … ." Griffin shook her head.

"If you'd take a moment to look at Aisling, you'd see that she's sitting there terrified that you're going to break up with her because she stole her father's car and ran headlong into danger," Maya said.

"I am not," I mumbled.

"Now, everyone here needs to accept the fact that Aisling is an adult," Maya said. "However impulsive she is, you guys helped create the problem. Now you have to deal with it."

"We are dealing with it," Dad said. "I'm locking her in her room and hiding the key."

"You might want to try a softer approach," Maya said.

"I'll give her pillows," Dad said.

Maya couldn't hide her smile. "I was thinking more along the lines of a compromise."

"Oh, you're cute," Cillian said, patting her hand. "Dad doesn't compromise."

"I compromise."

"When have you ever compromised?" Braden asked.

"Is Aisling thirty yet?"

"No."

"Well, her boyfriend is sitting at the table, and I vowed she wasn't going to date until she was thirty," Dad said.

"Oh, well, I stand corrected."

"How about a mutually beneficial compromise," Maya said, refusing to let the lead in the conversation get away from her.

"Like what?" Dad asked.

"Like Aisling agrees to stay here with you until this is settled," Maya said.

I opened my mouth to argue, but Maya silenced me with a look.

"And you all agree to let her go back to work," Maya added.

"No," Dad said. "She's not safe."

"If she goes out with one of her brothers she'll be protected," Maya said. "You can't lock her up like a prisoner."

Dad considered the offer. "Only if she agrees that she can go out only on daylight jobs and at places where there are a lot of people."

Maya glanced at me. "Aisling?"

"Only if Griffin can stay here, too," I said.

"Fine," Dad said.

"In my room," I added.

"Don't push me," Dad said.

I crossed my arms over my chest.

"We'll talk about it after dinner," Dad said. "I think you're getting ahead of yourself. Griffin doesn't look as though he wants to be anywhere near you right now. I can't lock him in the house just to make you happy."

A swift look at Griffin told me Dad was right. I had no doubt he'd be sleeping under a different roof tonight.

"YOU CAN'T STAY IN HERE WITH ME."

"I know," Jerry said, shifting on my bed to get more comfortable. "I just want to make sure you're okay."

"I'm great."

"You don't look great."

"Well, I feel great."

"You don't look it."

"Jerry, I'm going to beat you if you don't leave me alone," I threatened.

Jerry sighed dramatically. "It's going to be all right, Bug." He kissed my cheek. "Your skin really is soft. If I wasn't gay, I'd be all over you."

"Well, that makes everything better."

"Griffin didn't leave," Jerry pointed out.

"He didn't speak to me."

"No, but he didn't leave."

"I think that's just because Maya is staying the night again," I said. "He doesn't want her to be here alone."

"Oh, I can see there's no talking to you tonight," Jerry said. "We'll talk in the morning." He climbed off the bed.

"You're sleeping in Aidan's room, right? I don't want to find you crawling back in here in the middle of the night." I really just wanted to be left alone. Pouting is a lot more fun when you don't have an audience.

"I am," Jerry said. "I'll wake you for breakfast."

"I can't wait." I focused on the television when he left, the mindless sitcom playing out on the screen annoying me the longer I stared at it. I glanced up when I sensed a presence in the open door. Griffin was dressed in flannel sleep pants and a T-shirt, and his face was unreadable as he stared down at me. "I don't feel like fighting."

Griffin watched me for another moment, and then he walked into the room and shut the door behind him. That couldn't be good. He was going to start screaming, and there was no one here to protect me if he decided it was easier to strangle me than deal with me.

Instead of speaking, he stopped in front of the television and shut it off and then moved to the side of the bed. "Scoot over."

"What?"

"You're in the middle of the bed," he said. "I need room. Scoot over."

I did as I was told, watching curiously as he slipped under the covers and settled next to me.

"What … are you staying in here with me?"

"Yes."

"Aren't you angry with me?"

"Yes."

"Are you going to yell at me?"

"Would it do any good?"

"I have no idea," I said.

"I think you've been yelled at enough for one day," Griffin said. "I am still really angry with you, though."

"I know."

"Turn off the light."

I hit the switch on my side of the bed, plunging the room into darkness. I could feel his presence next to me, even though he wasn't moving. His breathing was even, and for a second, I wondered if he'd already dropped off.

"Turn your mind off, Aisling," he said. "You need your rest."

I pressed my eyes shut. After a few more minutes, I heard him sigh and then felt his body shift closer to mine. He wrapped his arm around my waist and pulled me so I was flush against him. "You make me really tired."

"I've heard."

He rubbed his cheek against my face. "We're probably going to have a big fight tomorrow. I'm going to try really hard not to say something I'll regret. You need to try to think before you act, though. You're driving me crazy."

"I … ."

"Don't speak," Griffin admonished. "You'll ruin the moment."

"What moment?"

"Go to sleep, Aisling," he said.

"Fine. Good night."

"Good night." He rested his head against mine. "Your skin really is soft."

"You should feel my butt."

"Maybe tomorrow," he said. "I'm too tired now."

That's not what a girl wants to hear. I squealed when I felt his hand.

"That's nice, too," he said. "Go to sleep."

"Yes, sir."

"See, you're ruining the moment."

34

THIRTY-FOUR

"You're going to be careful today, right?"

Griffin's face was serious, and even though he'd reneged on his promise to pick a really big fight after a much-needed night of sleep I knew better than to push him too far.

"It's only one job," I said, tentatively reaching out to touch his arm. He'd been affectionate this morning, but still slightly distant. I wasn't sure what was going through his head, but my imagination was running wild.

Griffin wrapped his hand around my fingers, his eyes contemplative. "Who are you going with?"

"Aidan."

"Where?"

"Detective, is this an interrogation?"

"Where?" Griffin pressed.

"It's one of the big Catholic churches down in the city," I said.

"Someone is dying in the church?"

"Someone is dying in the rectory behind the church," I said.

"A priest?" Griffin looked relieved. "That should be easy, right? A priest should be looking forward to the hereafter."

"Actually, it's a nun," I said. "It's the same principle, though."

Griffin sighed heavily. "Good. That's good."

"The worst that will happen is that she'll veto my outfit," I said. "Dad made sure that there was no possible way we could be in danger."

Griffin let go of my hand and wrapped both of his around the back of my head so he could tilt my chin up. "You're going to be careful, though. You're going to go in and get your soul, keep your mouth shut and then have a big lunch with your brother. That's going to be your day, right?"

"Yes."

"Okay," Griffin said, pressing a quick kiss to my forehead. "I have to go to work this afternoon. It should be for only a few hours, but I'll be back here in plenty of time to protect you from your family at dinner."

"You're staying here again?"

"Where else would I stay?"

"Some place where my Dad isn't going to be giving you the evil eye and where I'm not always fighting with my brothers sounds like just the kind of break you need," I pointed out.

"Maybe I don't want a break," Griffin said.

"Does mental illness run in your family?"

Griffin grinned. "It's going to be fine. While part of me finds your family crazy, the other part … likes the way you interact. You guys can say anything to each other – I mean really mean things – and yet it doesn't even phase you. It's kind of fun. Not everyone's family is like that. Some families hold grudges forever."

I made a mental note to question him about his family when all of this was settled. This was the second time he'd made an offhand remark about his family. "Okay."

"Now, give me a proper kiss."

He was too cute to ignore.

"And people say I never compromise," Dad said, strolling past us. We stood in the front foyer of Grimlock Manor, where I thought we were alone. Even though the house was huge, there were times it still felt small.

I separated from Griffin. "What's your problem now?"

"I swore you wouldn't date until you were thirty and now you're making out with your overnight guest right in front of me," Dad said. "Yes, I'm certain you thought I didn't know you two slept in the same room last night, didn't you?"

"I didn't care if you knew," I said. "Griffin is the one who fears your wrath."

"Obviously he doesn't fear my wrath sufficiently," Dad grumbled.

"Don't worry, there was no funny business," I said.

"I know. He was too angry."

"You're loving this, aren't you?"

"I'm loving parts of it," Dad said. "Now, you and Aidan have exactly one job. One. If you can't collect a nun, then we have bigger problems than your attitude and … ."

"Stupidity?"

"I promised not to use that word again," Dad said.

I smiled.

"But yes," he said.

"Now, kiss your … friend … goodbye and get to work. I'm not paying you to play kissy-face in the foyer."

Griffin covered my open mouth with a quick kiss – one that Dad couldn't possibly mistake for something sultry – and then patted my head. "Be good."

"I told you. It's a nun. What could possibly go wrong?"

"I AM NOT LETTING YOU SUCK ME UP IN THAT." SISTER MARY Angelica was like a tiny drill sergeant. She didn't take guff from the kids in her classrooms, and she wasn't about to put up with it from two reapers who invaded her spare bedroom to give her bad news.

"You're not going to live here," Aidan said. "We're going to transport you to your final resting place. And, good news for you, you're going to Heaven."

He said it like Oprah Winfrey did when she was giving away cars. *You're going to Heaven, and you're going to Heaven and you're going to Heaven.*

"Well, I'm happy I'm going to Heaven, but I'm not ready to go yet," Sister Mary Angelica said. "I'm still in the prime of my life."

"You're ninety-two," I pointed out.

"And I have plenty of life left to live."

"Well, God obviously didn't think so," I said. "He decided to call you home … early."

"Well, I'm not ready to go. Tell him I'll take a rain check and he can collect me in twenty years."

Twenty years? I glanced at Aidan. "I thought we weren't going to talk to her? I thought we were going to suck and run? Isn't that what we promised Dad?"

"I thought she would be excited to go," Aidan said, chagrined. "If anyone should be excited, it's this woman. It's like hitting the lottery for her."

"How is dying like hitting the lottery?" Sister Mary Angelica asked, hands on hips. "Am I going to get a mansion and a flat-screen television?"

That was a very good question. "I thought you took a vow of poverty?"

"That doesn't mean I don't like *Dancing With the Stars*," Sister Mary Angelica shot back.

I was starting to like this nun, her taste in television shows notwithstanding. "I'm sure you can watch it from Heaven." I had no idea whether that was true. I just wanted this job to be over with.

"What about cable? I can't miss *The Walking Dead*."

Holy crap! "Isn't *The Walking Dead* blasphemous where you're concerned?" I was genuinely curious.

"Why?"

"Because they die and they come back from the dead – and not in the same way Jesus did. They try to eat people. Doesn't that cast … I don't know … doubt on the Catholic faith?" Religion often confuses me. There are just so many of them to keep up with when you're a reaper.

"It's a television show," Sister Mary Angelica said. "It's not real life. You understand the difference, right?"

I was really starting to like her. "I get that. I didn't know you were allowed to get that."

"Oh, grow up."

Aidan smirked. "Sister, I know this has come as a shock to you. Obviously. It's just … we're on a bit of a timetable."

"Oh, so now I have to schedule my death around your life? What are you late for? Do you have a date with some hot trollop tonight? Some pretty little thing with narrow hips and a busy mouth?"

Aidan's mouth dropped open.

"His significant other does have narrow hips and a busy mouth, but he's not a girl," I said. What? I was trying to help.

"Oh, you're a homosexual. Well, good for you."

Aidan was flabbergasted. "Isn't that against your faith?"

"Why? Are you a bad man otherwise? Do you kick puppies and smack children?"

"No."

"Then I don't care who you love," Sister Mary Angelica said. "You need to grow up, too. Your sister obviously isn't the only one with insecurity issues."

"How did you know she was my sister?" Aidan asked.

The look on Sister Mary Angelica's face was almost comical. "You look like twins."

"We are twins."

"Well, you look it."

Aidan looked to me for help.

"What? We do look exactly alike. You should see our three other brothers. We look like a genetic experiment gone awry," I said.

"Okay, we need to get back on point here," Aidan said. "Sister Mary Angelica, I'm very sorry you're not ready to travel to your eternal resting place, but we can't stay here."

"Why not?"

"It's a long story."

"I have time."

"No, you don't," Aidan said. "You have to move on, and we have to get out of here. Some very bad people are trying to hurt my sister and she's not safe here. She's technically not supposed to be working, but she pitched a fit and my father gave in. He always gives in where she's concerned."

"That's because fathers dote on daughters. Why didn't you just say that from the beginning?" Sister Mary Angelica asked. "Is the Devil after her? She's got a face built for sin."

I think I'd just been insulted. "No. They're called wraiths."

"Minions of the Devil?"

I shrugged. That was as good of an explanation as any. "Kind of."

"And why do they want you?"

"We have no idea," I said. "We just know they want me. It's been a busy two weeks."

"Well, then I guess I should get going," Sister Mary Angelica said, resigned. "I'd hate for my death to cause yours."

"That would be a bummer," I said.

Aidan raised his scepter. "I have a feeling you're going to be really happy where you're going."

"Wait. I have two questions."

Aidan sighed. "Go ahead."

I left Aidan to answer Sister Mary Angelica's questions and wandered over to the lone window in the room. Since we'd entered the building through the front, it hadn't dawned on me what was in the rear. "Is that Eternal Sunshine Cemetery?"

"Yes."

"Is that where you're going to be interred?" I asked, gesturing to the prone body on the bed.

"Yes."

"I guess I didn't realize the church backed up to the cemetery," I said. "That's kind of … creepy."

"How do you figure that?" Sister Mary Angelica was nonplussed. "They're dead. They're very quiet neighbors."

"But … never mind. Have you ever seen any odd activity in the cemetery?"

"Define odd."

"Yeah, what are you getting at?" Aidan asked.

"I don't know," I said. "I just … I still think something is going on at the cemetery."

"Have you been back there since … ?"

"Since when?" Sister Mary Angelica prodded.

"Since she almost died there five weeks ago."

"Oh. You're having a run of bad luck, girl."

"I am," I said.

"It's about to get worse."

Three heads swiveled to the partially opened door in unison. One of them was dead, but equally interested.

"Fontaine," Aidan said, stepping forward. "This is our soul."

"Then you should have collected it," Fontaine said.

"That's what we're doing."

"Really? Because I've heard a lot of talk about *Dancing With the Stars* and *The Walking Dead*," Fontaine said.

"Were you eavesdropping?" That was so juvenile.

"I was mildly curious as to how you guys went about your daily business," Fontaine said. "I thought you might have some interesting moves. It turns out, you're both idiots."

"Hey!"

"Calm down, boogers. I'm not here for your soul."

"Why are you here?" I asked.

"I have a name on my list," Fontaine said. "It just happens to be here."

Aidan stepped between us instinctively. "You're not laying a hand on my sister."

"Oh, I don't want your sister, Aidan," Fontaine said, his grin evil. "I'm here for you."

"What?"

Fontaine grabbed Aidan roughly, whipping his body around so Aidan's back was pressed against Fontaine's expansive chest. He wrapped his beefy forearm around Aidan's throat and applied pressure. My brother is strong and fit, but he's no match for a mountain like Fontaine.

"Let him go," I raged.

"You had your chance, Aisling," Fontaine said. "We've moved on to Aidan now."

"You can't have him." I had no idea how to fight Fontaine. It's not as though there are weapons in a church. Sister Mary Angelica's room was so spare there wasn't even a nightstand to throw.

"It's too late," Fontaine said, dragging Aidan out of the room by his neck.

Aidan's eyes bulged as he gasped for breath. He fought Fontaine's bulk, but it was a losing proposition.

"You're crazy if you think I'm going to let you take him," I challenged.

"I don't see where you have a lot of options," Fontaine said.

I opened my mouth to argue but Fontaine cut me off by slamming the bedroom door in my face. It clanged loudly, echoing through the small space. "I am sorry it had to come to this, Aisling."

"I can't believe he thinks that will stop me," I grumbled, stalking toward the door.

I yanked on it, but it didn't open. "What the … ?"

I pulled again, figuring it was stuck. I raised my leg to use as leverage and tugged mercilessly, but the door wouldn't open and the handle was frozen. "How is this door locked? There's no mechanism to lock it." I studied the handle.

"It locks from the other side," Sister Mary Angelica said, her face drawn.

"What? Why?"

"Back in the day, everyone was locked into their rooms after dark."

"Was it the Dark Ages?"

"You're not very funny," Sister Mary Angelica said. "It was how this rectory ran. Don't judge."

"I'm not … I have to get to Aidan."

"Well, you can't get out through that door."

"So, wait. Are you saying there's no way for me to get out of here? Are you telling me that a madman just took my brother to do God knows what with him, and I can't get out of here?"

How does this keep happening to me?

35

THIRTY-FIVE

"You need to calm down," Sister Mary Angelica instructed. "You're going off the rails, girl."

"Did you see what just happened?"

"A bad man took your brother."

"He's going to take him to … ." I had no idea what Fontaine's plan was, but I knew it couldn't be good. "He's going to take him to the cemetery." How did I know that? Fontaine's appearance was too much of a coincidence.

"Eternal Sunshine? Why would he take him there?"

"They've been using one of the mausoleums," I said. "I was there about a week ago. It was empty, but there was a flower. Someone had been there."

"And you think it was these wraiths?"

"I think there aren't a lot of people comfortable with hanging around in a mausoleum," I said. "None of the guests in that mausoleum were fresh. So who would be visiting?"

"Fresh? You have a mouth on you."

"So I've been told." I rummaged around in my pocket for my cellphone. I had to get Aidan some help. Unfortunately, no bars appeared on the screen. "Do you not get cell service here?"

"This place is built like a fortress," Sister Mary Angelica said.

"Great," I snapped. "Now I can't call my brothers. This is your fault."

"How is this my fault?"

"You put up a fight. I am never talking to a soul again. Period. It always goes badly for me. It's so … frustrating."

"You're a defeatist," Sister Mary Angelica said.

"Excuse me?"

"Are you just giving up on going after your brother on your own?"

"I'm locked in here!"

"So, go through the tunnel."

I stilled. "Tunnel?"

Sister Mary Angelica pointed to her closet.

"That's a tunnel?"

"There's a door to one in there," Sister Mary Angelica said. "Even in the Dark Ages, as you like to refer to it, you couldn't lock someone in a room without an escape route. What if there was a fire?"

"And where does the tunnel lead?" I was already moving. I shoved the limited clothing to the side and studied the back of the closet. "Are there creepy-crawlies in there?"

"It's a tunnel," Sister Mary Angelica said, her tone dry. "It's not clean."

"Where does it go?"

"It leads to the side lawn," Sister Mary Angelica said.

I sighed and turned the handle on the door. It creaked as it opened, and the darkness on the other side was enough to squeeze my heart. "How am I going to know where I'm going? I won't be able to see anything."

"I'll lead you."

"You will?" I had a small glimmer of hope.

"You must have faith," Sister Mary Angelica said. "Now, come on. Your brother is far too pretty to die."

"I'VE NEVER BEEN SO HAPPY TO SEE A CEMETERY IN MY ENTIRE LIFE." I dropped to the ground and kissed it, not deterred in the slightest by my sense of drama.

The trek through the church's tunnels had been long and arduous. Without a physical touchstone, I'd had no choice but to hug close to the walls and follow Sister Mary Angelica's voice. By the time we found daylight, I was a filthy mess.

I reached for my phone again. Bars! I dialed Redmond out of instinct. I rushed through the story, despite the plethora of curses and colorful language pouring out of his mouth, and then waited for him to freak out.

"He's not going to a good place," Sister Mary Angelica said when I disconnected.

"He's just worked up." I climbed back to my feet and dusted the cobwebs and who knows what else from my shirt. "Are there spiders in my hair?"

"Just dirt."

Well, that was something at least. "Is there a back way into the cemetery? It's going to take me forever to go all the way around the wall."

"There's a back gate. It's usually locked, though."

No lock was going to keep me from getting to my brother. "I'll break it."

"Won't you get arrested for that?"

"The police can only help at this point." I broke into a run as I started moving toward the cemetery. "I'm coming, Aidan."

"WHAT MAUSOLEUM ARE WE LOOKING FOR?"

After watching me smash an antique lock with a rock, I figured Sister Mary Angelica would hang back. She was an unanchored soul. She didn't have a dog in this fight. She'd never left my side, though. She was invested in doing good. That's who she was.

"It's the Olivet mausoleum," I said. I scanned the cemetery. I was turned around. I'd never entered from this direction, and my brothers claimed I couldn't find my way out of a paper bag without a map, so I was lost.

"This way," Sister Mary Angelica said, pointing.

"Are you sure?"

"We helped maintain the grounds," she said. "It's this way. Trust me."

She hadn't led me astray yet. "We need to move faster. I need to get to Aidan."

"Can't you feel him?"

"What are you talking about?"

"You're twins and you're supernatural. I would think you should be able to feel him."

"We're not psychic," I snapped.

"He's still your blood."

I pressed my eyes shut. "I need to get to him. That's all I know."

"Let's go then," Sister Mary Angelica said. "Pick up your feet."

"That's easy for you to say," I grumbled. "You don't feel fatigue."

"Honey, I'm ninety-two years old, and even before I died I was in better shape than you."

"I'm joining a gym."

"You should," Sister Mary Angelica said. "Your body is a temple. God gave you only one."

"I get it," I said, pulling up short when we crested a familiar hill. "Oh."

Sister Mary Angelica ceased her forward momentum. "We're here."

I nodded, glancing around. The space in front of the mausoleum was empty. That didn't mean wraiths weren't hiding in the shadows of the trees. They'd done that before. "Can you do me a favor?"

"What did you have in mind?"

"Check out the tree groupings," I said. "The wraiths hide there. I don't want to approach the mausoleum if I'm going to get attacked from behind."

"You're smarter than you look. I'll be right back."

It took Sister Mary Angelica only two minutes to finish her loop. "There's something in those trees over there."

"Something?"

"It's really tall and it's wearing a black cloak."

"That's a wraith," I muttered. "Crap on toast."

"What should we do?"

I had no idea. "My brothers are on their way. They'll call my father and Griffin. It won't take them long to get here."

"Who is Griffin?"

"My boyfriend."

"Are you going to marry him?"

"I'm just trying to keep him from killing me on a weekly basis right now," I said. "Marriage is a long way off."

"He knows you're a reaper, though?"

"He does."

"That's the basis for a strong relationship," Sister Mary Angelica said. "Truth is always the most important thing."

"I thought faith was the most important thing?"

"They're both important. Do you really want to start arguing dogma now?"

I shook my head. "I have to go in there."

"Shouldn't you wait for your brothers?"

"I should," I said, "but Aidan needs me now. I can't leave him. There's no one to take his place if I lose him."

"Okay," Sister Mary Angelica said, squaring her shoulders. "Let's do this."

"You need to stay here," I said. "Wait for my brothers. You'll recognize them right away. Show them where the wraith is. Tell them … tell them I'm sorry, but I couldn't wait."

"I'm sure they'll understand."

I could only hope so.

I STUDIED THE MAUSOLEUM FOR THIRTY SECONDS LONGER. IT WAS out in the open. The expanse between me and the front door was mostly bare. Odds were good that I'd already been spotted anyway. It was now or never.

I broke into a run straight for the door. I had no idea what I was going to do if it was locked. I doubted Sister Mary Angelica had another tunnel handy. My hand closed around the cold brass of the doorknob and I turned it, hoping something would go my way this week. It gave without resistance and the door flew open.

I stepped into the sanctum, my hands clenched into fists, readied for an onslaught.

"I told you," Fontaine said. He leaned against the back wall of the mausoleum, arms crossed over his chest, a smug smile on his face. "I told you she would come after him."

"That still doesn't explain why you didn't take her at the church." Sylvia Dobbs stood a few feet from Fontaine, and she didn't look happy with the turn of events. "It's like you purposely had to make it dramatic."

"It's more fun this way."

I glared at them both, jerking my head away from the hanging oil-filled votive lantern on the wall. Setting my hair ablaze seemed counterproductive. "Where is Aidan?"

Fontaine pointed to the floor. I don't know how I'd missed him. He was sitting on the marble, his hands bound in front of him, leaning against the west wall. His eyes were bloodshot and glassy, the force of Fontaine's choking clearly taking a toll. He looked angry more than anything else, though.

"You are an idiot," he said.

"I love you, too."

"How did you get out of that room so quickly?" Fontaine asked. "I didn't think you'd be here for hours. We weren't quite prepared for your arrival."

In addition to Sylvia and Fontaine, two wraiths hung back behind their human counterparts. The one outside made three. I knew more would be coming. That was okay. I had reinforcements in transit, too. I just had to get a grip on the situation.

"I have many talents," I said. "They are varied and magical."

"You can walk through walls?"

"Sometimes," I said. I fixed Sylvia with a dark look. "So, you're Sylvia Dobbs. I saw you at the spa the other day. You look better in dim lighting. Harsh lighting makes you look older."

Sylvia's lip curled. "I see your reputation is well deserved."

"Yes. I'm a total bitch."

"And an idiot," Aidan said. "You should have called for help. You shouldn't have come here."

"My cellphone wouldn't work in the church. The walls were too thick."

"So you decided to be the hero and screw us both," Aidan grumbled.

He was getting on my last nerve. "I think the words you're looking for are 'thank' and 'you.'"

"Thank you for screwing us both."

I turned away from him. "So what happens now? You've caught me. I'm here for the taking. What's your grand plan?"

"What makes you think we have a grand plan?" Sylvia asked.

"Fontaine told me." What? I owe that man nothing. If they tried to kill each other that might be enough of a distraction for me to get Aidan out of here.

"What?" Sylvia knit her eyebrows together.

"Yeah. I followed you from the spa to the parking lot and listened to you two talk. He warned me after that I was in danger."

"You are unbelievable," Fontaine snapped. "Sylvia, she's exaggerating."

"No, I'm not. He's the weak link in your operation. You should kill him now."

"You shut your mouth!" Fontaine exploded.

I glanced back toward Aidan. "Are you hurt?"

"I'm fine."

"Are you going to sit there and pout?"

"Pretty much."

"Okay. Tell me when you're done." I turned back to Sylvia and Fontaine. "So, does anyone want to give me a hint here? I have a few questions, and I know you weren't expecting me for a few hours, so I figure now would be a good time to get my answers."

"Sit down and shut up," Fontaine ordered.

"Bite me."

"I'm going to … ." Fontaine mimed ripping my head off my shoulders.

I arched an eyebrow as I regarded Sylvia. "Do you want to answer my questions?"

"Sure," Sylvia said. "I don't have anything better to do. It's not as though I'm running a business or anything."

"Great."

"I was being sarcastic."

"Oh, I know. So, what's the deal with Morgan Reid?"

"Reid is an associate," Sylvia said carefully, her dark eyes never leaving my face. "He's handling a few financial issues for us."

"Who is trying to kill him?"

"Some guy he ripped off on the east side. He was supposed to take five percent, but he took ten, and it's a whole big thing. He's such an idiot. We told him he had to be covert for a few weeks, and then he went and did something stupid. He's a moron."

"So, his name appeared on the list, and you knew you had to keep him alive," I filled in. "Why use wraiths to do it?"

"Why not?" Sylvia asked. "They're hard to keep fed, and if I can hand over a soul to them and save the life of a business partner, it's a win-win situation."

"What is Reid doing for you, though?"

"He's handling our … investments."

"What kind of investments?"

"They're varied. You probably aren't capable of understanding."

I hate her. "How long are you going to protect him?"

"Not much longer," Sylvia said. "We're just waiting for our final payment. Then he's on his own."

Something about the story didn't jibe. "He doesn't know he's in danger, does he?"

Sylvia shook her head. "He has no idea. He's a financial whiz, but an absolute moron when it comes to reading people."

"Who does he think I am?"

"You'll have to be more specific."

"He's seen me several times at his place," I said. "He showed up at my home and asked me out on a date. I'm guessing one of you told him my real name. He clearly had other things on his mind, though. So, who does he think I am?"

"We told him you were an operative for one of his enemies," Fontaine said. "We figured he might be able to isolate you. He thought he was playing you – until you turned the tables on him at the restaurant that night – and now he's a little more suspicious."

"He's being a pain," Sylvia agreed. "He won't be our problem for much longer, though"

"I still don't understand why you guys need so much money."

"Money makes the world go round," Fontaine said, smiling wolfishly. "I love money."

"You're a pig."

"I'm also hung like a horse," Fontaine said, winking.

I wrinkled my nose. "You smell like one, too." I turned back to Sylvia. "Who do you work for?"

"What makes you think we work for anyone?"

"I heard you in the parking lot," I reminded her. "You mentioned someone else being unhappy. That has to be your boss, right?"

"We have a few other associates with whom we do business," Sylvia said. "That's not your concern – at least right now."

"Why do you want me?"

"You're a commodity," Sylvia said. "We have a bidder interested in your services."

That sounded gross. "What services?"

"It doesn't matter," Sylvia said. "That's between you and our ... associate."

"Why did you take Aidan?"

"To draw you in," Fontaine said. "I knew I couldn't take you without killing him, and I knew killing him would cause your father to amass an army to take us on. We needed a little time."

"It was a stupid plan," I said.

"You're here, aren't you?"

"Yeah, you're the stupid one," Aidan said. "You should have left me."

"Shut your mouth," I snapped. "I'll never leave you."

"That's why you're stupid." Aidan's face was drawn. I knew he was terrified. If they took me, there wasn't a thing he could do to stop them.

"You forgot one thing," I said.

"What's that?"

"I'm smarter than I look." I grabbed the votive lantern off the wall behind me and hurled it, covering my face as the glass shattered on the floor in front of Fontaine and Sylvia and the oil inside ignited into a ball of flames.

36

THIRTY-SIX

Taking advantage of the momentary confusion, I rushed to Aidan. I tugged on the ropes, frustrated when they didn't give. "I can't get them off."

"Run, Aisling," Aidan prodded. "Leave. You can't get me out of here."

I pulled him to his feet, irritated. "I will never leave you."

Aidan's face contorted with a myriad emotions, love and anger fighting for supremacy. "You have to go."

"Shut up," I said, pushing him in front of me. "Your feet work. Just … watch yourself. We have to … oh." I reached over and grabbed one of the small swords from the Olivet family crest on the wall. I yanked hard, freeing it, and then slipped the small piece of metal between his hands. "Cut yourself loose."

"What are you going to do?"

I pointed to the corner where Fontaine and Sylvia were busy beating at the flames with their coats. "I have to buy us more time. Start cutting!"

I strode to the other side of the front door and grabbed the second lantern. Because the mausoleum was so old, it lacked electricity. The only way to illuminate it was with fire, and fire was my friend today. I hurled the second lantern in their direction, smiling grimly as it shattered against the scared marble, and the fire exploded exponentially.

"I'm on fire!" Fontaine flapped his arms like a chicken.

"Stop doing that," Sylvia ordered. "You're making things worse."

"I'm on fire!"

"Good," Sylvia said. "You deserve it. This is your fault."

"Seriously, my pants are on fire!"

I shifted my gaze to the two figures behind Sylvia and Fontaine. The wraiths were shrinking, their gaunt bodies pressed to the back wall. There wasn't a lot of room to move in the small corner where they were trapped. I knew the fire wasn't big enough to trap them for long, though.

"Let's go," Aidan said, appearing at my side and rubbing his wrists. "You're a total badass, by the way."

"I'm going to want you to put that in writing when we're out of here," I said, moving toward the door.

"We'll have it notarized."

I paused when something in the corner of my eye caught my attention. I leaned over and grabbed the jug of lamp oil and straightened, casting a look over my shoulder as I considered my options.

"Are you going to burn them alive?" Aidan asked.

"There's at least one more wraith outside," I said. "Everyone is on their way."

"I thought you said your cellphone didn't work?"

"I said it didn't work in the church," I corrected. "I didn't say it didn't work outside of the church. I couldn't say that in front of them, though."

"How did you get out of the church?"

"Sister Mary Angelica. She's outside waiting for everyone so she can tip them off about the wraith. I'm sure there are more of them now."

"You are … always a surprise," Aidan said. He gave me a quick hug. "I love you. I'm going to beat your ass later for risking yourself, but I love you."

"I couldn't deal with an empty spot," I said. "Now back up."

"Are you really going to burn them alive?"

It was a tough question. He was really asking whether I was ready to kill two people. Killing wraiths was one thing. They should've died years before. They lived on borrowed time as it was. Killing people, even if they were evil, was quite another. "Yes."

"I'm not faulting you," Aidan said. "I think they need to die. I'll do it if you want me to."

"No," I said. "It's my job."

Aidan's face was unreadable. "Okay."

I uncapped the jug, meeting Fontaine's eyes as I readied for action. "I am genuinely sorry it came to this. You did try to warn me in your own way. You're too much of a danger, though."

"Wait!"

"You should have stayed away," I said. "You're a bottom-feeder. You always have been. You could have survived on someone else's turf, but your ego kept bringing you back here. You just had to beat my father, and it's coming back on you now."

"We can come to an understanding," Fontaine said, his eyes pleading.

"You can't be trusted, and I'm tired of looking over my shoulder."

My arms surged forward, and the liquid splashed out. The flames grew. I took a step back and repeated the motion. I was coating the area between Fontaine and Sylvia and the door, watching as the flames solidified and closed off any avenue of escape. "We'll be waiting outside to collect your souls."

I emptied the jug and then tossed it into the flames, taking a step back as the fresh air from outside washed over me. I risked one more glance at Fontaine, the blaze growing to a raging inferno between us. "I hope you find peace."

"LOOK OUT!"

I ducked as a body covered mine and forced me to the ground. The loud thud of metal meeting brick assailed my ears. I lifted my head, surprised to see Griffin shielding my body with his, and a thick knife resting on the ground near our feet. When had he arrived? "Hi."

"Hi yourself," he said, pulling me to the side of the mausoleum. He moved his hands over me, checking for injuries. "What's going on in there?"

"I … they're burning."

Griffin searched my face and ran his hand down the back of my head. It was as if he understood what I'd just done. "Okay. Stay here."

"Wait. Why?"

Griffin pointed to the scene in front of the mausoleum. The wraiths had multiplied in number, too numerous to count now. My brothers had arrived – and my father was cutting through black cloaks with reckless abandon – and a really big sword – but we were still outnumbered.

"I can help," I said.

"You've already helped," Griffin said. "Just … stay here."

"I … ."

"Stay here! For once in your life, just do what you're told."

"We're going to have a talk about this later," I warned.

He kissed my forehead. "I'm looking forward to it. I have a few things I want to talk to you about, too."

"Hey, I called for help."

"And then you ran headlong into danger, as you always do."

"I cannot possibly be blamed for this situation," I said.

"As much as I enjoy a lovers' spat, do you think you could help?" Braden moved in front of us and slammed a knife into the chest of an approaching wraith. "We still have a little work to do."

"Sorry." Griffin moved to Braden's side, a knife clutched in his hand. I had no idea where he gotten it, but my father fancied himself an antique weapons collector. Fighting supernatural beings in a cemetery probably seemed a good opportunity to dust them off and unsheathe them.

I fought the urge to join the fray, reminding myself that I was probably more of a hindrance than a help, but the inner argument wasn't going well. I crouched outside of the mausoleum, and despite the fight still raging outside, I couldn't push the reality of what I'd done inside out of my mind.

I hadn't just let Fontaine and Sylvia die. I'd killed them. I knew I should feel guilty, but that wasn't the emotion flitting through me. Don't get me wrong, I wasn't satisfied with my actions. I wasn't proud of myself. I wasn't angry, either. I was … confused.

I jerked when a hand landed on my arm, swiveling my head and expecting to find a wraith trying to drain me. I didn't have a weapon to protect myself.

The hand on my arm wasn't chalky. The fingernails weren't red talons. The clothing wasn't a black robe. It was hard to tell what I confronted. The flesh was an angry red in some places and charcoal black in others. The thing touching me hadn't attacked from outside, it had escaped from inside.

"Fontaine," I gasped.

His face was a mess, his features unrecognizable. He wasn't a threat, and there was no chance of his survival. I knew that. He still clung to life, though.

"I can't believe you did that," he rasped.

"Is Sylvia still alive, too? I thought for sure you guys would die in there."

"I used her body as a shield to escape," Fontaine rasped.

"Well, you always were a standup guy."

Fontaine had crawled out of the mausoleum, his legs no longer strong enough to hold him upright. He rested on his elbow, large swatches of his clothing burned away, revealing scarred flesh beneath. I settled on the ground next to him.

"I didn't think you had it in you," Fontaine said, a violent cough erupting from his mangled chest.

"People always underestimate me."

"I'm sure they do. I know I did."

He was winding down, but I still had questions. "Who is your boss?"

Fontaine chuckled weakly. "You're still looking for answers. Even now, when your family is fighting a battle, you still need to know the hows and whys."

"Tell me," I prodded. "You know you don't have much time. You crawled out here for a reason. I think you want to tell me."

"Maybe I'm just bitter enough to take my secret to the grave," Fontaine suggested, his head starting to droop toward the ground.

"You have a chance to do one good thing before you're judged," I said.

"There is that," Fontaine said. "Okay. I'll tell you."

His lips were cracked and bleeding. I leaned my head close to hear the last words he would ever utter. They were enough to send my world into a tailspin. I had never seen this coming.

37

THIRTY-SEVEN

"Is Aidan okay?"

"He's being checked out right now," Griffin said, rubbing my back as he stepped up behind me. "Maya and Cillian are in with him. Your father and Braden are with Redmond. He needs a few stitches. They're both going to be fine, though."

The cleanup at the cemetery had ended at the same time the sun began to sink on the horizon. I'd collected Fontaine's soul without letting it materialize. I couldn't bear to look at him. Not again. Then I had gone searching for Sylvia's soul. Instead of listening to her or questioning her further, I absorbed her ethereal remains while she continued raving about Fontaine's mistakes.

Sister Mary Angelica waited until everything was over, and then willingly said goodbye to the earthly plane. "You do a good thing here, girl. Don't forget that. Life is hard, and you have a lot of choices to deal with, but you can't second-guess yourself. What happened here today was a tragedy, but your family is safe and you all lived to fight another day. That's the most important thing. Never give up the fight." Her final words were busily going through my mind, even as Fontaine's final admission haunted me.

"Fontaine choked Aidan," I said, my voice hollow. "He should be checked out thoroughly."

"It's a hospital," Griffin said. "That's what they do here."

"Was anyone else hurt?"

Griffin furrowed his brow. He'd already given me an update. It just hadn't fully registered. "Everyone else is fine. How about you? Are you hurt?"

"No one laid a finger on me," I said. "Well … Fontaine did … but he was already pretty much gone."

"Do you want to talk about it?"

I lifted my head, meeting Griffin's concerned gaze. "I don't know."

"Okay," he said, ushering me toward one of the chairs in the waiting room. "Why don't you sit down and rest for a few minutes. You look dead on your feet."

That was an interesting choice of words. "Are you going to yell at me for going after Aidan alone?"

"No," Griffin said. "He's your brother. You couldn't leave him."

"I called before I went."

"I know."

"I had to go after him. I couldn't just leave him."

"I know."

"I … ."

Griffin pushed my hair out of my face so he could study me. "What did Fontaine say to you?"

"What makes you think he said anything to me?"

"He was dying," Griffin said. "He knew he was dying. He obviously felt he had something you needed to hear."

"He … he said he was surprised I killed him."

"Is that what's bothering you? Are you upset about … the fire? You didn't have a choice. You know that, right? It was either you or them."

"I know," I said. "I still feel weird about it."

"Well, that's probably a normal reaction," Griffin said. "You still didn't have a choice. I don't want you to feel guilty."

"I don't feel guilty."

Griffin was frustrated. "Then what's wrong? Your family just survived a war. You won. You're all in one piece, more or less."

"Fontaine did tell me something before he died," I said, my voice small.

Griffin waited.

"Sylvia and Fontaine were working for someone," I said. "They said they were acquiring me for a business associate. They were only interested in me for the money. That was their ultimate goal. It was their associate who really wanted me."

"Why?"

"They wouldn't say," I said. "Just that whoever it was had plans for me."

"You're worried because there's still someone out there, aren't you? Did Fontaine tell you who?"

I nodded, my lower lip starting to tremble despite my best efforts to remain strong.

"Who, baby? Tell me. We can't fight the enemy if we don't know who it is."

I sucked in a steadying breath and faced him, momentarily getting lost in the depths of his chocolate eyes.

"Aisling, tell me," Griffin pressed. "You're scaring me."

"He said … he said it was my mother."

Griffin's face drained. "What?"

"He said my mother is still alive, and she was the one who … she's coming for me."

Griffin drew me close, resting his cheek against the side of my head.

He didn't know what to say. That was fine, because I didn't know what to think.

"It's going to be okay, Aisling."

"How?"

"I don't know," he said, pressing his lips to my forehead. "We'll figure it out."

That was easier said than done.

Made in the USA
San Bernardino, CA
16 April 2020

67830614R00153